"

"It's a substance deadly to humans, Jean-Luc," Crusher said.

"*Bioweapons?* Dax, you haven't found some of this substance on Outpost V-4?"

Dax shook her head. "*No, and that's my problem. Yes, there's the presence of the stabilizing compounds. Yes, the Venetans have confirmed that the Tzenkethi have asked if they can stock certain 'resinous compounds' on the base. Yes, there's a large medical facility being run by Tzenkethi who could all be bioweapons experts for all I know. And, yes, the base is being refitted to cope with large Tzenkethi ships. Whether these will be merchant freighters or warships, your guess is as good as mine.*"

"That's a great deal of evidence," Picard said. "But all circumstantial."

"*Exactly. Every single element is innocuous by itself. But put it all side by side and it looks horrifically like the Tzenkethi are intending to put bioweapons along the Venetan border with Federation space. And given what Detrek said earlier, I don't think they'll be stopping with our border. This could affect most of the powers in the Khitomer Accords.*"

Don't miss these other thrilling tales in the
TYPHON PACT series!

STAR TREK®
TYPHON PACT

BRINKMANSHIP

UNA MCCORMACK

Based upon *Star Trek* and
Star Trek: The Next Generation®
created by Gene Roddenberry

POCKET BOOKS
New York   London   Toronto   Sydney   New Delhi

Pocket Books
A Division of Simon & Schuster, Inc.
1230 Avenue of the Americas
New York, NY 10020

This book is a work of fiction. Names, characters, places, and incidents either are products of the author's imagination or are used fictitiously. Any resemblance to actual events or locales or persons, living or dead, is entirely coincidental.

First Pocket Books paperback edition October 2012

POCKET and colophon are registered trademarks of Simon & Schuster, Inc.

For information about special discounts for bulk purchases, please contact Simon & Schuster Special Sales at 1-866-506-1949 or business@simonandschuster.com.

The Simon & Schuster Speakers Bureau can bring authors to your live event. For more information or to book an event, contact the Simon & Schuster Speakers Bureau at 1-866-248-3049 or visit our website at www.simonspeakers.com.

Manufactured in the United States of America

10   9   8   7   6   5   4   3

ISBN 978-1-4516-8782-8
ISBN 978-1-4516-8784-2 (ebook)

To the students of my Writing Short Fiction classes,
for their listening skills, wow words, and connectors.

Historian's Note

The events in this story take place in November of 2383 (ACE).

After Andor's shocking secession from the United Federation of Planets (*Star Trek: Typhon Pact—Paths of Disharmony*), the Federation president succeeded in persuading the Cardassian Union and the Ferengi Alliance to become signatories to the Khitomer Accords (*Star Trek: Typhon Pact—Plagues of Night, Star Trek: Typhon Pact—Raise the Dawn*). The tensions between Federation and the Typhon Pact—Romulan Star Empire, Tholian Assembly, Gorn Hegemony, Tzenkethi Coalition, Breen Confederacy, and Holy Order of the Kinshaya—are mounting. One small spark could set off an interstellar war.

For somehow this is tyranny's disease,
to trust no friends.

—Aeschylus, *Prometheus Bound*

Week 1

Expositions

1

FROM:
Civilian Freighter *Inzitran*, flagship, Merchant Fleet 9

TO:
Ementar Vik Tov-A, senior designated speaker, Active Affairs, Department of the Outside

STATUS:
Estimated time to border: 40 skyturns
Estimated time to destination: 45 skyturns

In the name of our most beloved and exalted Autarch Korzenten Rej Tov-AA, and in defense of the perfection of his borders, we serve and salute you!

The complex chatter of the administrators above, the silent attentiveness of her workmates around her—Neta Efheny spent her days with her head down, her mind empty, and her recording devices primed, and she did not speak or look around. Until today. Today, Neta Efheny was going to make a mistake that would change three lives forever and put whole civilizations at risk.

A few skyturns from now, as her mission to Ab-Tzenketh came to its violent and wholly unexpected conclusion, Efheny would have just enough time to reflect again upon the error she was about to make, the uncharacteristic lapse of attention that would cost at least one life. Sitting on a remote hillside, with a terrified workmate and a hostile and desperate ally, Efheny would think about the steps she had taken that had brought her to this pass. She would watch the twin moons silvering the dark expanse of the lagoon, and she would realize that something in her had changed that could not be changed back. She would suddenly understand the extent to which she had acclimated. She would understand that she had gone native. Step by incremental step, move by minute move, Neta Efheny had settled into her place in Tzenkethi society.

That was why she had missed the obvious, which, in retrospect, had been staring her in the face for the best part of four months. Initially, she had been dazzled by Ab-Tzenketh. She had learned to keep her head down, and had kept it lowered for so long that she was barely able to lift it again—it is difficult to see what is staring you in the face if you are looking at the ground.

There were good reasons why this had happened, reasons Efheny would understand very well. Tzenkethi society maintained strict boundaries between its echelons. The bioengineering programs instituted decades ago by the ruling cohorts were attempting to embed these distinctions down at a genetic level. As the programs bore fruit, generation after generation, it was a rare Tzenkethi service grade who found herself lifted by her test scores to a higher function.

These days, most Tzenkethi felt uneasy about too much proximity to those outside their echelon, an unease that surely went well beyond cultural taboo. One's pulse quickened and one's luminosity lessened at the sight of a steely skinned enforcer, not simply because one knew what an enforcer was empowered to do but also because one's body communicated it, physically.

Each year, the Tzenkethi leaders believed that they were coming closer to eradicating the effects of nurture upon their population, and that soon nature would control everything. So they would have been horrified to discover Neta Efheny, and for more reasons than the obvious. That she was a Cardassian spy who, for the last two years, had been successfully placed in one of the most sensitive government departments on the Tzenkethi homeworld would have been alarming. But to find something at the heart of their society that transgressed the natural order of things? That would be revolting.

Efheny had always been fascinated by the Tzenkethi and their rigid social system. Cardassian to the core (whatever her current physical appearance and bioreadings might suggest), she thoroughly approved of the stability achieved by such carefully designed and maintained hierarchies. The chaos of her own world's recent history made her crave that stability more than she perhaps understood. And she'd found, over the months embedded on Ab-Tzenketh, that what appeared from the outside to be a monolithic caste system in fact allowed for great variation: differences not just in dialects, for example, but also in tone of voice, or pronunciations of words, or the degree of light emitted from one's luciferous skin that conveyed deep subtleties. Not even the work that Efheny had done for the thesis that had won her this posting ("Toward a Typology of Social Stratification Among the Tzenkethi") had prepared her for the rich intricacy of everyday life here. This civilization, Efheny often reflected as she performed her mundane tasks, was like a great symphony in which even the lowliest server contributed to the great harmonic whole.

These were the kinds of thoughts that filled Efheny's head when she was not listening for instructions from her superiors or concentrating on her work. This was probably why she had almost forgotten herself, and was certainly why she had almost missed the obvious. She was too busy keeping her head down and too busy being dazzled. Because sometimes—just sometimes—Efheny forgot. Forgot that her cover identity designated her Ata, bred to carry out the maintenance work necessary to keep any empire going. Sometimes, when she was busy with her tasks, a Fel problem solver or Kre administrator would come down from his or her station on the superior deck, and Efheny would not be able to resist lifting her head just a little to catch a glimpse of these magnificent beings, with their phosphorescent skin and long, strong bodies. Sometimes, when her work was done for the day and she was traveling home to her billet, she would marvel at this glorious world—sun kissed, shining, and blessed with so much water that a Cardassian could not help but stare, however furtively. Stable, controlled, beautiful—no wonder the Tzenkethi systems were policed so jealously by their inhabitants. No wonder they would have been horrified to discover Neta Efheny in their midst, no matter how much she had come to love them.

That morning—the morning of her terrible, fatal mistake—Efheny inched slowly back and forth on her knees along the inferior deck of a conference room, rubbing nutrient gel into its intricate coral floor. This had been her function since arriving on Ab-Tzenketh. As Mayazan Ret Ata-E (Ret to designate her as one who received her orders directly from any Ter leader; E to indicate the quality of her genetic stock), Efheny was part of a work unit assigned to maintain a series of chambers that made up a division of the Department of the Outside. In these chambers, Fel problem solvers and Kre administrators of the governing echelon met and formulated briefing documents on Tzenkethi policy toward foreign powers to be passed farther up to the court, where they might even reach the ear of the Autarch himself. As an undercover operative for the Cardassian Intelligence Bureau, Neta Efheny's task was to keep as close to these discussions as possible, log everything on the numerous audiovisual recording devices implanted in her person, and transmit these files back to the analysts at the embassy. Neither task made much in the way of intellectual demands, although the maintenance work required physical activity, however repetitive. But as both Efheny and Mayazan, she was a function more than a person.

Pausing for a moment to examine her cloth, which seemed to be running low on the embedded chemical cleansing agents, Efheny saw, from the corner of her eye, the familiar figure of the leader of her work unit, Hertome Ter Ata-C. Hertome's genetic profile gave him a slight edge over lower-grade Atas when it came to height, and his Ter designation allowed him to emit a coppery hue to distinguish him from the duller browns of his Ata inferiors. He was also allowed to stand without formal permission when higher functions were nearby.

Today, he was waiting near the point where the gravitational field of the anterior deck met that of the superior deck. He had paused in his task of prepping the surfaces of the anterior deck for cleaning and was listening hard to all that was being said by the higher grades above.

Efheny gaped. What was he doing? Such an error might easily lead him to be censured. But Efheny's dismay ran deeper than that. Hertome's brazenness seemed almost inconceivable. No true C grade would imagine doing such a thing. Whatever those above were discussing was their concern, not his, and best left to their superior capabilities. Efheny, shocked out of maintaining her normal deferential stance, stopped what she was doing and stared at him.

It was an error that might well have proved fatal for

both of them. Fortunately for Efheny, the four other members of the unit were busy with their tasks and did not notice what occurred next between their two workmates. As if suddenly aware that he was being watched, Hertome Ter Ata-C turned his head and stared directly down at Efheny, kneeling on the inferior deck and staring up at him. He had green eyes, ovoid, and flecked with gold, ordinary enough for a Tzenkethi—but somehow, unmistakably, not . . .

Efheny clenched her jaw. Seeing the movement, Hertome blinked—once, twice—and then, from the narrowing of his eyelids, Efheny knew that he'd guessed that she too was not all that she seemed. She cursed under her breath. She had stared up at him for too long, far longer than any true Tzenkethi server of her grade would at a superior.

In a few short seconds, she had given herself away.

But then, so had he . . .

How had she not seen this? Hertome had been her superior for eight twin-months. How had she not known? He was *human*!

"Mayazan," said Hertome in a soft, firm voice pitched to convey his authority over her but not to interfere with the important business of their superiors working above, "am I to expect a request of you?"

The use of her name, the personal pronouns, and the formality of his sentence structure reminded Efheny of the parts they were meant to be playing. In fact, it was a most appropriate communication between them, mindful of the differences in their respective grades but granting her the opportunity to speak. Efheny made a gesture of respectful supplication, dimmed further what glow was emitting from her skin, and held up her cloth.

"Ap-Rej," she said, "this one must request a replacement in order to continue to perform her function satisfactorily."

For a moment, Hertome did not move, then he nodded toward their supplies. "An acceptable request," he said. "Take a new cloth, and be quick about it, Mayazan. Lazy hands serve no purpose."

"And this one's purpose is to serve." Efheny stood up and hurried across to their supplies. Within moments she was back on her knees, head down, furiously rubbing the nutrient gel into the coral of the inferior deck. Beside her, one of her workmates, Corazame Ret Ata-E, began to sing, softly, a tune that had been very popular among the Ata a twin-month ago. Soon the other two deck workers were singing along with her, and Efheny joined in too:

> *Like the moons that hand by hand traverse the sky,*
> *Like the waves that ebb and flow upon the shore,*
> *These ones know,*
> *These ones know,*
> *There is an order and a purpose for all things.*

Eventually Hertome and the other wall worker provided harmonies. By all outward appearances, they were a happy and productive unit, and no doubt the Fel and Kre work groups sitting above were comforted to hear the simple chant being murmured below them. Usually Efheny was soothed by participating in these songs, but today her stomach turned queasily, and her hands shook as she cleaned. Because she knew that her immediate superior in Maintenance Unit 17 at the Department of the Outside was not Hertome Ter Ata-C but a Federation agent, name unknown. The question now was: Which of them would be first to act on this new information? Which was going to blink first?

It's the little things that kill, thought Beverly Crusher, pushing her mug farther across the table, out of reach of René's questing, vulnerable hands. *The things you don't notice until they're hurtling toward you. The tiny things you forget about until all of a sudden they're critical.*

René, thwarted in his mission to take possession of her mug, began to frown. Expertly, Crusher picked up his small cup and put it down in front of him.

"Juice, sweetheart!" she said. Eagerly, the little boy took the cup. He drank thirstily and gave a wide smile that made his mother's spirits soar.

Across the table of the quarters that they shared on the *Enterprise,* a padd in one hand and his meal forgotten in front of him, her husband sighed deeply.

"Problem?" Crusher said.

"You could say that."

"What kind?"

"Cardassians," Jean-Luc Picard said brusquely. He put down the padd, stood up, and crossed the room to use the companel on the desk.

"Ah." Crusher followed him across the room. "Yes. I can see how that might be a problem."

The screen on the companel shimmered, and then Admiral Akaar appeared, stern and unyielding. Unconsciously, Crusher reached up to straighten her uniform, before remembering she was off-duty, in her quarters, and dressed for dinner with a two-year-old.

"Captain," Akaar said. *"There's been a little change of plan. Cardassians,"* he added, steely eyed and wry faced.

Crusher heard her husband sigh, just a little. A complication of Cardassians . . . Yes, that would be the collective noun. Picard opened his palm to invite the admiral to elucidate. "Please, go on."

"They want their people to come along on the mission. When you get to Starbase 66 to pick up the Ferengi and Federation representatives, there'll be a Cardassian diplomat and her team to pick up too. Negotiator Detrek. If it's any consolation, she's very experienced. A democrat too. First appointed during the Rejal administration, and then a favorite of Alon Ghemor. In other words, our kind of Cardassian."

To Crusher's eyes, her husband did not look particularly appeased by Detrek's impeccable credentials as a democrat. "Our preliminary exchanges with the Venetan government have been marked by a distinct frost, sir," he said. "It might not be wise to add more people at such a late stage. It could be construed as undue pressure."

"*Or construed as a signal of how seriously not just two but* three *other powers on their borders are taking their current dalliance with the Tzenkethi.*" Akaar sighed. "*I know this will be a tough sell, Jean-Luc, but I have our relations with the Cardassians to think of. As their ambassador is* constantly *reminding us, they are our allies these days. And when he's not banging that drum, he's indicated in innumerable ways—stopping short of saying it outright, of course—that his government will take the worst kind of message away from any refusal to allow their people to join in this mission to Venette. Since we're counting allies pretty much on the fingers of one hand right now, the president has agreed to their request.*" He frowned. "*She said she would throw in a brass band if they asked. So I'm afraid Cardassians are going to be there at the negotiating table, and you and the rest of the team will have to look as if that was the plan all along.*" Akaar's eyes flicked sideways slightly. "*Is Doctor Crusher there? I'd like to speak to her.*"

Picard, quirking up his eyebrows, gestured to Crusher. Quickly, she concealed a sticky bright blue plastic spoon in her pocket, and came into view.

"How can I help, Admiral?"

"*Doctor, I'd like you to take Lieutenant Chen's place on this mission.*"

"Excuse me?"

"*I know Chen would do a good job, but I want you there. You've been to Venette already, am I correct?*"

"Well, yes, but a long time ago. I was a *cadet*—" Crusher glanced at Picard, who shrugged his own confusion at the admiral's request. "Chen's the first contact specialist, Admiral. She's been preparing for this mission for several weeks—"

"No," said Akaar firmly. *"I want the perspective of someone who has been there before."*

"Of course, Admiral—although my perspective was pretty limited. I was fetching and carrying for senior officers most of the time."

"I'm sure things will start to come back to you when you're there, Doctor. Besides, there's another reason I want you there." He leaned toward the screen conspiratorially. *Surely this is a secure channel,* Crusher thought, even as she and Picard mirrored the admiral's move.

"Another reason?" she said.

"Or, to be more precise, I want a doctor there. This friendship between the Venetans and the Tzenkethi took us completely by surprise, Doctor. And our intelligence networks on Ab-Tzenketh are excellent. So how did we miss this?"

"I don't see how a doctor can answer that question," Crusher said. "You'd be better sending Choudhury—or, better still, send a specialist along, someone from Tzenkethi Affairs—"

"My specialist is on his way already. No, I have a particular purpose in mind for you, Doctor. I want to know whether the Tzenkethi are influencing the Venetans biochemically in some way."

"A biochemical influence?" Crusher was baffled.

"Aggression enhancers? Hallucinogens? Is that the kind of thing you mean?"

"I'll leave the technicalities to you, Doctor."

"Is that possible, Beverly?" Picard asked.

"Anything's possible, Jean-Luc. We know very little about Tzenkethi physiology, and even less about their medical science—"

"And, with your prior experience of the Venetans, you're the person best placed to judge any differences in their behavior, Doctor. Look around. Compare and contrast with your previous visit. Take tricorder readings—samples if you have to. But find out whether there's a biomedical reason for the Venetans' sudden shift toward the Tzenkethi and this new hostility toward us."

Crusher nodded slowly. She remembered the Venetans as welcoming. Perhaps this idea wasn't so far-fetched. "Very well, Admiral. I'll do my best."

"Good. What else? Oh, yes, you've still got that Cardassian glinn from the officers' exchange program, haven't you, Jean-Luc?"

"Glinn Dygan, yes—"

"Might be time for his moment in the sun. See what help he can be with the Cardassian contingent. All right, that's it. Keep the reports coming in, Jean-Luc. I'll be waiting to hear them. Beverly, enjoy revisiting Venette."

The channel cut off. Crusher exhaled. Beside her, Picard tapped the table with his fingertips—once, twice—and abruptly stopped. He gave no other sign that he was perturbed at having his plans thrown into disarray so late in the day. Crusher wasn't fooled.

"Well," he said at length, and calmly, "it seems that our mission to the Venette Convention is now rather more complicated than it was."

"Complicated by Cardassians, no less." Crusher perched on the side of the desk. "Do you really think the Venetans will be angered by their involvement?"

Picard leaned back in his chair and rested his hand upon hers. "I think there's a strong possibility. They're not well-disposed toward the Federation anyway. To bring the advertised diplomatic teams from the Federation and Ferenginar is one thing. To add representatives from another major power . . . As I said to the admiral—"

"The Venetans could see it as a last-minute attempt to put pressure on them."

"And without many reasons to take us at our word when we assure them that it's not."

Crusher nodded. The Federation had an unfortunate history with the three systems that comprised the Venette Convention. When she had visited the convention, as Beverly Howard, all those years ago, the Venetans had been in the early stages of establishing links with the Federation. All had progressed smoothly. Ten years ago, they had been on the verge of applying for Federation membership. Then the Dominion War had intervened, followed by the horror of the Borg Invasion, and the political destiny of these three small systems had quite simply been forgotten. Until they'd announced their new trading agreement with the Tzenkethi Coalition, that is. Now the Federation diplomatic service was scrambling to make up the ground lost in a decade. The Venette Convention bordered upon some interesting (not to mention sensitive) spots.

"Chen's going to be disappointed," Crusher said.

"I'd better inform her of the change of plans—" Picard started suddenly, and Crusher turned to look behind her.

At the table, René had lost interest in his own drink and had got hold of his mother's mug. His hands were too small to manage the weight, and the mug was now balancing precariously on the edge of the table. One small push and . . .

. . . *Down will go baby, cradle and all.*

Crusher crossed the room in a split second, catching the mug midway between table and floor.

"Nice save," Picard said appreciatively.

"An eye for critical situations," Crusher said, "and the reflexes to deal with them. Two more reasons why I should come along on this mission."

"So . . . this friend of yours," said Bowers.

"Not really a friend," said Dax. "More a friend of a friend."

"All right, this passing acquaintance of yours—"

"I wouldn't even call him a friend of a friend. I mean, Netara dated him . . . *twice,* maybe? Three times at the very most."

"All right, so you had a friend at the academy called Netara, and she dated this guy Alden three times . . ."

"Could have been four."

"Three or maybe four times . . ."

"But over several months," Dax said. "He was around a fair bit. I don't want you to think he was a complete *stranger* or anything . . ."

Bowers lifted his hand to stop the flow of information. "I get the idea. And what I'm getting at is this: why exactly are you pulling all the stops out for this guy, Ezri?"

Dax, who had been smoothing down her uniform and looking around the *Aventine*'s state-of-the-art transporter room to make sure everything was spotless (it was), stopped and thought, *Good question.*

"Given that by this point in your life he's surely no more than a minor footnote . . ."

"I guess . . ." Dax paused to think. "I guess, because he was around during an important bit. You know, right near the start, when you're not shy or nervous anymore, but the end isn't anywhere near in sight, and so you're just enjoying the freedom and the comparative lack of responsibility."

"I think I just about remember that," Bowers said wistfully. "Despite the rusting memory and the dimming haze of time."

"And Peter Alden, he was a year or two older than the rest of us. The crowd I went around with. It made a difference. We all wanted his approval, anyway, and then, to top it all, he was *brilliant,* Sam. A standout student. Obviously destined for great and important things."

"'Most Likely to Be Admiral Before the Rest of Us,' huh?" Bowers frowned. "I knew a few like that."

"No, not that type at all! Not pushy or self-important—the very opposite. Cooler, quieter. Modest, almost. But confident in himself. Like he had his eye on what was *really* important. Whenever one of us said anything—and you know 'youngsters,' too much to say most of the time—we always had half an eye on Peter Alden. What did he think of it? Did he approve? Was he disappointed? Everyone raised their game when Peter Alden was around."

Dax paused. What about shy, gawky, hapless Ezri Tigan, who had found Peter Alden yet another entirely daunting experience that the academy was throwing at her? Had she raised her game? Had she *ever* raised her game, before Dax?

"Even Ezri Tigan?" Bowers said gently.

Dax laughed. "Yes, I think that once or twice even *she* managed to shine for Peter Alden."

Bowers smiled. Dax twitched her uniform again. Trust Sam to know what was really going on in her head, to guess what it meant for her to be meeting someone who had known her before Dax.

It seemed a long time since Ensign Ezri Tigan, half qualified as a counselor and with slightly less than half a clue, had unexpectedly become the host of the venerable Trill symbiont, Dax. She'd been twenty years old. Time passed, and these days the people who had known her as Ezri Tigan seemed fewer and farther between. So when the *Aventine* had been assigned to collect Peter Alden, an intelligence expert on Tzen-kethi affairs, and take him to rendezvous with a dip-lomatic mission en route to the Venette Convention, Ezri had been struck by the name. The thought of glimpsing that girl again—through someone else's eyes, and someone whom that girl had admired—was tantalizing.

And to be able to show off the *Aventine* was the icing on the cake. "Most Likely to Be Admiral Before the Rest of Us"? Dax was still a player in that game.

Beside her, Bowers smiled. "I see," he said. "'Ezri Dax—My Success Story.'"

"Something like that."

"Then I'm honored to find myself part of the parade." Bowers cast an appraising eye around the transporter room. "So . . . does he have it?"

"Have what?"

"The glittering career that everyone predicted."

"I lost track. You know how it is. But I imagine Starfleet Intelligence hasn't been wasting his talents."

"I imagine not. Your uniform's perfectly straight, by the way," Bowers said. "Oh, and you're captain of one of Starfleet's most advanced vessels."

They exchanged grins. Dax patted Bowers on the arm. "Where would I be without you, Sam?"

"Here, probably. Hush. Your guest is about to arrive."

The *Aventine*'s transporter chief, Spon, operated the controls, and Commander Peter Alden of Starfleet Intelligence materialized before them.

He was a taut man in his midthirties, all lines and angles, with dark hair graying at the temples and a slight frown etched upon his face. When he saw Dax, a smile softened the tension at his mouth and eyes.

"Ezri," he said, offering her his hand. "Good to see you. It's been . . . what, ten years? Twelve?"

"Must be," Dax said, smiling back. She'd forgotten how good-looking Peter Alden was, and he had one of those faces that become more interesting with age and experience.

Alden glanced around the transporter room. "Your ship . . ." He laughed. "Well, it's amazing!"

"I know," Dax replied, beginning to laugh herself. Their hands were still clasped together. Gently, Dax detached herself from him. "Want to take a look around?"

Alden tucked both hands behind his back. "I'd like nothing better."

They smiled at each other. At Dax's side, Bowers cleared his throat. "Oh!" said Dax. "Yes! Allow me to introduce my first officer, Commander Samaritan Bowers."

"Sam will do," said Bowers, offering his hand. The two men exchanged pleasantries and handshakes.

Bowers turned to Dax. "Shall I accompany you on the tour of the ship, Captain? I know you were just saying that you didn't know where you'd be without me—"

"D'you know, Sam, I think I'll just about cope by myself."

Dax gestured to Alden to go ahead through the door, and she followed him out. "May I be the first," Bowers breathed into her ear as she went past, "to remark that your ex-roommate's ex-boyfriend is a *fox*."

"Shut up," ordered Dax.

2

FROM:
Civilian Freighter *Inzitran,* flagship, Merchant Fleet 9

TO:
Ementar Vik Tov-A, senior designated speaker,
Active Affairs, Department of the Outside

STATUS:
Estimated time to border: 37 skyturns
Estimated time to destination: 42 skyturns

Merchant vessel 3, hold temperature low but
stable. Monitoring.

Over the years, the *Enterprise* had hosted countless diplomatic receptions, and Doctor Crusher
and Captain Picard had evolved a system for working
the room. Starting at opposite ends, they would move
around the space in a figure eight, meeting briefly at the
center to trade information, before moving on to the
side of the room that the other had recently navigated.

"Make sure you speak to the Ferengi diplomat," Picard murmured, as they passed each other. "Madame Ilka. I think you'll find her very interesting."

Madame, Crusher thought. *Now that's something I've not seen before.* She glanced across the room to where a petite Ferengi female stood, twisting her fingers around the stem of her empty glass, observing the chattering guests with an air of distant amusement. Crusher extricated herself from her conversation with a junior member of the Cardassian team and began to move toward that end of the room. Picard, meanwhile, headed off in the direction of the lead Federation negotiator, Jeyn. Veterans of many similar missions together, they greeted each other with hail-fellow-well-met joviality.

Halfway toward Ilka, Crusher realized that the Ferengi woman had spotted her and had turned her gentle amusement to Beverly's nonchalant approach.

At last, Ilka took pity and beckoned to her. "Doctor Crusher," she called, "why don't you join me in my corner?"

Relieved to be able to abandon her futile attempt to sidle up discreetly on the other woman, Crusher grabbed two flutes of champagne and headed straight for her. Ilka took the proffered glass and sipped the liquid. She was middle-aged by Ferengi standards, with a higher than usual brow and perhaps slightly small earlobes. She wore a plain gray and silver dress, very elegant and conservative, that almost acted as camouflage against the ship's bulkhead. It was an interesting fashion statement. Most of the Ferengi women one saw in public tended to opt for bright, almost garish, colors, with plenty of decoration, as if celebrating their new freedom to dress as they pleased. Ilka's one concession to prevailing taste was a pair of long earrings. Crusher noted, however, that they did not join together at the bottom in the usual style. She liked this innovation. The old style had always faintly reminded her of chains.

Ilka stared at her with huge, bright, intelligent eyes. "Have you met our new Cardassian colleague yet, Doctor?"

"Detrek?" Crusher shook her head. "No, not yet. I believe she's not yet come aboard."

"She is something of a mystery," Ilka murmured.

"I gather it was a last-minute decision to send her along. She may well still simply be receiving her brief."

"Perhaps." Ilka took a sip of her drink. "Are you optimistic about the prospects of our mission, Doctor?"

"Beverly, please."

"Beverly."

"Am I confident about our mission?" Crusher pondered the question. "I have to say that I have mixed feelings. The news that the Venette Convention was seeking closer ties with the Tzenkethi came completely out of the blue."

"For us, too," Ilka said softly.

"We had such close links with them in the past. We had hoped to be welcoming them into the Federation—"

"But things change, and can change very quickly."

"They can indeed, Madame Ilka, but not always for the worst."

Ilka's smile broadened. She had long white teeth, meticulously sharpened. "I would call that typical Federation optimism!"

"And I would suggest that Ferenginar proves my point."

Ilka threw back her head and laughed, a frank, unforced laugh that warmed Crusher to the heart. She liked this small, clever Ferengi woman.

"Go ahead!" Ilka said. "Ask me whatever you like!"

"I wouldn't dream of doing that," Crusher said swiftly. "You must get tired of being treated as a specimen."

Ilka briefly closed her eyes, her gaiety changing in an instant into something closer to fatigue. She leaned toward Crusher and lowered her voice in confidence.

"You know our history," Ilka said. "As a girl I barely set foot outside my father's house. At the age of consent I was traded by him in marriage for a controlling interest in a shipping company. By good fortune, the man to whom I had been sold happens wholeheartedly to support the advancement of females. More than that, he was willing to put latinum behind that cause. By that happy set of circumstances, I am now the first Ferengi female to be appointed head of a diplomatic mission. I have come this far by keeping my ears open, my mouth shut, and my wit sharper than that of everyone around me. There are many on my homeworld eager to see me fail in this task." She considered this statement and glanced around the room to where several of her juniors were in conversation with members of the Federation diplomatic mission. "There are many on my *team* eager to see me fail in this task."

"You can trust me, Madame Ilka," Crusher said sincerely.

Ilka studied her with her bright, wary eyes. "I'd like to think I can. But I'll hold some of my latinum in reserve a little longer, I think."

"I'd be disappointed if you didn't," Crusher replied.

Smiling, Ilka polished off the last of her champagne. She twisted the stem of the glass between her fingers. "An interesting beverage," she said. "A kind of wine, is it not? Champagne, if I remember correctly?"

"That's right. Ruinart, to be exact," Crusher said. "You're very well-informed."

"I take an interest in the world around me," Ilka said. "The bubbles make it rather noisy, of course, but I rather like the idea of a drink that is as fun to listen to as it is to taste. One of my sons has an import company that deals in superior quality alien goods— there's a thriving market for them on Ferenginar these days. Our Bajoran first lady has set quite a fashion. I believe my son might be interested." Her eyes sparkled at Crusher like the bubbles in the drink she was holding. Demurely, she said, "You sound like you know what you're talking about. Do you happen to know anyone in the wine trade?"

Only my sister-in-law, Crusher thought. *What*

a remarkable coincidence! Ilka certainly did take an interest in the world around her. She'd also done her research quite thoroughly.

Crusher lifted her glass and gave a traditional Ferengi response to such a question. "I may well have some information that could bring you profit."

Ilka smiled broadly. And Crusher, looking around a room where the representatives of three powers were mixing freely and good-humoredly, was suddenly cheered—that in a climate of such mistrust, and amid such fear, there were great powers lining up against them, a friendship such as this could still be made.

When her shift ended, Neta Efheny did not linger, as she sometimes did, to chat with Corazame and the other deck workers. Instead she hurried down to the water shuttle that ran across the lagoon around which this city was built.

Efheny sat in the back, the part of the craft designated for Atas. The shuttle set off at a gentle pace, creeping along the shore and stopping regularly to drop off passengers. Efheny watched them as they scuttled down the narrow coral lanes that ran through most Tzenkethi cities. They were heading for their homes, tucked behind the blank walls of tenements turned inward around central courts. Even relatively superior echelons such as the ones Efheny was watching preferred to crowd together. Open spaces, being alone—these things caused Tzenkethi considerable discomfort.

The evening sky was purple, and a gentle breeze ruffled the water. The shuttle, after its last stop on this side of the lagoon, accelerated out into open water, heading toward the distant district where Atas such as Efheny had their billets. The canopies began to rise automatically, shielding the passengers from the great outdoors. Before the sky was completely hidden, Efheny caught a glimpse of the Royal Moon, a pale pink pearl above. All the passengers, Efheny included, raised their hands to touch their chests and then signal up to the moon, acknowledging the blessing of their Autarch, looking down from his palace upon his loyal servants. The canopy reached its full height, and the moon could no longer be seen, although its presence remained.

Efheny leaned back tiredly on the low bench and subvocalized instructions to begin transmitting the day's data to her superiors at the embassy. Once the task was under way, she pondered her current predicament.

Much as she would have preferred to ignore what had happened, Efheny knew she had to speak to Hertome. She was terribly afraid that someone else had noticed their exchange, the sudden slip of their masks. Perhaps Hertome, with the advantage of his higher designation, would be able to alleviate her fears. But she would have to be careful. Hertome might be the representative of an ally, but Efheny was wary of humans. They were unpredictable. Take the meeting this evening. To arrange it, Hertome had simply walked past her and told her when and where to come as casually as if he had been instructing her on her next task. She'd had to hurry to switch on the audio-disruption devices that were part of her bioengineering, and even then she wasn't sure that Karenzen Ter Ata-D, Hertome's assistant, hadn't noticed their unusual exchange.

Efheny disembarked two stops before her usual place, at a busy interchange that served as a covered market. Here Gar traders of the lower sort plied their wares to those Ata with a little more standing and a little more credit to their names. Slipping between stalls bearing *ilva* fish and *pana* stones and the sweet-smelling dyes with which many of the Ata grades liked to pattern their skins below their work wear, Efheny came at last to a tiny eatery. She came here once every other skyturn chiefly because the food was bland enough for her tastes, being largely free of the saltiness that all Tzenkethi, regardless of grade, seemed to believe was a necessary flavor to any meal.

Hertome (or whatever his name was in Standard) was already there, head down, reading the evening bulletin tickertaping across the tabletop. Efheny clicked her tongue. This was a risky meeting, out in public, but perhaps, given his slightly higher grading, it was less noteworthy than if he had come to her billet, or she had gone to his. Quietly, unobtrusively, she went to the table behind his, arranging herself on the low seat so that they had their backs to each other. The retinal scanner on the table, identifying her grade and function, changed the tickertape over to the

E-bulletin. Efheny switched on her audio-disruption devices and waited.

After a moment, Hertome leaned back. "Not quite what you seem, are you, Mayazan?"

A frank opening move, too frank for her taste. These humans, thought Efheny (conveniently forgetting her own people's recent history)—their proclivity for gambling would surely plunge the whole quadrant into chaos one of these days. Doggedly, she continued playing her part.

"This one can only offer her services to you, Ap-Rej."

"All right, stay in role if you want to."

Hertome twisted his neck slightly, so that from the corner of her eye Efheny could see the side of his face. The bioengineering was flawless. There was no sign now in his eyes of that unnerving alien humanness that had been so visible before. Now there was just an expression of patient, limpid sedateness that all the Ata seemed to bear.

Before Hertome could say anything else, a server approached their tables. His dull flesh and arm markings designated him EE. This made speech between them inappropriate, so Hertome signaled his order and Efheny did the same when he came to her.

When the server had left, Hertome spoke again. "I acknowledge your willingness to serve," he said, "and commend you on your readiness. But what I really want to know is if you're going to blow my damn cover."

"This one acknowledges with gratitude your commendation," Efheny said quickly. "She assures you of her dutifulness." He could take that, she thought, whichever damn way he wanted.

Their cups of steaming *leti* arrived together, with two savory biscuits for Hertome and one for her. Hertome drank the shot of *leti* in one go but left the biscuits. He tapped his fingers against the cup, then stood up abruptly, knocking the biscuits to the ground as he did so. Efheny, as her status required, bent to pick them up for him—and, shockingly, he did the same. Their heads almost touched below the level of the tabletops. Efheny almost shuddered to think of the number of taboos that were being violated.

"It's not so bad, you know." His eyes were alien—human—once again. "We're in this together. Perhaps we should think about working as a team."

He stood up, keyed his credit code into the table, and left. *Perhaps we should,* Efheny thought. *But we still have to be careful.* She didn't watch him leave and sat holding her mug in both hands, keeping her lowered eyes on a Ter Ata-B workman sitting at a far table. Had he been watching them throughout their meeting? Or was she simply being paranoid?

Glinn Ravel Dygan spruced up his uniform and headed toward the transporter room to meet the Cardassian delegation to the Venette Convention. This was a significant day for Dygan, who was looking forward to welcoming his compatriots on board. He felt welcome on the *Enterprise,* but nothing compared with having your own people around you, sharing jokes about the same childhood holovids, complaining about the same politicians, understanding the Cardassian way. Moreover, Dygan was quietly proud of the work that he had done on the officer exchange program to build bridges between Cardassia and the Federation. He wanted to introduce more of his people to this remarkable ship and its exceptional crew. Like many before him, Dygan was honored to be serving on the *Enterprise.* Unfortunately for the young glinn, his day was about to take a turn for the worse.

When Dygan reached the transporter room, Commander Worf was already there. He acknowledged Dygan's arrival with a curt nod and his customary frown. "The cruiser *Ghemor* docked at Starbase 66 half an hour ago," Worf said. "Your people are on their way."

A quick communication between the transporter chief and his counterpart on the starbase established that the Cardassian contingent was ready to come aboard. The transporter chief operated the controls and the Cardassians materialized.

Four Cardassians. One too few. Worf's frown shifted down a level from "situation normal" to "potential problem." Dygan's day began to go off the rails.

One of the insufficiency of Cardassians stepped forward and offered his palm in greeting to Worf. "I am Sub-Negotiator Gerety of Cardassian External Affairs," he said. "On behalf of my government, I would like to thank you for accommodating us on this mission."

"You are one fewer than we were expecting," Worf said brusquely, pressing his palm against Gerety's as quickly as he could. Dygan squirmed, guessing the commander's thoughts. *Cardassians. Always a complication.*

Gerety gestured apologetically. "Our head of mission, Negotiator Detrek, has been called to take an urgent message." Gerety jerked his thumb upward. "From the powers above."

Worf glanced up at the overhead.

"I think he means the castellan," Dygan murmured.

A low growl, barely audible except to the trained ear, escaped Worf's throat. His frown-level plunged to "irritated." Dygan quickly said, "I imagine Negotiator Detrek will inform us as soon as she's ready to come aboard?"

"Naturally," Gerety replied.

"Then, Commander, perhaps we should simply proceed as planned and escort our guests to the reception?" Dygan said. "I'll be happy to return here as soon as Negotiator Detrek arrives."

"That, ah, may be a while," said Gerety.

"I'll be available," Dygan said, avoiding Worf's eyes, and starting to shepherd his four compatriots toward the corridor. In the turbolift, Worf loomed over them all like clouds over the Andak Mountains, but the new arrivals were impervious to his disapproval and made cheerful small talk. Reaching the reception, Dygan let them loose among their Ferengi counterparts and glanced worriedly around the room.

Captain Picard, seeing him, beckoned to Dygan to join him.

"I don't see your head of mission, Dygan. Has Negotiator Detrek lost her way?"

"I'm afraid she's not yet come on board, sir. I understand she's taking a message from the castellan."

Picard's lips pursed. Dygan frowned. The captain liked things to be orderly. Dygan shared this attitude, as he'd found over the months that he shared many of the captain's ideas. Dygan's respect for Picard bordered on the devotional. He most certainly did not like to contribute even in a small way to making Picard's life more disorganized.

"Well," Picard said, with a slight sigh, "I'm sure she—or perhaps your castellan—has a very good reason for the delay."

"I'm sure that must be the case, sir."

Picard looked around the room and gave a brisk nod at what he saw. "The rest of the delegation seems very much at ease," he said, watching two junior negotiators in lively conversation with their Ferengi opposites and some distance away from Commander Worf. "Good work, Dygan."

With that praise ringing in his ears, Dygan was at last prepared to relax. The reception passed smoothly. Dygan had an entertaining conversation with a junior Ferengi negotiator called Rekkt, who pressed him unsuccessfully for information about the Federation team and tried to sell him a tasting holiday at a *kanar* distillery. He introduced some of his colleagues from the *Enterprise* to the members of the Cardassian team, and a more informal gathering in The Riding Club was arranged for later. This gathering, when it occurred, transformed rapidly into a good-naturedly competitive and synthol-fueled six-handed *kotra* tournament that Sub-Negotiator Entrek lost only narrowly to the *Enterprise*'s senior counselor, Doctor Hegol. (Hegol, a Bajoran, even managed not to make the Cardassians feel as if they'd lost the Dominion War all over again.) All in all, Dygan thought, as he rolled into his quarters some hours later than usual, it had been a good start to the mission, fully in the spirit of interspecies friendship and cooperation. He could sleep happy.

But even the just, dedicated, and hardworking are not always rewarded with their beauty sleep. Dygan's day was not over yet. Thirty-six minutes after his head touched his pillow, he was pulling his uniform straight and sprinting down the corridor toward the turbolift. Negotiator Detrek was finally putting in an appearance.

Dygan sped into the transporter room and came to a halt at Captain Picard's left shoulder. Picard glanced at him, up and down (Dygan now looked immaculate), and grunted approval.

"Perfect timing," Picard murmured—presciently, since Detrek immediately materialized.

She was a tall, stern woman—iron haired and flint eyed—exactly the kind of strong-minded individual that had come to populate the upper ranks of the Cardassian civil service since the end of the Dominion

War. Cardassia was currently in the hands of resolute and principled public servants who fully understood the nature of the calamity that had befallen their beloved home and were determined never to let it happen again. Dygan wholeheartedly approved of her and her kind. This was why he had applied for the officer exchange program. Cardassians had to be serious about their desire for change, serious about their desire to participate in the affairs of the quadrant as reliable allies. It was the responsibility of all Cardassian citizens to show that they could be trusted.

Picard stepped forward and raised his palm in a formal but friendly greeting.

"Negotiator Detrek. I'm Captain Jean-Luc Picard. Welcome aboard the *Enterprise*. May I introduce Glinn Ravel Dygan, who has been serving with us recently? He is a credit to your military, and I'm delighted to be able to attach him to you for the duration of our mission as an aide-de-camp."

Detrek gave Dygan a brisk brief nod. She shifted the pile of padds that she was carrying to her left arm and pressed her free palm quickly against Picard's.

"Captain Picard, I owe you a double apology," she said. "First, I hope you will forgive my last-minute inclusion in this mission. I must surely have thrown your preparations into disarray—"

"Not at all, Negotiator," Picard said smoothly, although everyone on the *Enterprise* guessed how frustrated the captain had been by this sudden change to their well-made plans.

Detrek smiled. "That is very kind of you. But I must apologize for my subsequent delay in coming aboard. All will become clear very soon." She looked around. Her voice went low. "Where can we speak? Privately, of course."

Picard showed no outward sign of being disconcerted by the speed at which Detrek was moving and gestured toward the door. "The observation lounge is of course at your disposal," he said.

"Thank you." Detrek began to move in the direction Picard had indicated. "May I impose upon you with one further request?"

"By all means," said Picard. Dygan, attuned to him by now, caught the merest hint of dryness in the captain's tone.

"I must speak to the other chief negotiators."

"We have a briefing session scheduled for the morning—"

"Immediately, Captain. Please."

Picard turned to Dygan. "Perhaps," he said softly, "you could convey my apologies to Madame Ilka and Ambassador Jeyn for waking them, and ask them to join me in the observation lounge as soon as they are able."

"Of course, Captain. Right away."

Picard, pausing in his pursuit of Detrek, added, "I'd like you at this meeting too, Dygan." His eyes flicked sideways imperceptibly, toward the newly arrived negotiator. "I'd like your perspective on what's happening."

Dygan nodded his understanding. He contacted both Ilka and Jeyn, and then hurried to join the captain and Detrek.

Detrek seemed to have made herself at home in double-quick time. Her padds and data rods were spread out across the table, and she was standing, hands clasped before her, studying a large holodisplay of the border between Cardassian space and the Venette Convention that was projected on the nearest bulkhead. When the other two negotiators arrived— Jeyn in slight disarray, Ilka meticulous—Detrek turned to speak to them.

"Forgive me for waking you," she said to her colleagues. "Forgive me also for moving past the formalities of introduction. We have all familiarized ourselves with each other's names, careers, histories, strengths, and weaknesses. We all know our business here. But we have very little time and we must move forward quickly."

Through the displayed star chart, Dygan and Picard shared a surprised look. Cardassians loved protocol: it was a game, a delight, the warp and weft of their social interactions. To forgo protocol completely implied that something was badly wrong.

"Our mission to the Venette Convention has become more critical than any of us were prepared for," Detrek went on. "This is no longer a matter of making overtures to the Venetans and offering them an alternative to friendship with the Tzenkethi. Events have overtaken us, and we find ourselves already long past that point." She sighed. "The castellan regrets to inform you that today our intelligence sources within the Venette Convention learned that the convention has agreed to lease three of its starbases to the Tzenkethi Coalition. When I show you the location of these bases, you will understand our concerns—and the urgent need to wake you."

Detrek moved her hand across the display. As she did so, the border between Cardassian and Venetan space lit up, a thin golden sheet between the two domains. Jabbing at a point close to the frontier, Detrek made one red light come up.

"The Venetan trading station Outpost V-15," she said, "forty hours from Cardassian space. Here"—she moved her hand again and another glowing surface appeared, cutting through the void—"the border between Ferengi and Venetan space. Look." She tapped a fingertip to make a second red light appear. "This is the second of the bases to be leased to the Tzenkethi. And *here*"—a third red spot appeared—"the third base. Captain Picard, I'm sure I don't need to point out to you its proximity to—"

"—to Starbase 261," Picard said, moving around the display to join her. Dygan drew in a quiet breath.

"Quite, Captain." Shifting her hand again, Detrek made the three red dots connect. To Dygan's eye, they looked uncomfortably like a net.

"Three bases," said Detrek, "at the disposal of the Tzenkethi Coalition, each one of them"—she drew her finger around the red lines—"on the border of a

Khitomer power." She looked around at the assembled team. "I can see that you understand the importance of this. If the Venetans lease these bases to the Tzenkethi Coalition, then a Typhon Pact power will have established a significant presence on the borders of each one of the governments represented here today."

"Not only that, surely," said Picard. "They will have also established a direct supply line between those borders and their military bases."

Ilka's hand went up to cover her mouth. Jeyn drew in a sharp breath.

"That, to my mind, and to the mind of my castellan," said Detrek, "is enough to constitute a significant military threat." She gave a slight smile. "I hope now that you understand my presence here. The Venetans are no longer simply offering friendship to the Tzenkethi—"

"No," said Picard, coming to stand beside her, gravely studying the golden net. "They are handing them the means—the infrastructure—to militarize the whole Venetan border against us."

And even a Cardassian, Dygan thought, would forgo the pleasures of protocol when delivering news like that.

3

FROM:
Civilian Freighter *Inzitran,* flagship, Merchant Fleet 9

TO:
Ementar Vik Tov-A, senior designated speaker,
Active Affairs, Department of the Outside

STATUS:
Estimated time to border: 34 skyturns
Estimated time to destination: 39 skyturns

Fleet course correction calculated to compensate
for ion winds. Executing at next waypoint.

Over dinner in her quarters, Dax pressed Alden for details of his career. He proved slippery as *gagh*.

"So," she said, as they picked over the remains of dessert and sipped their *raktajinos,* "Tell me more about what's brought you here, Peter."

He gave her a crooked smile. "Orders have brought me here. What else?"

She frowned at him through the steam of her coffee. "You don't get off that lightly. A specialist in Tzenkethi affairs? Some pretty interesting material must cross your desk."

"Just the usual paperwork. But what about you, Ezri?" He gestured around her quarters. "This ship—I wonder where it's taken you."

Dodged again, Dax thought. The lid was screwed on tightly. The habit of years, she guessed—although she had been hoping that their long friendship and the privacy of her quarters might have made him open up. "You know how it is, Peter. Excitement. Adventure. Really wild things."

"Not what you signed up for when you entered the Academy."

"No—but then neither was Dax."

"No," he said. "Life throws up some strange twists." He swirled his coffee around in his cup.

"What are the Tzenkethi like, Peter?"

He started at her question; no, he *jumped*. "What on earth makes you ask me that?"

"Mission specialist? Come on, we all know what that means. How long were you there?"

He smiled. "What makes you think I was there?"

She tilted her head. *Come on. Give a little.*

He put down his cup and propped his head on his hand. He looked very tired and Dax suddenly regretted pressing him so hard.

"They're beautiful, Ezri. Impenetrable. Terrifying." He rubbed his eyes and sighed. "Do you mind if we don't talk about this tonight? Let's talk about something else. Do you ever hear from Netara?"

She let him take her back again to reminiscence, although quietly a part of her wondered whether his weariness was genuine, or a feint to stop discussion. But by the time Bowers, coming off-shift, joined them, they were relaxed, well back into the past, and they entertained him with stories that were old to them but made fresh again by telling him. As they talked and laughed (and drank), Dax easily remembered why Peter Alden had been so admired as a young man. His wit was sharp, his intelligence undoubted, but he never turned these talents on anyone, not in a way that would do harm. And then there was his self-containment, his slight reserve, which only added to the appeal.

"It's good to see you, Peter," Dax said, at the door to her quarters, when at last he went off to bed. They hugged, for a moment or two longer than one might usually hold on, as if to make up for lost years.

"Good to see you too, Ezri. Good to see you soaring."

The door closed after him. Dax remained standing there, tapping her fingers against the bulkhead.

"Now there's a man with secrets," Bowers said. "What do you think? Is he hiding anything?"

"Oh, I should think so."

"Anything we should be worried about, Ezri?"

Dax looked around at the ruins of dinner, spread across the table. "I don't know yet, Sam. Sure, he was closed, but that's what spies are like."

"Even the foxes?"

Dax smiled and opened the door again. *Dismissed, Commander.* As Bowers passed her on his way out, she said, "Especially the foxes."

She didn't waste more time that night worrying, but went straight to bed—only to be woken three hours later by the persistent chime of the shipboard computer.

"Message from Commander Alden," the sleek voice told her.

She rolled onto her back. "What's up, Peter? You can't be in need of another nightcap."

The beat before Alden replied put her immediately on alert. She levered herself up onto her elbow. "Computer, lights. What is it, Commander?"

"Change of plan, Captain. We should meet in your ready room. Now, please, Ezri."

Eight minutes later—washed, uniformed, and partially caffeinated—Dax strode into her ready room, Bowers as ever at her back. Alden was already there, studying a holoprojection of a star chart that displayed a sizable portion of the border between the Venette Convention and the Federation. Starbase 261 gleamed in one corner of the display. Alden's shirtsleeves were rolled up and there was a mug of cooling coffee by his right hand, forgotten and forlorn. Padds were scattered across the table. Alden looked sober and unrested, and had evidently not yet been to bed. Dax sympathized.

At the sound of the door easing shut, Alden's head snapped up. His eyes narrowed at the sight of Bowers.

"What are you doing here?" Alden said sharply.

For a moment, Dax wasn't sure how to reply. "Peter," she said, baffled, "Bowers is my XO . . ."

Alden gave a quick shake of the head, as if to bring himself into focus. "Of course. Yes. Well, I'm sure you have clearance, or we can get you clearance."

Dax and Bowers exchanged puzzled looks. "I certainly hope so," Bowers said, taking his usual seat. Dax went to her chair, forcing Alden to move around the desk and take the remaining seat next to Bowers. She relaxed deliberately back in her chair and folded her hands in front of her. The dim lighting was giving the small room an unusually stifling atmosphere.

"When shall we three meet again . . . ," she murmured, then, crisply and louder, "Computer, lights!"

The room brightened. Alden rubbed his eyes against the sudden glare.

"That's better," Dax said firmly. "Go ahead, Peter. What's happening?"

Alden gestured toward the display. "Things have moved on. The Venetan government is about to announce that it intends to lease three of its starbases to the Tzenkethi for . . ." He gave a sharp, bitter laugh that surprised Dax in the level of its cynicism. "Well, they *say* that they'll be used for refitting and refueling purposes only, but let me show you their location and perhaps you'll see why our government—and not only ours—is unconvinced by this claim."

Across the star chart, three bright red points lit up.

"This one on the left is Outpost V-27," Alden

said. "You'll note its proximity to the border with the Ferengi Alliance, as you'll note the proximity of *this* base to the border with Cardassian space. And this one . . ." He gestured toward Starbase 261.

"Certainly doesn't look good," said Dax. "But is there any evidence that the Tzenkethi intend to use these bases other than, well, 'as advertised'?"

Alden gave a thin smile. "Why these bases, Ezri? Why not, for example, these?" The first three red lights disappeared and another three lit up. "Three more Venetan bases. Each as conveniently close to regular Tzenkethi trade routes but not a single one near the border with any power within the Khitomer Accords."

"It's circumstantial," Bowers said, perhaps still piqued at Alden's earlier dismissal. "And it strikes me that accusing the Tzenkethi of planning to militarize these bases when there might not be sufficient reason could *start* that militarization."

"That could even be the intent," Dax said. "Get us to fling around an accusation or two, take umbrage, and there's your excuse to weaponize." She shook her head. "Listen to me! If we start on that line of thinking, we'll keep going back and forth until everyone is blaming everyone else for the slightest move."

"Yes, indeed," Alden said seriously, "these are complicated times. There's not much in the way of trust going around." He picked up his cup of coffee, studied it closely, and put it down again. "Which is why my mission has changed, and I've been ordered to find out exactly what is going on at Outpost V-4." He raised his hand to his face and rubbed at his eyes once again. "Tired, tired, tired . . . ," he muttered. He shook his head and seemed once again to try to pull himself back into focus. "It's been pretty busy since you went off to bed."

So why the hell didn't you wake me? Dax thought. A glance at Bowers, eyebrows raised, confirmed that he was wondering the same thing.

"Communications have been flying around between my superiors and the Venetans," Alden went on. "They say they've nothing to hide, and they've agreed to allow Federation observers to visit Outpost V-4." He gestured at the scattered padds. "I've been trying to get up to speed with Venetan politics and culture . . ."

"But the immediate upshot of this is?" Dax cut in. "For the *Aventine,* I mean. That being my primary responsibility."

"My instructions are now not to join the *Enterprise* on its diplomatic mission to the convention but to go to Outpost V-4, meet the Venetan representatives, and learn as much as possible about the Tzenkethi presence there. You're to take me to Outpost V-4 and give me whatever assistance is needed."

There was a brief pause while Dax drummed her fingers on the tabletop. "Yet I haven't received any direct instructions from Starfleet—"

As if on cue, the comm by her seat chimed. *"Priority message from Admiral Akaar. Security code alpha-2."*

"I guess," said Bowers, "this will be our summons."

It was. A brief conversation with Akaar confirmed everything that Alden had said and directed the *Aventine* away from the Venetan homeworld and instead toward Outpost V-4. Still, Dax thought, as she relayed instructions for the new course to the bridge and made her way down, there were ways of doing things—and receiving her orders from a junior officer (no matter that they'd known each other as students) wasn't one of them. Sitting in her chair on the bridge, she watched Alden from the corner of her eye: the hard-achieved focus, the barely hidden fatigue. *I've certainly changed,* she thought. *Why wouldn't he?*

Crusher refreshed her memory of her brief, long-ago visit to the Venette Convention from Chen's briefing documents and her own logs, virtually dusty and half-forgotten. As she read, she was struck by how unlikely the three systems that comprised the convention were as candidates for finding themselves at the center of a diplomatic storm. Tucked away in a quiet part of the quadrant (but adjacent to several powers), and peaceable (but not particularly isolationist), they were home to several long-lived humanoid species that shared a distinctive ancient and venerable culture that valued moderation and tolerance and placed great emphasis on cooperation and mutual respect. But, as she'd said to Ilka, things changed.

In retrospect, Crusher thought, the clues to their current frostiness toward the Federation and their allies had been there. The Venetans—cautious and deeply proud of their enduring and successful way of life—clearly believed they had been snubbed by the Federation when their application to become a member state had been sidelined as a result of the traumas of the previous ten years. The longevity of the various Venetan species only complicated the matter. The discussion on Venette over closer ties with the Federation had lasted the best part of two centuries, and many of those who had promoted those links were still very much alive and active. No wonder they felt snubbed! But rather than turning inward, the Venetans were turning toward the Tzenkethi Coalition and, therefore, toward the Typhon Pact. And that surely merited this intervention, no matter how embarrassing it was for the Federation's diplomatic corps. Perhaps Akaar was right and there was some deeper, more injurious Tzenkethi project under way. Crusher recalled hospitable and no-nonsense people. Not hostile and suspicious. Why had the Venetans been drawn to the Tzenkethi?

"In many ways," Ilka said, as if guessing the direction of Crusher's thoughts, "Venetan culture is a better fit with the Tzenkethi than with the Federation. Both civilizations are very stable and achieve that stability through a certain degree of conformism on the part of their members rather than through encouraging individualism." Her clever eyes gleamed. "You Federation explorers and we Ferengi entrepreneurs are perhaps somewhat baffling to the Venetans. An enduring civilization of long-lived people, content with the habitable worlds of their systems—no wonder our outward-focused cultures seem at odds with their values. I'm surprised they ever wanted to join the Federation at all." Her eyes crinkled with a smile. "Perhaps they thought they could teach you something, Beverly?"

Crusher laughed. "I've no doubt that they could. That they still can."

"But breaking your promise to bring them into the Federation. *Tsch!*" Ilka made an odd clicking noise with her tongue that Crusher took to be a sign of disapproval, but the Ferengi woman's eyes were still full of humor. "Most unwise! Your government has stored up a great deal of trouble for us."

"So it seems," Crusher replied. "But I'm not so sure the Venetans place as high a premium on conformity as you suggest. Certainly that's true of the Tzenkethi—or what we know of them—but the Venetans? Cooperation is their key word, not compliance. Sure, they might try to channel individuality toward a greater good and away from excessive competition, but I don't think they want to eradicate competitive urges entirely. It's simply that they've found it less useful in maintaining a society with the kinds of values they most admire. Whereas the Tzenkethi—as far as I can tell—want to remove self-interest from the gene pool altogether. But if it came down to coercing someone into living her life against her own interests simply for some greater good . . ." Crusher shook her head. "My instinct is that the Venetans would find that unacceptable."

And that, perhaps, might be the key to finding common ground again with the Venetans, Crusher thought. That must have been why the Federation had seemed an attractive option in the first place: a diverse community of many cultures, living (mostly) successfully together, much like the Venetans' own arrangement. Perhaps the very liveliness of the Federation's diversity had seemed attractive too: the fractious debates and heated quarrels that sometimes characterized the council. Perhaps it had reminded these ancient people of their own childhood.

We've been beaten back and battered for so long now, Crusher thought. *War after war, the Andorian secession . . . We should try to remember what's good about us, about our way of life, even when we're at low ebb. Because if we don't care any longer, why should anyone else?*

Beside her, Ilka gave a little tilt of the head that set her long earrings jangling. "We'll see," she said. "I'll have a better idea once I've heard Rusht speak." She clicked her tongue again. "*Tsch!* I wish they would use titles as well as names! It feels so *wrong* simply calling her 'Rusht.' So ill-mannered! Titles make everything so much clearer."

Crusher and Ilka were waiting with the rest of the diplomatic teams for the Venetan negotiators. Arriving by transporter in Guwine, the Venetan capital, the members of the mission found themselves in the atrium of a sunlit honey-stone building that their guide called the Hall of Assembly. Taken quickly via curving corridors to what Crusher guessed was the center of the building, they were brought up one level to a pleasant chamber that was clearly a meeting room of some kind, although the organization of the space had been causing some confusion to the members of the various delegations. Two large tables, each shaped like a huge letter C, were hooked around each other, and while there were many chairs in the room, none of them had been arranged at the tables, and no places had been designated for the diplomats and their aides.

Their guide seemed baffled when Detrek asked where they should sit.

"Sit wherever you like," she replied, which caused a great confusion of activity among the junior aides of the three parties, as they tried to organize places for their superiors and themselves. The situation was not helped by the fact that Venetans were constantly coming into the room in twos and threes, picking up chairs as they entered and putting them down again wherever it suited them.

"Are you not concerned with the seating arrangements, Ilka?" Crusher asked her colleague. She and Ilka, on walking into the room and observing the chaos, had immediately gone over to a large bay window where refreshments were laid out, helping themselves to drinks and watching rather than participating in the mêlée. They'd sort themselves out in the end, Crusher thought (although poor Jean-Luc, trying to impose some calm and order on the proceedings, was clearly hating every second of this undignified scrum).

"I'm sure my colleagues will determine an arrangement that suits them best," Ilka said cheerfully. "I shall be happy to oblige them."

Crusher nodded toward a junior Ferengi diplomat, who was engaged in a very lively dispute with one of the Cardassians over ownership of a chair. "Your associate doesn't seem to share your indifference."

"Sub-Dealer Prott," Ilka said sharply, "needs to understand who exactly is in charge of this mission and to take direction accordingly. Nevertheless"—she demurely sipped her drink—"if he wants to wear himself out before discussions have even started, he is quite welcome to do so. And I am content to observe, thereby learning more about the dispositions of my allies and the Venetans than Prott will learn in a lifetime. Ah!" She smiled. "I believe the matter of the chair will shortly be resolved."

Crusher laughed. Glinn Dygan—tall, solid, broad, and exactly *not* the kind of person one argued with—was, on Picard's instruction, moving ominously toward Prott and the Cardassian. Soon the chair was placed behind Detrek, with the Cardassian junior sitting firmly upon it and Prott sent in search of another.

Crusher turned to look out the window. Although they were only one floor up, this building seemed to be the tallest in the capital and consequently gave her a good view out across Guwine. Long avenues curved around the city, with short spirals of smaller roads branching out. Low buildings and little gardens were gathered haphazardly around these roads such that it was difficult to see where the greenery ended and the buildings started, as if nature and culture were indistinguishable. It gave the whole settlement a serene, pastoral quality. Crusher saw children playing in a large green space across the nearest avenue, and wondered whether "park" was the right word, implying as it did some sort of barrier between it and the rest of the city. She wondered what life must be like for Venetan children, surrounded by so many wise and ancient elders. She smiled. Perhaps not too different from René, growing up on the *Enterprise*.

"It's a beautiful place," Ilka said.

"Reminds me of Paris," Crusher said absently, refilling her glass with a pale yellow sparkling liquid that tasted pleasantly like elderflower. Ilka, accepting a refill, sipped and wrinkled her nose.

"Not a patch on your champagne, Doctor," she said with a dismissive sniff.

The chatter in the room from all the Venetans now present was very noisy. They made an interesting sight. Four of their species were easily distinguishable either by their heights (varying from petite to imposing) or by the soft fur upon the bodies of two of them. Everything else was simply a matter of counting fingers. They mixed together freely and, having taken their seats, seemed amused if rather perplexed by what their visitors were doing. Crusher, wondering who they all were, realized that they must simply be ordinary people interested in seeing firsthand the visitors from other worlds.

Looking around the room, something on the far wall caught her eye. She tapped Ilka on the arm and pointed. "Recording devices," she said. "These aren't closed proceedings, are they?"

"The Venetans have a completely open society," Ilka said. "Closed proceedings would make no sense to them. First to the room gets a seat; everyone else can watch live." Ilka nodded across the room to where Picard, his frown deepening with each moment, was in whispered conversation with a very unhappy-looking Detrek. "Shall you inform Captain Picard, or shall I?"

"I'll pick my moment, thanks."

"Then in the meantime," Ilka said very softly, "may I ask whether your government has yet taken advantage of the offer from the Venetans to inspect Outpost V-4?"

Crusher, circling the remains of her drink around the base of her glass, considered the question and the potential reasons for asking. *Remember that she's an ally—but she's not Federation. You don't have to tell her everything.*

"I understand that the offer is being seriously considered." Crusher smiled at her new friend over the rim of her glass. "I'm just the doctor, Ilka. They don't tell me half of what's going on."

"Beverly, I don't believe that for one moment!"

Their amiable fencing halted when a set of large double doors at the far end of the chamber swung open. Even the Venetans went quiet as Rusht swept into the room.

Rusht was on the very imposing end of the Venetan height spectrum, nearly two meters tall. Crusher checked immediately for high heels but couldn't see below the hem of Rusht's long pale-green gown. Nor was her hair adding any extra height: it was pulled back sharply from her brow to give the effect of a dark peaked cap. In fact, Rusht's whole style was unornamented to the point of severe, as if dressing up was something that took attention away from more serious business, something that children might do. Ilka murmured under her breath and reached up to touch one of her earrings in an almost nervous gesture. Not for the first time in her career, Crusher was grateful for the low-pressure anonymity of a uniform.

Another Venetan, smaller and covered with beautiful gold fur with darker stripes along her arms and temples, followed Rusht into the room. Rusht's aide, perhaps? Did the Venetans have aides? How was this going to work? But Crusher's attempts to guess how this already bewildering meeting would play out stopped when the third figure entered the room and her startling beauty nearly took Crusher's breath away. This tall, glowing woman, fluid in movement and yet clearly very strong, was surely a Tzenkethi.

Crusher exhaled slowly. She had never seen one in person before. The aesthetic effect was remarkable, and the inclusion of a Tzenkethi in the Venetan diplomatic team sent about as strong a signal as possible about the strengthening ties between their world and the bigger, more powerful empire at their border. The Venetans really were angry.

What's behind that? Crusher wondered. *Why such depth of feeling? We were careless, perhaps, but we were also preoccupied. We were at war, for heaven's sake! Surely our lack of attention was understandable. So why was the snub felt so deeply?*

"Well, Beverly," murmured Ilka, "I believe we are outclassed—visually, at least."

Rusht and her companion spoke quietly to the Tzenkethi for a few moments. The Tzenkethi moved to one end of the table and, with infinite grace, rearranged her body so that she was comfortably seated on the floor. Her face was a mask, unreadable. Rusht took a seat near her at the end of the same curved table. Her colleague sat beside her.

"I am Rusht," she said simply. Her voice was low, but it carried. She gestured to her companion. "This is Vitig. We've decided that we'll be the ones to speak to you." She looked around the room at the confusion of delegates, sighed, and said, "Sit wherever you like. We should begin."

The chaos among the delegates, which had subsided when Rusht entered the room, did not pick up again. The members of the three delegations, much subdued, quickly organized themselves around three points across the two tables, with Jeyn and Picard diagonally opposite Rusht and Vitig, and Detrek and the Cardassians along the curve to their right. Dygan, sitting behind Detrek, was making an effort not to look anxious and instead ready and eager to respond to any request his government's representative made of him. The Ferengi took their place to the left of the Federation representatives, around from the Venetans on their table. Ilka put down her glass and went to join her delegation. As she moved away, she murmured to Crusher, "First point to Rusht."

But Crusher wasn't too sure. Yes, on the surface it seemed that with one well-judged entrance and a few well-judged words, Rusht had managed to take control of the proceedings, but something about her demeanor suggested that she found the behavior of her guests rather wearying. She seemed . . . *tired* by their antics. Much like Jean-Luc, in fact, Crusher reflected. Still, it was true that whatever Rusht's intention, the delegates from the Khitomer Accords were now on the defensive.

Crusher picked up a chair and put it down behind Jeyn and Picard, and found herself beside a cheerful Venetan who offered her his bag of sweets. At his insistence she took a couple, putting one in her pocket for later. Rolling the other slowly around her mouth (it had an almost peppery flavor—surprising, but not unpleasant), she leaned back so that she had a good view of the opposing parties—or, rather, a good view of the Tzenkethi behind Rusht.

In fact, everyone who wasn't a Venetan was goggling at the Tzenkethi, or pretending not to. Rusht said, "I should introduce a good friend of the convention, Alizome Vik Tov-A."

An approving murmur rose up from around the room as the Venetans welcomed their guest. Crusher flipped mentally back through the briefing documents she had read en route and tried to decipher the mysterious code of the Tzenkethi naming system.

Alizome Vik Tov-A . . . Alizome was a personal name. Tov was a status marker, indicating her importance as part of the governing echelon, the ruling class. Vik, as Crusher understood it, was a functional designation, indicating her specific purpose within that echelon. It meant Alizome was a speaker, permitted to conduct negotiations on behalf of her Autarch and speak in his voice. Was she sanctioned to do that today, Crusher wondered, or was she here simply to observe and then report back to her masters? As for A, well, the genetic grading spoke for itself. Altogether, if intelligence on Tzenkethi naming conventions was accurate, Alizome Vik Tov-A was a very prestigious member of Tzenkethi society. This person might even have the ear of the elusive and mysterious Autarch himself.

Ambassador Jeyn, taking the lead for the allies in their negotiations, got the nod from Ilka and Detrek. Jeyn stood up and smiled across the table at Rusht. The Venetans, politely, went (mostly) quiet. Crusher relaxed. Jeyn was as much a veteran of this kind of occasion as Jean-Luc.

"On behalf of my own government," Jeyn said, "and on behalf of my two colleagues, I'd like to thank you formally for your welcome today, Rusht—"

A raised palm from Rusht stopped Jeyn in midflow. "You are mistaken," Rusht said.

Jeyn, who had simply been warming up, blinked at her in surprise. "I'm sorry?"

"You are mistaken. I have offered no welcome. It would be better for all of us if you were not inaccurate. This has caused difficulties between our governments in the past and brought us to the unfortunate situation in which we find ourselves now."

There was a short, charged, and extremely embarrassed silence. Then the Venetans began to murmur to each other. There was no glee or schadenfreude in them, but Crusher rapidly got the impression that they agreed with what Rusht had said. Again, it was not that a point had been scored but that something necessary and accurate had been said. Across the room, Alizome glowed gently and turned an impassive golden eye upon Ambassador Jeyn.

Jeyn was completely at a loss as to what to say in response to such blunt hostility. Not so Detrek, however, who, eyes flashing, leaned forward and said, "This is outrageous! You invite us to your world simply to *insult* us—?"

Dygan, seated behind her, flinched. Crusher saw him throw an anxious look across the table at Picard.

Who swiftly intervened. "You are correct, Rusht," he said, "that you have made no formal welcome. Yet in the hospitality that has been shown since our arrival— the rooms, the refreshments—and in your simple willingness to meet us after the disappointments of the past, I fear we must be forgiven if we misconstrued these signs as a welcome. Our gratitude for this my colleague has, I think, accurately conveyed on behalf of all of us."

That voice, Crusher thought fondly. *Who could possibly be immune to its charm? I know I'm not.*

And Rusht, if not charmed, seemed at least prepared to be persuaded by the sentiment expressed.

"Skillful words," she said with a slight smile. "We knew that already about the Federation, of course. Words came easily, although action did not. But I'm ready, for the moment, to hear more." She glanced briefly across at Detrek (was that contempt in her eyes?) and then looked back at Picard. "From you, Picard, at least."

Crusher breathed out slightly and relaxed. She saw Dygan do the same. *Nice save, Jean-Luc. That's why they send you on these missions.*

4

FROM:
Civilian Freighter *Inzitran,* flagship, Merchant Fleet 9

TO:
Ementar Vik Tov-A, senior designated speaker, Active Affairs, Department of the Outside

STATUS:
Estimated time to border: 32 skyturns
Estimated time to destination: 47 skyturns

Waypoint 42. Fleet course adjustment executed successfully.

The next time Efheny went to the eatery at the covered market, there was no sign of Hertome. She was able to enjoy her *leti* and biscuit in peace. She watched the bustle of the crowd and observed the servers, moving silently between tables, signaling orders back to the kitchen with a kind of finger poetry that made her xenoanthropologist's heart sing. She needed this moment of solitude. She was still uncertain what to do about Hertome.

She had thought of killing him, of course, but murder was unusual on Ab-Tzenketh, and the enforcers investigated any instances fiercely and effectively. Far too risky for an undercover spy. She had debated working with him, as he'd suggested, but she could not bring herself to trust a human, even one as highly trained as Hertome must be. She'd already seen him slip too easily out of his role. She couldn't request a transfer from her work unit. The whole point of her presence on Ab-Tzenketh was to be in the rooms used by the civil servants in the Department of the Outside. They could keep up the pretense indefinitely, but Hertome was a problem that wasn't going away. So what should she do? She went into work the next day still undecided, keeping her head down and rushing to obey Hertome's every order.

That evening she went back to the eatery. To her dismay, Hertome was there. Worse, the only available space was at the same table. With a sigh, Efheny began the complex series of supplications that would allow someone of her grade to request permission to sit opposite someone of his comparatively elevated status.

"We *can* speak freely, you know," he said rather impatiently, when at last she lowered herself down to the ground. "My bioengineering enables audio disruption, as I'm sure yours does too. I activated it when you sat down. Anyone listening will hear us exchanging prerecorded pleasantries. But keep your eyes down, Mayazan. You still have to look the part."

She did keep her eyes down and she did not reply, simply signaled her request to the server. Hertome's fingers, darkly stained with the cleaning agents that they both used, fiddled with his cup as she ordered.

"I saw on the C-bulletin the other day," he said chattily, as if they were old friends soaking up the heat in some city stone room, "that the Ret Ata-EE genome is under revision. Some of the Yai scientists have suggested that the next generation of servers should be bred not to speak. They're arguing that such a feature is redundant in them because they can perform all of their functions perfectly adequately without. They don't need to speak to serve. What do you think of that, Mayazan? Or whatever your name is?"

"This one would not question the decisions of superiors. Whatever is decided will be best for her."

Hertome sighed deeply. From beneath her eyelids, Efheny could see him watching her.

"Cardassian," he said at last. "You have to be. You didn't even blink. Genetically manipulating an entire class so that they no longer have speech? If you were Federation, if you were Ferengi, certainly if you were Klingon, there'd have been a muscle twitch at the very least. Revulsion is almost impossible to suppress." He leaned back in again, close, and spoke very quietly. "But Cardassians? You're made of colder stuff, aren't you? Bet you'd have done it yourselves if you were able, at several points in your history."

Stung, Efheny looked up—yes, looked directly at him. "This one suggests," she said softly back, "that her training might simply be better than yours."

"I thought about that," he admitted cheerfully. "Thought about whether you were Federation and nobody had bothered to brief me. Even wondered whether you were from another Typhon Pact power— no reason why you wouldn't all be spying on each other, after all—but when I woke up the morning after our little tête-à-tête here and I *wasn't* dead, I figured you were probably an ally. So the question then was, what kind? Ferengi? Klingon?" He shook his head. "The thing is, I've worked alongside you for months. You *like* it here, don't you, Mayazan? You like how calm it is, how ordered. I've seen you staring out across the lagoon as if it was a glimpse of paradise. You're Cardassian, or my name's not . . ." He smiled crookedly. "Well, my name's not Hertome Ter Ata-C."

Her *leti* arrived. She sipped it.

"How did you know I wasn't Tzenkethi?" Hertome said conversationally.

Efheny thought, *How do you think? Because humans are a menace and we are trained to watch out for them in case their impulsiveness gets us killed.* She said, "That doesn't matter. What matters is that we need to be careful. I wouldn't be surprised if this meeting hadn't already attracted attention. It's not illegal for an Ata-C of breeding age to associate outside of work with an Ata-E of a similar age, but it's not usual, and a biomedical check is considered appropriate first—"

"So take my hand."

Startled, she looked up at him over the rim of her cup. "What did you say?"

"Take my hand. If we're already marked, we might as well give them a reason to mark us. But it's surely better if it's nowhere near the truth."

She considered his words, weighed them, moved the *kotra* pieces of their game around in her mind. Then she came to her decision about what to do. *Keep him close. That's all you have to do for now.* She put down her cup and reached across the table to clasp his hand.

"If it becomes necessary," she said, looking deep into his alien eyes, "this one *will* kill you."

He smiled. "Mayazan," he said, "I think that might be the most romantic thing anyone has ever said to me."

With the *Aventine* under way to Outpost V-4, Ezri Dax called her senior staff together to brief them on the new mission. Peter Alden sat at the opposite end of the table. No, not sat. Slumped. He looked exhausted.

"Seeing as you're all bright and able graduates of Starfleet Academy," Dax said, "I imagine you've already gathered that we're no longer delivering Commander Alden to the *Enterprise*. Our mission instead is to take him to the Venetan Outpost V-4, where the Tzenkethi are currently making free with the outpost's facilities."

"And all within spitting distance of Starbase 261,"

Security Chief Kedair noted, as Alden brought up the relevant star charts. "What exactly do you mean by 'making free,' Captain?"

"That, as they say, is the question," Dax replied. "The purpose of our journey is to observe what's going on. The story the Venetans are putting out is that it's a trading agreement, plain and simple. Goods coming in, goods going out. Everyone happy. However, Commander Alden and his colleagues"—she nodded down the table and he nodded back—"fear darker purposes behind this arrangement." She stared again at the star chart. "It is *damned* convenient that these bases all lie on the border . . ." She shook herself. *Remember, Ezri, we know nothing yet, nothing substantial.* "But we need proof of any plan to militarize these bases. The Venetans insist they have nothing to hide, but it's a delicate situation, and we can't simply blunder in waving our phasers around and kicking over consoles to search for long-range weapons."

"Our visit will be highly stage-managed," Alden said. "The only consoles that we'll get anywhere near, whether we're kicking them over or not, are likely to have been tidied up for the occasion."

"That's a possibility," Dax agreed ruefully. "So I need strategies for investigating whether Tzenkethi weaponry is already on the station, or whether it's anywhere near the station." She glanced at Leishman and Helkara, her engineering and science officers, who both nodded back. Leishman even began thumbing away at a padd.

"Unobtrusive strategies, I assume?" asked Helkara.

"You bet," said Dax. "The Venetans have long since decided we are belligerent. I don't want them discovering that we're running all kinds of scans and so giving them even *more* reasons to distrust us. Sure, they'll suspect that we're doing it, but I don't want them to have proof."

Around the table, her senior staff began to murmur to each other. Dax threw up her hands. "I know, I know, it's crazy! But it seems everyone's out to take offense these days. So we've got to make damned sure that we don't give them any opportunity to do so."

They got down into the minutiae of the mission: their time of arrival at Outpost V-4, who exactly would be in the away team sent over to the base. Alden briefed them on how best to deal with the Venetans (frankly) and Tzenkethi (cautiously). When Leishman threw in a few preliminary suggestions as to how the weapons scans might work based on what she knew of Venetan technology, and Helkara started to shoot her ideas down, it was clear they were moving from general business to specific tasks, so Dax halted the discussion and dismissed them. They all got up to leave, Leishman and Helkara still deep in conversation. Bowers hung back just in case but, at a nod from Dax, left with the rest. Only Alden remained.

Dax came around the table and sat in the chair next to him.

"You're convinced, aren't you, that we're going to

find something there?" she said. "Some proof that the Tzenkethi intend to use this base to threaten our borders?"

"Yes, I'm convinced."

"But why would they do that? It would be absolute madness! In this climate, how much more provocative could you get? The Tzenkethi must know that none of the members of the Khitomer Accords could possibly allow them to put weapons so close to our borders. So why the hell would they even try?"

"Why?" Alden looked bewildered that she would even ask. "Why do you think? Because they don't trust us. And because our bad luck has brought them together with the Venetans, who have their own reasons not to trust us either." He gave her a tired, rather hollow look. "I'm telling you, Ezri, there'll be weapons on that base, or there'll be weapons on the way to that base. Not just this one. All three of them. We'll hear the same from the Cardassian and Ferengi observers at the other outposts."

"Okay, I'm going to stick my neck out and say I think you're wrong. I've read up on the Venetans. It doesn't sit right with my sense of what they're like. I think the Tzenkethi have pursued this friendship simply because it embarrasses us. They're there to rub our noses in what we lost. That's enough for them. I don't think we'll find anything."

"Ah," he said, lifting a finger and smiling, "I covered myself on that already. If there aren't weapons there now, there will be soon, I said."

"But again I come back to the fact this is madly, *insanely* provocative. Why do that? *Why?*"

Alden eased back in his chair. "You ever met a Tzenkethi?"

"You know I haven't. Have you?"

"You know I have. I was there once." He looked past her, down the table, at nothing. "On Ab-Tzenketh." He shrugged. "You know how it is . . ."

"Actually, Peter, no, I don't."

"I'll tell you about it one day."

"I hope you will."

"But my point is, I got a fairly good sense of what the Tzenkethi don't like about us. Because make no mistake about it, they despise us." His face clouded and his eyes went distant. "Physically, the Tzenkethi appear humanoid, but their outside shape masks a fundamental fluidity of form. You're the counselor, work it out."

"Former counselor."

"You know enough. What do you think the effects might be of that?"

Dax shook her head. "I don't know . . . Anxiety about dissolution? Fear of collapse? I'm guessing here. You can't extrapolate directly from biological form to psychological state. Nurture counts at least as much as nature."

"Well, I would say that you're bang on the mark. Tzenkethi social systems are designed to stave off exactly such collapses. You've read about them, Ezri. You know the rigid nature of their social stratification, for example, and their convoluted codes for interacting with each other."

Dax nodded. She'd read about the strict naming conventions and the complex linguistic codes that communicated and reinforced function and status.

"But you said 'despise,' Peter. That's a strong word. Lots of worlds within the Federation have formal structures and ritualized interactions. *Starfleet* has formal structures and ritualized interactions. Why would that make them despise us?"

"Because to the Tzenkethi, the Federation is chaos personified—their worst nightmare, their greatest fear. What are we, after all? An unruly mishmash of people, all shouting out noisily in our own voices, all bringing our own particular culture to the mix. For the Tzenkethi, it's the monster under the bed. And, even worse, that chaos is right next to them and has a fleet of warships at its disposal. They must live in terror of what such unstable people as we are might do with all that firepower. The Venetans were a propaganda gift to them. A civilization that looked at Federation membership and then turned away . . ."

"Now hold on," said Dax. "The Venetans didn't turn away. The whole process got delayed by . . . oh, *minor* issues like Borg invasions and a war or two. But they *were* going to join the Federation."

"But they didn't."

"Not because we turned them down, or they turned us down—"

"That doesn't matter. They didn't join, and that's

all that counts." His eyes shadowed. "I have to wonder how long the Tzenkethi have been working within the Venette Convention. Working on the Venetans. Reminding them why they shouldn't trust us, whispering about how dangerous we are, seeding doubt upon doubt . . ." He gave a slight laugh. "That's what I would have done in their place. That's what I *know* they've been doing. I know what they're like."

Dax realized she had been listening as if mesmerized. He was so persuasive, always had been. "Peter, you can't talk this way. You can't *think* this way! So much suspicion. We've got to . . ." She opened her palms. "We've got to keep on hoping that we can build trust. Otherwise . . . well, I don't want to think where it might take us. But we've got to go to Outpost V-4 with an open mind. No, I know what you're going to say," she said when he frowned. "I'm not saying that we blind ourselves to the possibility that something might be happening there, something that we don't want. I'm not so naïve! But even while we're watching our backs, we've got to hope that we'll be surprised—and in the best way possible. We've got to *hope*, Peter."

He smiled at her. There was only the faintest sign of the confident young man that he had been. This was someone weary of the world, someone crushed by the weight of experience, whose early bloom had been crowded out by weeds. The thought of that—the sight of that—saddened her.

"Hope, Ezri?" he said. "You'll have to take care of that, I think. All I can do is keep watch."

They smiled at each other. "In fact, mister," she said, "there's one other thing you can do."

"Oh, yes?"

"Go to sleep. We've got hours yet."

"Sleep." He stretched in his chair and stood up. "Yes, I think I remember that . . ."

"Then reacquaint yourself with it. That's an order. Good night, Peter," she said as he headed for the door. "Sleep well. Don't dream of Tzenkethi under the bed."

He laughed and left.

Dax sat for a while staring at the star chart that was still displayed. Counselor. She hadn't thought of herself that way in a long time. Ezri Tigan had barely started on that role when Dax had come into her life, turned her upside down, and left her standing on her head. Now she was Ezri Dax, and Ezri Dax was a captain: a captain who had been a counselor who had eight lifetimes of experience to draw on. She was surely qualified to know when she should be worried about someone under her command.

Quickly, Dax stood up. She went back to the head of the table and put through a private communication to the ship's senior counselor. "Susan, meet me in my ready room. I want to talk to you about a friend."

If Dygan had been troubled by Detrek's flash of temper at the start of negotiations, it was nothing compared to his mounting alarm as the morning progressed. Negotiator Detrek seemed not to be in the mood for negotiation. Every word spoken by Rusht earned a sneer from Detrek; every suggestion by Rusht that the Venetans had the right to lease their bases to whomever they chose brought from Detrek blunt warnings that such choices came with consequences. The other members of the negotiating teams were too well trained to show their anxiety, but Dygan could see it: in the nervous twitch of Jeyn's left hand, in Ilka's twisting of the long chain of one earring, in Captain Picard's increasing reliance upon formality and politeness.

And then there was the evident displeasure of all the other Venetans in the room. They'd taken a dislike to Negotiator Detrek, no doubt about it, and they weren't afraid to make their opinion known. In the main they let Rusht do their speaking for them, as she'd been tasked to do, but there were many whispered conversations among them and sore looks directed at Detrek, not to mention the occasional catcall when she spoke.

The only person in the room who seemed unaffected by what was happening was the Tzenkethi observer, curled at the far end of the table, within her bright impenetrable glow, silently watching everything that was happening. And what was happening was that Negotiator Detrek was throwing the whole mission from the Khitomer Accords into disarray, leaving her allies badly flustered and the Venetans infuriated.

"However often I repeat myself," said Rusht, late in that long morning, "you seem unable to understand that these bases will be used for supply and refitting purposes only. We have invited you to send observers, who are already en route. The *Starship Aventine,* carrying Commander Peter Alden from Starfleet Intelligence, is now merely eight hours from Outpost V-4. Ferengi observers will be docking at Outpost V-27 within the hour. And your own ship, Detrek, the *Legate Damar,* with people from your own intelligence bureau, is only two hours from Outpost V-15. If we had something to hide, do you really think that we would invite you to come and see what operations are being established by the Tzenkethi on our bases?"

There was a ripple of approval from around the room.

"Why," Rusht concluded, "would we engage in such a pointless charade?"

"Because you'll have had plenty of time to clean up before any of our observers arrive," Detrek shot back. The disapproval from all around got louder as she continued. "What do you take us for, Rusht? You . . . and your new friends"—she gestured angrily toward Alizome—"must think we're fools. But we are *not* fools!"

A deep, communal growl rose up. Detrek, clearly rattled, nevertheless continued in a louder tone, "Cardassians recognize threats when we see them, and I am here to tell you that we will *not* accept this!"

She slammed her hand down upon the table. The room fell suddenly silent. Every Venetan present seemed to stare at Detrek with scorn at such a childish outburst from an adult. Dygan closed his eyes. This was a nightmare, the kind of bombast and posturing he would have expected from the guls when Central Command ran Cardassia. Weren't those days meant to be over now? Weren't they all meant to be striving to create a new Cardassia?

Picard eventually broke the silence. "I believe," he said, "that we are unlikely to progress much farther at this point. We should take a short break."

Rusht exchanged a few quiet words with her companion, Vitig, and then nodded. "We agree that would be for the best." She rose from her chair. "Perhaps when we reconvene," she said, looking steadily at Detrek, "more constructive conversation will be permitted to occur."

Rusht and Vitig departed, with their Tzenkethi adviser in their wake. The Venetans in the room immediately broke into lively debate. Dygan watched as Ilka raised her hand to her brow, and Picard and Jeyn leaned together for a few private, rapid exchanges. He saw Crusher, sitting behind the captain, thoughtfully study Detrek, and her calm, intelligent gaze fell on him. Dygan dropped his head. He felt ashamed to be Cardassian.

Captain Picard came across to speak to Detrek. Dygan busied himself with his notes and tried not to listen, but it soon became difficult, as Detrek's voice rose again.

"No, Captain," she said. "I am *not* unjust. I am *angry*. This is provocation on the part of the Autarch, nothing more. If he wants to send his trading ships through Venetan space, he can choose routes that keep him far away from Cardassian borders." She gathered up her padds. "What you and our friends from Ferenginar decide to do about the bases on your borders is up to you. But this point is nonnegotiable as far as the Cardassian Union is concerned. A strong Tzenkethi presence so close to our borders is *not* acceptable."

Her voice carried. There were a few more catcalls from around the room, and Detrek, gathering her dignity and her padds, strode out. Picard went over to where Crusher was sitting, and from the way they glanced over at him, Dygan realized that they must be talking about him. Again, he looked away, too embarrassed to meet the captain's eye. After a few minutes, Crusher came over and sat next to him.

"Hey, Ravel," she said. "How's *your* morning been?"

Dygan couldn't help but smile. His shoulders relaxed. He was about to open up to the doctor, tell her about his concerns, when he realized that the Ferengi diplomat, Madame Ilka, was hovering at Crusher's shoulder.

Crusher might be friendly, but Ilka was an unknown quantity, and he had to remember that he was here as a member of the Cardassian deputation and not as part of the crew of the *Enterprise*.

"Excuse me," he mumbled, jumping to his feet and hurrying away. He heard Crusher sigh, but she greeted Ilka affably. Dygan didn't wait to listen to what they had to say to each other. He ducked out of the convening room and ran down the corridor to the private office assigned to Detrek.

He tapped on the door. She called out to him to enter, and he slipped inside.

"Dygan," she said, a small smile twisting her lips. "Here to give me a message from Picard, by any chance?"

"No, ma'am. I'm here of my own accord."

She gestured to a chair, and he sat down. She seemed gentler, sadder, very unlike the person she had been at the negotiating table. He placed his hands on his knees and took a deep breath. "May I speak freely?"

"Of course you may." Her eye ridges twitched up. "Don't you know that we live in a democracy now? Speak freely. But"—she lifted a warning finger—"I'm going to ask you not to question me. Not yet."

Dygan pondered that for a moment. "Not question you?" he said. "That's not something you should ask me, ma'am. To ask for my obedience, without any explanation as to why?" He shook his head. "No, that's not right. You shouldn't ask me to do that."

"No, no," she said quickly, "not your obedience, Dygan. Your *trust*. Is that unreasonable of me to ask of you?"

"Ma'am, we have hardly met—"

"You trust Picard, don't you?"

"Well, yes, but—"

"Why? Why do you trust him?"

Dygan thought about that. There were many reasons. Picard was wise, and just, and experienced, and he looked for peaceful solutions. He would not push his Federation into war for the sake of patriotism or pride . . .

The companel on Detrek's desk chimed. She looked down and frowned.

"I'm sorry, Glinn Dygan, I have to take this in private. I know you're worried," she said, as he stood up, "and I do understand the reasons why. But you *can* trust me. And for exactly the same reasons that you trust Jean-Luc Picard."

Dygan left her office and went in search of a quiet corner, where he sat for a while and thought. *Trust her? Why should he trust her?* Not so long ago, Cardassia had almost been destroyed by the blind faith its people had put in their superiors. Where had that trust brought them? It had brought the Jem'Hadar down on them; it had led them to the Great Burning. His duty to Cardassia was *always* to question and to keep questioning until the answers he received were satisfactory. That was another reason why he trusted Picard—because the captain was always prepared to explain. And when there was no time for explanations, Dygan would still readily do what Picard ordered, because eventually the explanation would be forthcoming, and he knew it would be good. That was what Dygan wanted from Detrek. But he was disappointed. To ask him to trust her blindly? A Cardassian should know better these days than to ask.

A bell chimed. The meeting was about to resume. Dygan hurried back to the meeting room and took his seat. The room seemed even fuller now, and the doors had been left open. People were crowding outside in the corridors, trying to get a glimpse of what was going on inside. Clearly word of the extraordinary alien and her anger had got around.

Detrek, entering last, smiled as she passed Dygan. "Trust me, Glinn Dygan," she whispered as she sat down.

But then he watched her put aside the face of the wise elder that she had presented to him in private and become the rigid combatant she'd been since arriving on Venette. He watched the Venetans' contempt toward the representative of his people, and the silent scrutiny of the Tzenkethi Alizome. He watched Ilka fret, and Jeyn twitch, and Picard struggle to keep everyone calm. And as the afternoon went steadily downhill, Dygan felt afraid, terribly afraid, to see matters slipping beyond even Picard's control, sure that when they did, something bad, something irrevocable, was going to happen—like the fire that had once taken Cardassia.

5

FROM:
Civilian Freighter *Inzitran*, flagship, Merchant Fleet 9

TO:
Ementar Vik Tov-A, senior designated speaker, Active Affairs, Department of the Outside

STATUS:
Estimated time to border: 29 skyturns
Estimated time to destination: 34 skyturns

No message.

To anyone serving on the *Aventine*, the composition of the away team to Outpost V-4 must have looked distinctly odd. Leaving Sam Bowers in command, Ezri Dax took, along with Peter Alden, her chief of security, Lonnoc Kedair, and the ship's counselor, Susan Hyatt. Dax could only hope that her intention in including Hyatt was not too obvious. While she, Alden, and Kedair were observing the Venetans and the Tzenkethi, Dax wanted someone on the spot to observe Alden.

The Venetans operating the base had chosen from among their number someone named Heldon to speak on their behalf. Heldon, small as a Ferengi, rounded, and with lustrous silver fur, received the away team with exactly the coolness that Dax (up-to-date on Picard's reports from Venette) had been expecting. She made it abundantly clear that the presence of these Federation visitors might be tolerated but was hardly welcome.

"I suggest we begin with the docking circles," she said with a sigh, waving to them to follow her. Alden, walking beside Dax, gave her a look: *What else did we expect?*

As they went along, Dax studied her surroundings with interest. The lighting on the base was clear as daylight, with a faint green-gold tint, and the air seemed as fresh as a spring morning. With the slight concave bow in the walls, Dax felt faintly as if she was walking through a forest. She knew that Venetan design emphasized concord between natural and artificial elements: in fact, it did not admit the existence of such a distinction. But that gave the base a rather unsettling impression of having been woven from natural fibers.

"Is it just me," muttered Hyatt from behind Dax's shoulder, "or has this place been *knitted?*"

When they came to the docking circles, all seemed ordinary and orderly, but Dax hadn't exactly been expecting to be taken directly to the weapons sites. Coming to a halt by a large viewing window, she looked out across the base's primary ring to where zero-*g* building crews were busy at work. Most were wearing EV suits of Venetan design, with an almost barklike exterior, but here and there Dax saw the distinctive phosphorescent glow of a Tzenkethi suit. She couldn't decipher the markings on the shells, but she hazarded a guess that they signified that their occupants were engineers, overseeing and directing the work. The whole display was a model, Dax thought, for peaceful cooperation between species and friendship between a larger power and its independent allies.

If only the Tzenkethi engineers were standing over the Venetan construction workers with whips, Dax thought. *If only they were Federation engineers. If only I knew why these docking facilities were being expanded in the first place . . .*

"Why all this work?" she asked Heldon. "What's wrong with the docking facilities already here? They look fine to me." *If crocheted.*

"Tzenkethi freighters are larger than anything we have previously had to accommodate," Heldon said. "Our facilities were insufficiently able to cope with the demands that will be put upon them by Tzenkethi supply ships."

From the look of them, these new facilities would certainly be able to cope; they were large enough for Tzenkethi freighters. The question was, would they also be large enough for their warships? Dax sighed, leaned back against the transparent aluminum, and folded her arms. Heldon gave a dry smile. She had ice-blue eyes and dark streaks of fur that ran back from her brow up her forehead, giving her a permanently quizzical and amused look.

"I know what's at the forefront in your mind, Dax. Why don't you ask?"

"Because I don't want to give offense," Dax said. To her surprise, Heldon's smile actually broadened.

"At last," Heldon said, "an honest response! Frankness goes a long way with us. I'll pay you the compliment of being frank with you. We're not warmongers, whatever you're telling yourselves. We're an old people, looking to share everything we've learned with the wider quadrant. We offered the hand of friendship to your Federation first. You refused that offer, but the Tzenkethi have welcomed it." Seeing that Dax was about to object, Heldon went on, "Be honest, Dax. Would you be bothering with us if we weren't drawing closer to your enemies? Would *you* be here now, to meet me, to learn more about me and my culture, if the Tzenkethi weren't here?"

"No," admitted Dax. "I probably wouldn't."

Again Heldon smiled. "Less than an hour in our company, and already you have a much better idea of how to deal with us. Perhaps more time is all that you need. Come," she said. "According to our schedule, I now have to show you our medical facilities. I think you'll be impressed."

Dax *was* impressed, and for more reasons than she'd anticipated. The medical station was larger than she would have expected for a base of this size; moreover, it was staffed entirely by Tzenkethi. Five of them, moving around the space like highly trained dancers, taking measured, careful steps. Dax heard a noise overhead and looked up to see three more Tzenkethi, upside down, apparently hanging from the ceiling.

Dax's stomach lurched giddily before she realized that some sort of local gravity devices must have been installed to enable the Tzenkethi to use all available surfaces. Certainly it was efficient, but the effect of several of them at once, and from all angles, was almost overpowering. Their luminosity drowned out the naturalistic lighting of the room and, furthermore, their skin tones seemed constantly in flux, altering slightly as members of the team passed each other. Dax assumed that these variations constituted some form of communication, like body language and gesture in other species, and found herself quite dazzled by the shimmering display all around her. She had only a moment to admire it, however. Alden, standing beside her, muttered something under his breath and then retreated from the room. Quickly, Dax made her apologies to Heldon and followed him out.

Alden was propped up against the wall, bent double, hands pressed against his thighs, head down, and taking deep, shaky breaths. Dax recognized a panic attack when she saw one and put her hand on his shoulder.

"That's right, Peter," she said gently. "Deep breaths." After a moment or two, his breathing steadied, and he straightened up.

"Sorry," he said. "Don't know what came over me."

"Vertigo, I imagine," Dax replied cheerfully, although she didn't think that was even the half of it.

Hyatt came out to join them. She looked worriedly at Alden. "Everything okay?"

"Vertigo," said Dax. "You know those gravitational envelopes, Susan. They can play merry hell with the inner ear."

Hyatt's eyes narrowed, but she nodded, and Dax patted Alden's shoulder. "Coming back in, or staying out here?"

"I'll come back in."

They all turned to go back into the sickbay, but before they could enter, Dax's communicator chimed. She tapped her fingers against it.

"Dax, here."

"Leishman. Any chance of a quick word in private, Captain? There's something you should know."

"That," said Ambassador Jeyn, "was a disaster."

Crusher, Picard, and Jeyn had retreated to the private suite assigned to the senior Federation delegates in the Hall of Assembly. The main room was a pleasant circular chamber with comfortable couches arranged around a small pond. There was even a fountain, although it was not currently operating. Flower beds were set between each of the couches—not potted plants, Crusher noted, but patches of earth set into the stone floor, merging the line between interior and exterior. It made the room feel fresh, and under other circumstances would have been relaxing. Crusher, sitting on one of the couches, kicked off her boots, tucked her feet beneath her, and took a swig of wine. Picard, sighing, lowered himself into the seat beside her.

"Cardassians," he muttered darkly. "It's not as if I wanted them along in the first place." He tapped his fingers against the arm of the couch and burst out, "What the *hell* is Detrek playing at?"

"Who knows?" Jeyn said. "I've tried to speak to Admiral Akaar, but he seems to be permanently unavailable. His office has promised he'll get back to me within the hour."

Picard grunted and sipped his wine. "Did you get a chance to speak to Dygan, Beverly?"

"Only in passing at the end of the afternoon session." *If you could call what had happened a session. "Debacle" is more accurate.* "But I don't like to press him too hard, Jean-Luc. He's in a difficult position."

"Hmm." Picard frowned, but she could see that he agreed. Dygan was loyal, and it was unfair to exploit that loyalty. But he was their best chance of making sense of the approach the Cardassians were adopting.

"To be honest," Crusher went on, "my impression is that he's as confused as the rest of us as to why Detrek has gone in all guns blazing. Ilka's the same. Cardassian ways are proving enigmatic once again." She rubbed the sole of her left foot, trying to ease some of her tension. "Of course, the problem is that the crowd is against Detrek now, and she seems not to know how to handle it."

"I can't say that I was delighted to learn that the proceedings were open to anyone who was interested and could fit into the room," said Picard, and Crusher suppressed a twinge of guilt. She hadn't been able to warn him before it became manifestly clear what was going on.

"What about your own mission, Doctor?" Jeyn said. "Have you observed anything out of the ordinary?"

Crusher shook her head. "The Venetans seem much as they were before. Lively, interested, engaged. Admittedly, the crowd isn't exactly on our side. That's new. But I have no evidence to suggest that it's anything other than disappointment at how we treated them." *And, if I'm being honest, I'm not exactly sure how to go about acquiring any evidence to the contrary.*

"Of course," Jeyn said morosely, "it'll only get worse tomorrow. More people coming to watch, more chance for Detrek to lose her temper. Perhaps I should try to see Detrek tonight. Remind her that this is supposed to be a *diplomatic* mission—"

Jeyn's words were cut off by the chime of a communicator. Picard pulled himself out of his seat and went over to receive the transmission.

"With luck," Jeyn said, "this will be Akaar instructing us to whip Detrek into line . . ."

Crusher, settling back further into the deep comfort of the couch, felt something small and hard in her pocket. She drew out the candy she'd been given earlier by the Venetan sitting next to her. She held it in her palm. *I could test it,* she thought. *See if there's something wrong with it. Perhaps the Tzenkethi have sabotaged food production in some way. Or the water supply. It would show up in this, surely . . .*

She shook her head. Madness. She popped the candy into her mouth and savored the delicate, floral flavor.

Across the room, Picard sighed.

"What does it say, Captain? Is it from the admiral?"

"Well, yes, it *is* from the admiral," he said. "But he says: *At all costs, keep the Cardassians sweet.*"

The day after her second meeting with Hertome, Efheny arrived at the Department of the Outside to discover that sections of the building were sealed to anyone without a Ret Ata-BB rating or higher, the entrances no longer even visible to the lower grades. In the parts of the building to which she still had access, the people on the superior floors were dashing to and fro, whispering to each other in low, urgent tones. Efheny, mindful of her purpose on Ab-Tzenketh, quickly subvocalized instructions to her data collection devices to pick up and record as much of these discussions as their range allowed.

Efheny and Hertome did not speak that day. With the Ata maintenance units unable to enter sections of the building, Hertome broke his team into smaller groups, to work as best they could in those parts which remained accessible. Efheny was assigned to Hertome's immediate junior, Karenzen Ter Ata-D. Their task was to clean a series of conference rooms that had been used throughout the night as a result of whatever panic was currently on. The rooms were full of the detritus of the hasty meals taken by the problem solvers and administrators still camping out in them.

It made for a hard day. Karenzen had only recently received a Ter designation, granting him authority to give orders. He delighted in his new status and enjoyed lording it over people who had until recently been his workmates. At least he inadvertently did Efheny a favor: he refused to speak to her beyond the bare minimum required to order her about, and, as a result, she was able to record much more of what was happening in the building than if she had been working with the whole unit. But he kept her nose to the deck for the whole skyturn, and at the end of her shift Efheny was relieved to drag her aching limbs and sore back down to the Ret washroom in one of the subcaverns below the building.

She showered slowly. Efheny would never tire of how much water was available to her here. She would miss this bliss when she was ordered back to Cardassia.

She came out of the shower into the low cerulean changing room. She dried herself quickly and dressed in her everyday clothes, a long-skirted green dress that the E-bulletins currently prescribed fashionable for her grade. As she packed away her work wear, a hand grabbed her shoulder. Efheny reacted as she was trained to react, grasping her assailant's wrist and twisting hard until the hand released its grip on her.

"Ow! *Ow!* Let go. Mayazan, it's me! Let *go!*"

Hertome, of course. Who else? Efheny released her hold and turned to face him.

"Are you *mad*?" he said, rubbing his wrist. "Assaulting a superior is a serious crime. If you did that to any Ter other than me, you'd find yourself sent for reconditioning."

"No other Ter would come here," she hissed back. "No other Ter would be as . . . as . . . *indecent* as to come to the Ret washroom."

"Indecent, eh?" His alien eyes glimmered with humor, before turning sharp again. "But enough of our games, entertaining though they are. What do you know about what's been going on around here today?"

"Hertome—whatever your name is—this is going too far. You shouldn't be in here. You're putting us both in danger—"

"We're already in danger, Mayazan. So let's share our information and try to lessen that danger however we can. What do you know about what's been going on today?"

Efheny paused to consider. The truth was she knew nothing. Agents of her rank, in such deep cover, were under strict instructions not to examine the data that they had been sent to collect. If they were captured and interrogated, their only defense was exactly how little they knew. Efheny had been schooled to think of herself as a data transmission tool, nothing more. The analysis was done at the embassy, or else back on Prime itself. The only reason a live asset such as Efheny was placed there was that she was mobile and responsive. She could see ad hoc conversations taking place and move to record them.

But there was certainly a scare happening at the Tzenkethi Department of the Outside, and given that it was happening shortly after two undercover spies there had discovered each other's existence . . . Well, if her cover *was* in imminent danger of being blown, Efheny wanted to know. She said, "What do *you* think is going on?"

Hertome gave a short laugh. "If I knew that, I wouldn't have to ask you. But since you ask, there's been a flurry of communications with your lot today— yes, between this place and the Cardassian Embassy. I picked it all up when I was washing the walls on the seventh level. Come on, Mayazan, spill. What's happening?"

She swung her bag up onto her shoulder. "I don't know," she said.

"You must know something!"

"They don't tell me much. I'm just here to collect information."

"When do you see your contact again?"

"My contact?"

"Your superior," he said. "Whoever it is at the embassy that you report to."

Efheny shook her head. She didn't go anywhere near the embassy. At the end of each skyturn, the data she had collected was automatically transferred there via a secure channel. She had never met or spoken to anyone at the Cardassian Embassy on Ab-Tzenketh. She'd seen colleagues passing through on official business every so often. Only last week she'd been cleaning floors on the eleventh level and spied a tense meeting between four Cardassian attachés and their Fel opposite numbers. None of them had paid the Ata on the nearby deck any attention, of course. She doubted the attachés knew anything about her. The only communication she would receive from her superiors would be an automated warning twenty-five skyturns before her extraction from this world. But was this not the procedure followed by the humans? Did Hertome actually meet with them from his embassy? Efheny could hardly believe it. No wonder he ran so many risks with her.

"Come on, Mayazan. You must know when you're likely to see your contacts again. Will they know what's happening? Will they be able to tell you whether we're in danger here? We've got to know whether we're in danger!"

Efheny stood up. This had gone far enough. She'd been out of her mind ever to break cover. Only the fear that he might expose her had convinced her of the necessity of talking to him. She made to move past him.

"You're not to speak to me again," she said. "Not outside the context of our cover stories. I'll obey you— as Ret must obey Ter—as long as I have to while I'm still on this world, but you're to forget that we ever spoke to each other in any other way. This one is here to serve her Ap-Rej and through him serve her most exalted and beloved Rej, the beneficent Autarch himself. That's all. So let her past."

Deliberately, Hertome put himself in the doorway, blocking her exit.

"Let her *past*, Hertome. Or shall this one finish what she started with her Ap-Rej's wrist?"

He took a step forward, as if ready to take her up on her challenge, and then they both froze.

There were footsteps in the corridor, coming toward them. They looked around, but there was no way out except for the single door through which they'd entered. They were trapped. Was this the moment that every one of their kind dreaded: exposure, arrest, everything that came after?

"This one regrets to inform her Ap-Rej," Efheny hissed, "that she intends to tell her interrogators everything she knows about him."

The figure coming through the door did not have the steely silver luminescence of an enforcer but the dulled glow of another Ret Ata-E. It was Corazame, Efheny's fellow deck worker in Hertome's unit. Seeing her workmate and her immediate superior together in the washroom, Corazame's eyes widened in fright. Frantically, she signaled her deference to Hertome by further dimming the soft light emitting from her skin.

"This one . . . ," she stammered, "this one . . . Ai!" she cried, backed away, and fled down the corridor.

Hertome said something that Efheny's translator

couldn't quite catch—a curse, presumably—and then he turned to her.

"What now, Mayazan? What the hell now?"

In the end, Dax decided it was easier to return to the *Aventine* than to try to make sure that their communications would happen without scrutiny. She thought about making an elaborate excuse to Heldon as to why she had to go back to the ship but then decided to go for honesty.

"I trust you not to listen," she told Heldon. "But I cannot wear this uniform and trust that the same is true for the Tzenkethi that are here on this base."

Heldon soberly reflected on this. "I don't believe you're right about the Tzenkethi," she said, "but I believe that you're acting in good faith. That's all I can ask from you."

Excuses made, Dax went back across to the ship, taking Alden with her. They hurried to the conference room, where Leishman, Helkara, and the ship's doctor, Simon Tarses, were waiting for them.

"Talk quickly," Dax said. "I can't stay away without it looking like there's something serious going on." She glanced at her three senior officers. "I assume there *is* something serious going on?"

"There is," said Helkara, "but not what we thought."

He quickly handed around a number of padds. Dax scanned through hers while Helkara began briefing her.

"Leishman and I carried out a number of long-range scans designed to detect the movement or presence of Tzenkethi weaponry in the area. It's helpful to know that most Tzenkethi weapons leave a faint but distinctive trail of"—Helkara looked almost embarrassed—"sodium chloride."

"Sodium chloride?" said Dax. "*Salt?*" She slumped into her seat. "You're kidding me."

"I'm not kidding you, Captain," Helkara said earnestly.

"Makes sense," said Alden, "if you've ever seen Tzenketh."

"Makes sense?" said Dax.

"Lots of water," Alden explained.

"All right," said Dax. "Salt. Good. Fine. So we're looking for . . . what? Too much salt in the area?"

"That's pretty much exactly what we were looking for, Captain," Leishman confirmed. "But we didn't find it."

"So let me get this straight," said Dax, pressing the heel of her hand hard against her forehead. "Outpost V-4, being insufficiently salty, is not likely to have played host or currently be playing host to any Tzenkethi weaponry that we know of?"

"That's right," said Helkara. "However—"

"You say anything about pepper, Commander, and you're in the brig."

Helkara didn't even blink. "I have no data on pepper," he said. "What I *am* going to draw your attention to, however"—he leaned over to place his finger on a line of text on Dax's padd—"is this."

Dax saw blue figures, red figures, and green figures. Some of them were numbers and some were letters. Some of them looked suspiciously like they were upside down.

"Tell me what this means," Dax said. "I'm a busy woman with a ship to run and a crisis to handle and I've surrounded myself with smart, dedicated people for the sole purpose of interpreting unintelligible squiggles for me."

"It's the chemical formula for a set of compounds generally known as P96 solvents," Leishman explained helpfully. "Those figures mean that we've detected unusually high levels of these around Outpost V-4."

"Again," said Dax, "a little more interpretation will go a long way with me. Much like salt, in fact."

"P96 solvents," said Helkara, "are used to stabilize certain other compounds. One of them is navithium resin."

Alden started. Dax, alert at once, said, "What is it?"

Helkara glanced at the doctor, sitting next to her, and sighed. "Simon, perhaps you could explain about the navithium resin?"

Tarses nodded. "Navithium resin, Captain, is a substance deadly to humans. Its most common use is in bioweapons."

"Oh," Dax said, and then she thought of the medical facility on Outpost V-4, staffed entirely by Tzenkethi. "Oh!"

"I knew it," said Alden. He almost sounded excited. "I *knew* it!"

"All right, Peter, hold on a moment," Dax said quickly and held up a hand before he could say any more. "Let me work through what's going on here and what other explanations there might be."

"Ezri, it's obvious what's going on—"

"Not to me," Dax said sharply. Alden, frowning, looked ready to say something equally snappish back but then pressed his lips together, folded his arms, and walked slowly across the room, his back to the rest of them. Dax didn't miss the surprised glances her three senior officers exchanged at the severity of her response. But it was critical that they got this right. Dax put the padd down on the table and pushed her hand through her short hair, trying to think clearly.

"All right," she said. "So we've found nothing to suggest that there are any Tzenkethi weapons on or around Outpost V-4."

"None that we know of," Leishman confirmed. "I guess there could be a new generation of weapons that we know nothing about and can't detect." She glanced uncertainly at Alden. "But surely we have people on the ground finding out about this kind of thing, and that information would have cascaded through to us by now?"

There was a pause. "Commander Alden," Dax said. "Can you confirm or deny this?"

Alden didn't reply.

"Commander," Dax said, calmly and firmly, "you're here to offer the captain of this ship your specialist advice. Advise."

Alden turned around slowly. His hands were clasped behind his back and he didn't make eye contact with anyone. "Yes, we do," he said crisply. "And yes, it would."

"Thank you, Commander," Dax said. Again her senior officers gave each other worried looks. "So," Dax said, pushing forward decisively in her chair, "based on everything we know about Tzenkethi weaponry, we don't think there's anything hidden on Outpost V-4 right now. But while we were making sure of this, we discovered the presence of a compound used as a stabilizer for navithium resin." She considered this. "But you didn't find any *actual* navithium resin?"

"No," said Helkara. "Although that would be hard to pick up on a scan."

There was a pause. Dax propped her chin against her hand. Alden turned around and walked back to where she was sitting. He leaned down by her shoulder.

"Ezri," he said quietly but urgently, "this is what we were sent here for. This is exactly what we were sent here to find. You said you wanted my advice. You need to *listen*—"

She swung her head up to look at him. "And what exactly *have* we found, Commander? Evidence of some solvents? What else can they be used for? Leishman, Helkara, what are P96 solvents used for other than stabilizing navithium resins?"

"Oh, all kinds of things, Captain," Leishman replied.

"Hear that? All kinds of things. Their use might

be obvious to you—and to Starfleet Intelligence—but I've not yet heard the evidence."

She watched his hand clench into a fist. White knuckles. One slow, shuddering breath. *What is this? Why are you so keen to push me to take such a hard line? Are you concealing something? Do you—and your superiors—know something you're not telling me? Well, mister, you're going to have to tell me if you want me to risk war.*

"Ezri," he said too softly, "have we just been over to the same base? Did we see the same things? I saw Tzenkethi engineers extending the capacity of the docking circles to cope with their warships. I saw Tzenkethi medics refitting a facility stocked with stabilizers for compounds used in bioweapons. Do I have to remind you of the proximity of this base to our borders?"

"You don't have to remind me of anything, Commander!" Dax shot back. "You just have to show me *proof.*"

Alden pulled back as if bitten and went back across to the bulkhead. An uneasy silence settled on the room.

Dax took a deep breath and collected herself. "I've talked to Heldon," she said. "I don't believe she'd be complicit in something like this. In fact, I don't believe the Venetans en masse would be complicit in something like this. Making Federation visitors feel uncomfortable? Fine. Leasing bases to Federation enemies to embarrass us? Yes, I believe they'd do that. But *bioweapons*?" She shook her head. "No. So here's what we're going to do. We're not going to fling around accusations. We're going to keep calm.

Mikaela, Gruhn"—she glanced over at Leishman and Helkara—"go back to those scans and see if there's anything else you can learn from them."

Both officers nodded.

"Simon, any information you can supply about navithium resin, I'm sure I'll find that useful."

"Naturally, Captain."

"Commander Alden," Dax said.

A long moment passed before he turned around to face her.

"Yes, Captain?"

"Contact Starfleet Intelligence. Let them know what we've found. Tell them that we're not certain yet whether it means anything. I want to know if there is anything they are not telling you . . . telling us. Have you got that?"

Suddenly he relaxed. "Yes, sir. Of course. I'll get right onto it."

"Good," she said softly. "Thank you."

She glanced around at the rest of her senior officers. "Thank you all. And while you're all busy with that, I'm going to speak to Heldon. I want to give her every opportunity to explain what's happening here before any of us does anything that we might regret."

They left, somewhat subdued. Dax, exhausted, fell back into her chair. *It's bad enough fighting enemies,* she thought. *I don't want to have to fight my friends.*

6

FROM:

Civilian Freighter *Inzitran*, flagship, Merchant Fleet 9

TO:

Ementar Vik Tov-A, senior designated speaker,
Active Affairs, Department of the Outside

STATUS:

Estimated time to border: 26 skyturns
Estimated time to destination: 28 skyturns

Escort vessel D3 suffering engine malfunction.
Maintenance crew dispatched.

To Dax's astonishment, when she returned to Outpost V-4 to ask Heldon about the presence on the base of the solvents, the Venetan woman was completely frank in her response. Was there no subterfuge with these people? Did they have *any* secrets?

"Yes, we have a large stock of P96 solvents," Heldon said. "They're needed to stabilize certain resinous

compounds that the Tzenkethi intend to bring here."
She gestured to her colleague, Entrigar Ter Yai-A, the
Tzenkethi in charge of the new medical facility, who
signaled his agreement.

Ask a stupid question . . . Dax thought. From the
corner of her eye, she saw Alden shake his head and
open his mouth. Hyatt quickly intervened. "The resinous compounds, Captain," she said.

"Yes," said Dax, also trying to cut Alden off. "Heldon, do you know what their purpose is?"

"Of course I do," said Heldon. "Nobody brings
anything onto this base without full disclosure. You
must understand—as our Tzenkethi friends here
understand—that this is still a Venetan base, operating according to our principles."

"I do understand that," Dax replied. "So, in the
spirit of your principle of frankness, are you willing to
disclose the purpose of the compounds to me?"

"Naturally," said Heldon, and Dax was pleased to
see a twitch of a smile. "Chemicals that we have added to
the air here on Outpost V-4 make it comfortably breath-
able for our Tzenkethi friends. Unfortunately, they also
make it rather dry for them." She turned to Entrigar.
"You'll be able to explain this better than I can."

"You've seen us, Captain Dax," Entrigar said.
"You've seen how complex an organ our skin is." A
pulse of lights passed across his pale blue flesh, as if to
prove his words.

Dax watched in fascination. "This is part of how
you communicate, isn't it?"

"Yes," Entrigar said. "The resins are an emollient, nothing more. They're needed to treat skin conditions likely to arise from the arid air quality here." He turned to Alden. "You can confirm this, can you not, Commander? I understand that we are your . . ."—he lingered over the word—"'*specialism*.'"

Alden almost audibly snapped. "Do you think we're *idiots*? Ezri," he said, turning to her, "this is *ridiculous*!"

"Peter—"

"How much longer are we going to carry on with this bloody ridiculous charade?"

"Commander, be quiet!" Dax looked over at Heldon, whose eyes had widened, pushing the dark stripes farther back up her gentle face and giving her an expression of considerable alarm.

"As for *you*," Alden said, jabbing his finger toward Entrigar, whose skin crackled in response, "don't think I don't know what your game is!"

"Commander Alden. Outside. Now!"

Dax, grabbing Alden's arm, practically shoved him out of the room. Hyatt followed them out into the cool, forestlike corridor.

"What the *hell* do you think you're doing?" Dax said.

"What do *I* think I'm doing? Ezri, they're assembling the materials to make biogenic weapons! They're refitting a base to make it suitable for Tzenkethi warships! They are within *strike range* of Federation space! Why are you doing *nothing*?"

"I am listening to *everything* they have to say before I accuse them of intending to commit unimaginable crimes against us."

"They are feeding you a lie! A lie so transparent, it's practically an insult. I'm warning you, Ezri, don't make me go over your head—"

"Over my *head*? You need to be careful about what you say, mister. You're not in command here."

"I warned you about the Tzenkethi." Alden pressed his hands against his head. "I thought I could trust you, Ezri."

There was a rising note of desperation in his voice that stopped Dax from replying. She glanced at Hyatt, who was gesturing with her hands, palms down, toward the floor: *Calm it down. Calm it down.* Dax eased her posture slightly and moved backward, making herself less threatening.

"You *can* trust me, Peter," she said. "You can trust me to do everything in my power to try to stop a war breaking out. But I need to be able to trust you to keep your cool. Entrigar is playing you. Don't give him the satisfaction of seeing you blow up."

Slowly, Alden drew his hand across his face. "Of course. Of course. Damn it!" He slammed his hand against the wall, and the soft pliable material accepted the blow and absorbed it. "I should have seen it. Yes, yes, you're right, Ezri. You're right."

Dax glanced at Hyatt. *Better,* she mouthed. *A bit.*

"Don't worry about it," Dax said. "We're all tired, and we're all twitchy. But now comes the hard part. I need you to go back in there and apologize. I'll follow you back in a moment, by which time I know you'll have everyone in that room smiling again."

"Yes. Of course. I'll do that. I'm sorry."

"That's okay. Tense days. Everyone's tense."

He pushed himself up from the wall and went back inside Heldon's office.

"Captain," Hyatt said, "a word in your inner ear . . ."

"Fire ahead."

"Get Alden back on the ship. Now. He's not helping."

"You *think*?" Dax breathed out. "Look, can you give me a diagnosis?"

Hyatt raised her eyebrows. "Oh, come on. You trained long enough to know that I can't do that. I'd need to sit down with him, talk to him, do some tests . . ."

"Right, and any suggestions on how I go about persuading him to do that? 'Peter, I know we haven't seen each other for a long time, but don't take it the wrong way when I say I think you may be exhibiting symptoms of mild paranoia, and so Susan here would like a quick chat—'"

"You can *order* him, sir."

Dax didn't reply. She *could* order him, but she knew she wouldn't. That would be too cruel.

"I can't give you a diagnosis," Hyatt said, "but at the very least, it's my judgment that Commander Alden is suffering from stress, exhaustion, and tension, and as a result his reactions to the Tzenkethi are verging on phobic. That's the best-case scenario."

Dax sighed. "And the worst case?"

"At the worst, we have someone with incipient paranoia on our hands, for whom the Tzenkethi presence is a significant stressor. There's the possibility that he might take preemptive action against them."

"Preemptive *action*?" Dax said in horror. Visions of Alden running amok on the base ran horrifically through her mind. "Should I confiscate his phaser?"

"I don't think it would be anything so direct. He might simply collapse. Ezri, this is all conjecture. I can't diagnose simply from observation; I'd have to talk to him. But get him back on board the *Aventine*. He's not doing anyone any good here, himself least of all. And I can't promise that he'll be able to keep himself together much longer."

"All right, yes. I'll do that." Dax took a deep breath. "First, though, Heldon."

She went back into the room. Entrigar had gone, but Alden and Heldon were there: Heldon sitting at her desk and Alden standing rather sheepishly to one side.

"Alden has made a charming apology," Heldon said, "which I was glad to accept and which I shall pass on to Entrigar." She eyed Alden thoughtfully and, Dax realized, with considerable compassion. "We're all under a great deal of strain," Heldon said after a moment. "Perhaps it would be best for you and your crew to return to your ship for a short while."

Cool down, she means, Dax thought. *And get Alden out of here.* She was touched by Heldon's kind and tactful suggestion. The Venetan tendency toward bluntness certainly did not prevent them from seeing when face needed to be saved. Heldon glanced over at Dax and gave her a knowing smile. She seemed to be saying, *These young people, Dax. You and I, we are both so much older. We have so much more patience, so much more resilience.*

"I'm aware that there are still questions in your mind about the solvents, Dax," Heldon went on. "I'll speak to Entrigar and see what we can do. Perhaps another visit to the medical facility can be arranged."

Dax nodded. "Thank you, Heldon. Thank you for everything."

Parts of the Department of the Outside were still in lockdown, so Efheny found herself assigned to Karenzen again the next day. She saw Corazame only briefly in the washroom at the start of their shift, and they didn't get a chance to speak before Karenzen's voice came booming down the corridor, demanding to know what purpose the Ret Mayazan thought she served by standing under the shower all morning. Dashing to obey his summons, Efheny was hardly surprised when Corazame reached out to touch her hand and whispered, "I'll come by later."

Corazame arrived at Efheny's billet early in the evening. Efheny made a pot of *kela,* an expensive but friendly gesture. Corazame salted hers freely, while

Efheny added enough not to attract comment. They curled up on the floor to savor it and chatted about the new songs that had been released earlier in the day on the E-bulletin. Then Corazame lowered her eyes and fell silent. *Here it comes,* thought Efheny, bracing herself.

"I know," said Corazame at last, staring down into her *kela.*

"What do you mean, Cory?"

"You know what I mean! I know about you and Hertome Ter Ata-C. I know that you've been meeting." Quietly, almost inaudibly, Corazame added, "And I know the kinds of risks that you're running."

For one brief, terrifying moment, Efheny thought that Corazame really did know. But no, no, she couldn't *possibly* mean the truth . . .

Corazame reached out to take her hand. "What I really wanted you to know was that I understand, Maymi," she said shyly. "I've been where you are now. An Ata-CC. It was the best thing that has ever happened to me. It made me feel . . . special."

Efheny didn't know what to say. She knew that Corazame was entrusting her with a great secret, one that could bring her to the attention of the enforcers. All romantic and sexual liaisons were scrutinized before being given official permission (or refusal) to proceed, in order to ensure that no errors or impurities crept into the genetic-screening programs. If Corazame and her lover had been discovered, Corazame Ret Ata-E would not be here now. She would be in a reconditioning camp, and when she was allowed to leave she would no longer have even an E classification. She would be graded 0, null, contaminating stock, unfit for breeding, the greatest badge of shame a Tzenkethi could bear.

"The funny thing is," Corazame went on, "that all the time it was happening, I worked much harder. I sang more too . . ." She shook her head. "But it couldn't be, not given who I was. I know our purpose is to serve. I know that. It's a great comfort." She looked up. Her eyes were very bright. "But I wanted you to know that I understand, Maymi, and that your secret's safe with me. You'll have only a little time together. Enjoy it while you can. And I'll be here for you when it ends."

They sat there for a while, simply holding hands. Corazame was emitting a gentle charge from her skin that they both found comforting. Efheny tried to think what was best to do. Should she deny that she and Hertome were lovers? But then Corazame would be hurt. She'd seen them together, after all, and it would seem that her friend Mayazan was lying to her after she had confided in her. Or should she say that she and Hertome *had* been lovers, but that the affair was over now? In the end, she fell back on the spy's best tactic: sit still and say nothing.

Eventually Corazame stirred. She smiled at Efheny, who smiled back, and she was just about to say something comforting to her friend when a red glow, undetectable from the outside, flooded her eye filters, and data began to stream past her eyes. It was her superiors at the embassy, giving Neta Efheny twenty-five sky-turns' warning before her extraction and issuing her instructions on how to get to her pickup point.

Xenoanthropologists studying all the major (and minor) powers frequently remark that there is one social ritual that cuts across all the cultures that fall within their purview. When asked what this is, they darkly reply, *The knock on the door in the middle of the night.*

If you ask them to explain why this phenomenon is found across so many and such different civilizations, they give you a variety of answers utilizing an impressive arsenal of professional technical language (or, as some would call it, jargon). But the gist of their responses is this: that social control relies ultimately on fear of the power that others have over you, and that consequently the shocking display of power required to hammer on a door in the middle of the night, knock down that door, and drag out whoever is behind while you kick and scream and beg for mercy, has been universally shown to have the desired effect on anyone listening. They might hide beneath the covers, or turn up the volume on their holoviewer, or try to sing their loved ones back to sleep, but they will know what is happening nearby. And they will be afraid.

That, most xenoanthropologists will tell you, is an almost universal experience.

Like many assertions made by social scientists, it's not entirely accurate. The explanation it gives of the phenomenon is very good but not the claim that such experiences are to be had across all civilizations at some point in their history. It is not, for example, found within the Venette Convention (and never was). Neither is it to be found on Ab-Tzenketh.

On Ab-Tzenketh, as experts such as Neta Efheny or Peter Alden could tell you, enforcement relies less on inducing terror than on maintaining compliance. Tzenkethi remain docile, they would tell you, because they feel content. On Ab-Tzenketh, a ritualized display of force serves little purpose. It would not make people feel happy. It would not make them feel loved. It would only make them feel afraid, and frightened people dream of escape. That is not what the Autarch wants for his servants. Who would want to escape from Ab-Tzenketh, where one's function is clear and life is so beautiful and so safe?

Take this particular situation unfolding now. The two enforcers in the air car hovering above the Ata tenement on the far side of Velentur Lagoon could, if they chose, switch on sirens, set searchlights flaring, lower their car into the courtyard with the screech of high-grade entimium gears (enforcer air cars are state of the art), and, as a result, the whole surrounding area would be shocked from its slumber and lie awake in terror. But that is not what they want to achieve. All they want is the removal of the individual currently sleeping in a seventh-level billet.

So, instead, they drop the air car's lights and put the engine into a low-power mode. They descend into the small courtyard with a gentle, almost soundless *whoomph*. Before leaving the car, they dim their silvery flesh tones to a dull iron. Naturally, they check their weapons. They are not fools. They know the danger that their target might pose.

They cross the courtyard silently to the correct stairwell. They use their master codes to find and unseal the entrance. They pass like ghosts upstairs. At the door to the target's billet, they pause to check what is within. It is like many other billets in this district: there is the seating space, the holoviewer, the heater, the gravity pocket on the anterior deck where some personal possessions are stacked, the bed, with its sole occupant fast asleep after the day's labors. There are no surprises. Unsealing the door, they enter quickly and without fuss. The occupant, waking suddenly, cries out, but they are already there to muffle the sound. The contents of a hypospray are used to make the occupant unconscious, whereupon the comatose body is carried downstairs (this is the most awkward part) and secured in the back of the air car. The car lifts noiselessly, and not long afterward, the enforcers deliver their charge to the basement of the Department of the Outside, where numerous people are very eager to ask this particular individual numerous questions.

An efficiently executed, almost routine job, carried out by experienced people. And if anyone nearby heard a thing, and consequently felt fear, he did not call it that but instead reminded himself how much the Autarch must love his people to bless them with enforcers whose function was to keep his servants safe and sleeping.

Day two of talks with the Venetans got off to an equally rocky start. Not because of anything Detrek was doing but because of her absence. The Venetans in the room muttered away, but Rusht sat silently in her seat, her expression becoming more severe and remote with every passing minute. Vitig exchanged a few quiet words with Alizome and then also sat and waited in quiet and dignified silence.

Crusher eased forward in her seat and tapped Picard on the shoulder. "What's going on? Where is she?"

"I wish I knew."

"Want me to go and ask Dygan?"

They glanced across the table to where Dygan and the other Cardassian juniors sat huddled together, whispering.

"I'm not sure he knows much more than we do."

After about fifteen minutes, Rusht slowly began to gather up her data files. The assembled Venetans indicated their approval. The cheerful and friendly Venetan from the previous day leaned over to Crusher and said, "She's not going out of her way to win any friends, is she?"

On the whole, Crusher agreed. And when, three minutes later, Detrek did finally put in an appearance, her demeanor was hardly that of someone who wanted to apologize for her tardiness in arriving for a critical set of talks. She strode into the room, a padd in one hand, and pushed her way magisterially through the crowd to get to her place. She didn't sit down. She stayed standing and looked around the room witheringly. The buzz of Venetan dislike rose, peaked, and then simmered down.

"I'm glad I have your full attention," Detrek said.

Crusher's heart went out briefly to Dygan, who seemed to be shrinking into his chair at every word.

"And I hope that the whole of your convention is listening to this." Detrek held up her padd. "I have been in conversation with my government this morning. The observers we sent to Outpost V-15 reported back last night. Based on their observations, and information supplied to us by . . . *alternative* sources here on Venette, we are in no doubt that Outpost V-15 is being fitted out for military use—"

Picard started. "Has she quite lost her senses?"

Crusher put her hand over her mouth. Had she heard that correctly? Alternative sources? Had Detrek all but come out and said that the Cardassian Intelligence Bureau was operating within the Venette Convention?

The whole room was in an uproar. Detrek's voice grew louder to compensate for the racket. "This is an *outrage,* Rusht!" she cried. "We came to your world in good faith. We have no history of disagreement with you, and this is how you choose to repay us—"

Rusht rose from her chair, a tall woman with at least as much steel in her as in her Cardassian accuser.

The room fell silent, and yet Crusher was left in no doubt of the respect in which the Venetans held this woman, and of their trust that she would know how to respond on behalf of them all.

"I shall not dignify your accusations by asking you to prove them, Detrek," she said softly, and the room agreed with her. "You were indeed invited here in good faith, but from the moment you entered this room, you have done nothing but demonstrate yourself unworthy of any trust." She leaned down to speak quickly to Vitig and then looked over to Alizome, who nodded. "We shall not continue with this," she said. "Not while you and your contingent remain in this room."

She turned to leave. Vitig followed, and Alizome, uncoiling from her place, took up the rear. The Venetans cheered and stamped their feet in support of the delegates, and booed loudly when Detrek strode out of the room. Over the noise, Crusher could hear Jeyn curse.

"That's it," Picard said. "Detrek's effectively removed herself from these negotiations. If we're going to keep on talking to the Venetans, it will be without the Cardassians here."

"Akaar is going to hit the roof," Jeyn said.

Picard pulled himself out of his seat. "I'm going to speak to Dygan, get him assigned back to the Federation mission. I think we're going to need him more than ever now. Jeyn, see if you can get to see Detrek. We need to meet with her about this at once. Damn it, she could have warned us about this!"

He went around the table to where a shell-shocked

Dygan was sitting. Crusher, standing up to go speak to Ilka, felt a tap on her arm. It was the friendly Venetan.

"You need to find some better friends!" he said, and Crusher very nearly found herself agreeing with him.

The backroom negotiations got nowhere. Rusht confirmed what Picard had guessed: the Venetans were no longer willing to speak to the Cardassians. Detrek had gone too far, and not even an apology was likely to make Rusht agree to speak to her again. Detrek, meanwhile, had shut her doors and was, seemingly, in conference with her castellan. And the day was not over yet.

Captain Dax contacted the *Enterprise* to brief them on the presence of the P96 solvents and their significance in relation to navithium resin.

Picard frowned. "Navithium resin?"

"It's a substance deadly to humans," Crusher said. There was a cold, horrible sensation in her stomach, as if she was suddenly carrying a great weight. "It's used in bioweapons."

"*Bioweapons?* Dax, you haven't found some of this substance on Outpost V-4?"

Dax shook her head. "*No, and that's my problem. Yes, there's the presence of the stabilizing compounds. Yes, the Venetans have confirmed that the Tzenkethi have asked if they can stock certain 'resinous compounds' on the base. Yes, there's a large medical facility being run by Tzenkethi who could all be bioweapons experts for all I know. And yes, the base is being refitted to cope with large*

Tzenkethi ships. Whether these will be merchant freighters or warships, your guess is as good as mine."

"That's a great deal of evidence," Picard said. "But all circumstantial."

"Exactly. Every single element is innocuous by itself. But put it all side by side and it looks horrifically like the Tzenkethi are intending to put bioweapons along the Venetan border with Federation space. And given what Detrek said earlier, I don't think they'll be stopping with our border. This could affect most of the powers in the Khitomer Accords."

Bioweapons. On three borders. It was too easy, Crusher realized, to imagine the horrors that could follow. Far too easy. *We've seen too much in these last years.*

"But what does your mission specialist have to say about all this?" Picard asked. "What's his opinion?" A pause followed Picard's question. He frowned. "Captain Dax, what does Commander Alden have to say?"

Dax sighed. *"This is very difficult, Captain, and what I'm about to tell you I'm saying in the strictest confidence. Again, I have no evidence, but . . ."*

"Go on."

"I've got serious doubts about Peter Alden."

"Doubts?" Picard said in alarm. "About his loyalty?"

"No, no, nothing like that. About his judgment. He's certainly suffering from stress—"

"If we weren't suffering from stress after the last

few years," Crusher said softly, "we'd all be very ill indeed."

"This is something else."

Crusher looked at Dax in sympathy. "Just say it, Dax. It might turn out not to be true, but you've got to put it out there. You know it won't go farther than us."

"I think it might be possible—just possible, mind you—that he's suffering from a mild form of paranoia. I mean where the Tzenkethi are concerned. I can't say for sure, my counselor hasn't interviewed him at all, but . . ." Dax shook her head. *"Something isn't right. I can't entirely trust his judgment where the Tzenkethi are concerned. He sees a threat where there might not necessarily be any."*

"And he therefore presumably believes that the evidence is not circumstantial but definitive proof," Picard said.

"That's right."

"But is it not possible, Dax," said Picard, "that despite any irrational response on Commander Alden's part to the Tzenkethi around him, his assessment of the situation may be correct?"

"Of course it's possible. It's also possible that he's wrong. You've met the Venetans now, Captain. Do you think they want to rain bioweapons down on us?"

"No," Picard said immediately. "No. I think they are angry with us, and that they are often confused or even shocked by us, but I don't believe they have murderous intent."

"Nor do I. The Venetan I'm dealing with here, Heldon, she's intelligent, aware, principled, sometimes she's even friendly. Like anybody rational, she's appalled at the thought of biological warfare."

"Which leaves us stuck," said Picard. "Either we accuse the Tzenkethi outright of intending to weaponize Outpost V-4—"

"In which case we no doubt find ourselves thrown out of negotiations like Detrek," said Crusher.

"Indeed. Or else we wait for something else to happen that gives us grounds to make this accusation."

"While any preparations that *are* being made to weaponize Outpost V-4 continue unhindered," Crusher concluded. "Jean-Luc, we have to stop this."

"How, Beverly? What firm evidence do I have?"

The chime of Dax's combadge prevented their discussion going any further. They heard her exchange a few brief words, and then she turned back to them, looking serious.

"Captain?" said Picard.

"You know that 'something else' we were worried might happen? I think it's happening. That was my XO. He's just informed me that our long-range sensors have picked up twelve Tzenkethi merchant ships en route to Venetan space. They're twelve days from crossing the border and fourteen from arriving at Outpost V-4. Call me suspicious, but I have a feeling that's the navithium resin on its way."

"Twelve days before crossing the border," said Picard. "And slightly more than a fortnight before the Tzenkethi Coalition might have the capability to assemble bioweapons and launch them at Starbase 261. And from there . . ."

Crusher put her hand on his arm. "From there, on into Federation space."

Week 2

Confrontations

7

FROM:
Civilian Freighter *Inzitran*, flagship, Merchant Fleet 9

TO:
Ementar Vik Tov-A, senior designated speaker, Active Affairs, Department of the Outside

STATUS:
Estimated time to border: 23 skyturns
Estimated time to destination: 28 skyturns

Instruments indicate that the fleet has been scanned by long-range detectors.

FROM:
Captain Ezri Dax, *U.S.S. Aventine*

TO:
Admiral Leonard Akaar, Starfleet Command

STATUS OF TZENKETHI FLEET:
ETA at Venetan border: 11 days
ETA at Outpost V-4: 13 days

Picture embassies on red alert. Analysts and policy makers and specialists up to their necks in data and up to their eyeballs in stimulants, trying to see some sort of pattern through the mist. Picture tired and fractious people trying to second-guess what other tired and fractious people are doing. Frightened politicians shouting for answers before they make decisions that are going to have consequences for millions. Picture being the one tasked to come up with the answer. Picture getting it wrong.

The problem is, you can't know the whole of other people's minds. You can't know whether they're being frank, or dissembling, or clueless, or triangulated somewhere in between. In the end, you have to make a judgment call. Do you believe what they say? Or do you think they're lying? What do you do when your allies are causing as much trouble as your enemies?

Whom can you trust?

At last, after several hours spent (presumably) in conference with her government, Detrek indicated her readiness to speak to her allies. She came to the private suite in the Hall of Assembly that the Federation delegates were using as their conference room. The fountain was working now—a steady, gentle bubble of water that Crusher could only hope would have a soothing effect on the quarreling allies.

Detrek was not late for this meeting, Crusher noted. She arrived at the Federation suite on the dot, her aides and Dygan following anxiously behind her. Crusher gave the unhappy-looking glinn a small wave, her hand close to her body. Dygan returned the gesture and gave her a rather sad smile.

Detrek didn't waste any time getting down to business, nor did she seem particularly contrite about blowing their negotiations out of the water.

"My government is very clear that this insult is unacceptable. To refuse to speak to us? Completely unreasonable!"

"Nonetheless," Picard said mildly, "the Venetans do seem to believe that the possible presence of spies among them is a grave insult in turn. Perhaps some form of words can be found that will allow the Venetans to feel that they have received an apology—"

"An *apology*?" Detrek shook her head vehemently. "Captain, *we* are the injured parties here, not the Venetans!" She eyed her colleagues one by one. "You are our allies. What do you intend to do about this?"

"Negotiator Detrek," said Jeyn, rather impatiently for a diplomat, Crusher thought, "what do you imagine we are able to do? You seem to have gone out of your way to offend our hosts at every opportunity!"

Ouch, thought Crusher. The water of the fountain bubbled blithely in the silence.

Ilka shifted uneasily in her chair. "I think what

Ambassador Jeyn means to say is that we have not, perhaps, presented the most united front—"

"I know what Ambassador Jeyn meant to say," Detrek replied. "That the only surprise is that the Venetans didn't throw me out of the room sooner? That's it, isn't it, Jeyn?"

Picard lifted his hand. "Negotiator, please! We achieve nothing by quarreling among ourselves other than to serve the purposes of those who seek to sow discord among us. You have come to us because we represent governments allied to your own. I agree that nothing is gained by your absence from these discussions, and I would prefer to have you alongside us. We all hope for a peaceful resolution to this crisis, and we hope that this is your desire too."

Crusher leaned forward. "We're all on the same side, Negotiator. We all want to do what's best. We want to strengthen our alliances, not strain them. What do you want from us?"

"A show of loyalty, Doctor," Detrek said. "A statement, in the strongest possible terms, that our friends in the Federation and Ferengi Alliance find this insult to their ally unacceptable, and they require our return to the negotiating table."

Frankly, Crusher thought, *I think she doesn't have a chance.* A quick glance at her husband suggested that he was thinking much the same. But he just sighed and tugged down his uniform.

"We'll certainly do our best, Detrek," Picard said.

Detrek slowly exhaled. Perhaps the sound of running water was beginning to have the desired effect.

"I appreciate, Captain," Detrek said in a much calmer voice, "all that you have done for me throughout this mission."

"Thank you," said Picard. "Now, these Tzenkethi ships approaching the Venetan border near Outpost V-4 are a further worry, but they may also provide us with the means of applying pressure to the Venetans. As long as our questions about what exactly the Tzenkethi are delivering to Outpost V-4 remain unanswered, we can try to insist upon your continued participation in our discussions." He frowned. "But don't expect miracles, Detrek."

Which was, Crusher thought, exactly how Jean-Luc would say: *Not a chance.*

Rusht agreed to meet Picard and Crusher in the atrium in the Hall of Assembly, where the Federation mission had materialized only a couple of days before. It was public space, with people passing through all the time, and a small family was sitting nearby when the three of them took their seats. Three parents and a little girl who did not look much older than René. She stopped playing with her blocks to stare curiously at the Federation officers. Crusher gave her a little wave.

"Hey, sweetie!" she said. The little girl frowned, and then gave Crusher a gorgeous grin. One of her parents, seeing the exchange, put a protective arm around her. All three adults listened to the conversation that followed quite openly. *Jean-Luc would surely prefer this meeting to be in private,* Crusher thought. *But does Rusht even have a private office? Do all such sensitive meetings happen in such public places?*

"These medical supplies en route to Outpost V-4," Picard said quietly. "They are a grave concern to us—"

Rusht tutted. "Heldon has explained this to Dax," she said. "They are necessary for the Tzenkethi stationed there. I do not understand why you keep returning to this, Picard. Again and again we've said that there is nothing suspicious about the cargo these ships are carrying. Each time you come back to this matter, you are, in effect, calling me a liar—"

Crusher, recalling Dax's notes on her interactions with Heldon, and how an almost naïve honesty seemed the best approach, said quickly, "We have your assurances, yes. But we're still afraid. Some of the resins associated with these solvents are particularly dangerous for humans—"

Rusht waved her hand impatiently, angrily, even. "Yes, yes, this too has been said, Crusher. I was puzzled the first time it was said, and when I understood the implication, I was horrified. What kind of people do you think we are? Do you think that we would use or permit the use of bioweapons against other species? We are not *monsters,* Crusher!"

The little girl watching opened her mouth into a wide *oh!* She turned and buried her face in the lap of one of her parents. Her parent picked her up and cuddled her, shushing her, and giving the humans an admonishing look.

Crusher tried to keep her voice soft. "I know that, Rusht. But we have responsibilities—"

"And," Rusht continued over her, "we have not yet received a satisfactory explanation from the Cardassians of what Detrek meant by her 'alternative sources.' We reject utterly the claim that the base is being turned over to military use. Until we are shown the evidence that Detrek claims to have, and receive a full explanation as to how she obtained it, I cannot see how we could welcome the Cardassians back to the table—"

The portable comm on Rusht's lap buzzed. She read the message and then looked at Crusher and Picard. Her face was very serious. "We must return to the hall. Alizome informs me that she's received some urgent news and wishes to address the gathering."

What could possibly have happened now? Crusher wondered, as the three of them made their silent and somber way back to the hall. *Why are we constantly being caught out like this?*

The mood in the hall was equally subdued. The gathering seemed to sense that something was afoot, and Rusht's expression only seemed to confirm it. She took her place in silence, and then Alizome Vik Tov-A rose to address the company.

She was an impressive sight as she uncoiled her strong and radiant body and placed her hands upon the table. Her voice was sonorous and yet seemed to Crusher like the clang of a warning bell.

"My friend Rusht," she said. "Thank you for gathering all our visitors together." She glanced over at Detrek's conspicuously empty seat. "*Almost* all our visitors . . ."

Ouch again, thought Crusher. Really, Alizome was in danger of showing the Venetans how much she enjoyed this.

"I have been in communication with my government," Alizome said. "It is my unfortunate task to inform you that a spy has been arrested on Tzenketh, in one of our major cities, engaged—as these people often are—in criminal activities designed to undermine the security of our people. The spy, I am sorry to say, is a Federation citizen."

Crusher's heart skipped a beat and then went out to the unlucky agent. She heard, rather than saw, Jean-Luc take a deep and steadying breath. The hush around the room was now almost tangible.

"This is a calculated insult to our people," Alizome said. "On behalf of our most exalted and beloved Rej, the beneficent Autarch himself, I must register our deep disgust and dismay at such a shocking revelation."

Oh, come off it, Alizome, Crusher thought impatiently. *You're laying this on far too thick. You know that we have spies on your world; we know that you have spies on our world. So why this performance?*

But even as Crusher thought this, the whole espionage business suddenly seemed like utter nonsense to her. *Why do we do this? Why do we carry on with these games? It's a kind of delusion. We pretend that we don't watch them; they pretend that they don't watch us. And when we discover each other's spies, we feign outrage. If René did this, I would tell him how silly he was being, how phony. When he got a little older, I'd tell him he was a hypocrite . . .*

Crusher glanced across the table at Ilka, expecting her too to be rolling her eyes. But Ilka's head was turned away from her. She was looking intently at Rusht. Crusher shifted in her seat to be able to look at her too.

It was a revelation. From Rusht's appalled expression, Crusher could see that the Venetan woman was genuinely shocked by this news.

But what did she expect? Crusher thought in bewilderment. *All right, so perhaps the news of the arrest came out of the blue, but she must have known that there would be Federation spies on Tzenketh. There'll be Cardassian spies, Klingon spies, Ferengi spies, who the hell knows what other spies! Not to mention all the ones from the Typhon Pact powers, keeping an eye on their allies. Don't we all know this about each other? Why is this news such a shock to her?*

A murmur was rising among the Venetans. Rusht rapped on the table for silence.

"This is very alarming news," she said. "I hardly know how to respond." She sat back in her chair, and the rest of the room waited silently to hear what she had to say. Crusher caught Ilka's eye. Yes, the Ferengi *was* thinking the same thing: *Why this amount of shock? Why is Rusht so surprised?*

At last Rusht spoke. Her voice was very quiet, as if she had been shaken. "All that I can do for the moment is express my bewilderment that anyone would choose to behave in such a way."

A gentle ripple of approval rose throughout the room. Rusht seemed to take heart from it. "I have to wonder why any person, or group of people, would choose to organize themselves in such a corrosive and counterproductive fashion. The idea that all the time we have been speaking, a Federation spy has been at work on the homeworld of our Tzenkethi friends is repulsive to me. Deeply repulsive."

"To me too, Rusht," Alizome said softly (and now Ilka did roll her eyes, although Alizome's words were evidently playing well with all the Venetans).

"Coupled with my belief that there has been a Cardassian spy on Venetan territory this whole time too," Rusht said, "I cannot see what can productively be said here, with such duplicity at work. I think it's only right that I close this session for the day."

She rose slowly from her seat. To Crusher's eyes, she seemed very old indeed, an ancient person who had not believed that the universe could hold any more surprises for her and had been unpleasantly proved wrong. Crusher had wild thoughts of Tzenkethi poisoners—but her long medical experience told her the real cause. Rusht had been profoundly shocked by this news. As the old woman left the room, every single Venetan present began to applaud, a furious applause that communicated not only their outrage but also the respect in which they held Rusht and their sense that she had spoken for them all. It was terrifying. *We've lost them,* Crusher thought. *We've lost them for good.*

Eager to press the case for a second visit to the medical facility on Outpost V-4, Dax took to the privacy of her ready room and opened a communication channel to Heldon. Bowers came with her. He sat on the opposite side of her desk, out of Heldon's view but able to hear everything.

Dax had something of a shock when Heldon finally appeared on-screen. The kindly, cheerful woman from their last encounter was gone, replaced by someone remote and angry. Whatever rapport had been established between them had disappeared. The gaps between them were suddenly shown to be immense; their different viewpoints seemed suddenly incommunicable.

"*I'm horrifed, Dax,*" Heldon said, "*at the idea that there might have been Cardassian spies on my world—that there might still be! I'm equally distressed to learn that there are Federation spies on Tzenketh.*"

Dax blinked at the screen. *But* are *you?* she thought. *Are you* really? Bowers too looked baffled by Heldon's reaction. Dax took a deep breath. Honesty: the best policy.

"In that case, I'm not sure what to say to you, Heldon. You know our history. Only twenty years ago, we were at war with them. Now they've allied themselves with powers that have long been hostile toward us."

"Yes, yes, and no doubt they could say the same about you."

"Well, yes, they could, so let's think about that. Did you really believe we wouldn't be trying to find out their intentions toward us? Did you seriously think that we could simply *ask* and get a straight answer?" She paused, then moved in for the kill: "Surely you realize that the Tzenkethi have been spying on us. *Are* spying on us."

Heldon pulled away in disgust. *"I haven't asked Entrigar. I wouldn't insult him in that way—"*

"Don't bother asking," Dax said bluntly. "I'm sure he'll be able to tell you with complete honesty that he knows nothing about any Tzenkethi operatives within the Federation, or within any of the Khitomer powers. I doubt he's been briefed with such information."

As she watched Heldon digest this, Dax thought back to the conversation she'd had with Alden the night that the *Aventine* had been redeployed to Outpost V-4. She took another breath and hoped that this wasn't pushing too hard. She glanced at Bowers, who nodded his encouragement. *Push on. Push harder.*

"Allies spy on each other; you know that, Heldon. In all likelihood there've been Tzenkethi operatives on your world for some time now. Observing you. Learning about you. Seeding ideas." She watched Heldon's face closely. "And doubts."

"Doubts?"

"Doubts about us."

Heldon shook her head. *"We already had doubts about you, Dax. About your reliability, your trustworthiness."*

"But you were not hostile toward us. Yet somehow what were straightforward doubts—and, yes, I admit, reasonable doubts, given how we failed to continue negotiations with you to enter into the Federation—somehow these reasonable doubts have turned into something that's brought you to the edge of outright war with us—"

Heldon recoiled at the word. *"We have no interest in war!"*

"Perhaps not. But war might have an interest in you."

There was a pause. Across the table, Bowers seemed to be holding his breath. *"Is that a threat, Dax?"*

"A threat?" Suddenly Dax felt all of her nine lives. She was weary, sick of this game and angry at how this conversation had to be. She liked Heldon, plain and simple, and yet they were talking as if they were on the verge of becoming enemies. "Of course it's not a threat. It's the truth. It's a hostile galaxy out there. Not everyone means me and my compatriots well."

"Now you sound like your colleague Alden."

Dax sat back in her chair. *Do I?*

"I am sure you're aware of this already," Heldon went on, *"but Peter Alden is a troubled man. His fearfulness, his suspicion, his sense of dread when our friends the Tzenkethi are around—and these even manifesting themselves as physical symptoms. Within the convention,*

people exhibit such symptoms only rarely, but when they do, those closest to them, who love them the most, don't shy away from telling them the truth about themselves. Peter Alden would be encouraged to put aside his day-to-day life. He would go away and rest for a while, relieve his mind of whatever worries are making him so fretful, so agitated, so out of kilter with the world." She shook her head sadly. "*Why is he here, Dax? Why was a man suffering like that allowed to come on a mission like this? Not only is it counterproductive, it is unkind.*"

Dax put her hands to her face and rubbed her forehead. "I've been asking myself the same question."

"*I thought maybe you had.*" Heldon paused for a moment to gather her thoughts before continuing. "*I've only been able to observe you for a few days, Dax, but it seems to me that there's a sickness gripping your Federation. A sickness caused by terrible fear . . .*"

"Well, it's been a difficult few years, Heldon."

"*I know that. And I'm afraid that the convention will learn this way of being from you.*" She stopped, catching her own words. "*Yes,*" she said. "*Already, I am afraid.*"

"I swear, it's not us you have to be afraid of."

"*Are you sure about that?*"

I'm not sure of anything right now, Dax thought. "Watch your back, Heldon," she said. She reached out to cut the comm, but before she did so, she took one last risk.

"I've liked dealing with you," Dax said frankly. "I think that in another time we could easily be friends. I really regret that time isn't now."

"So do I, Dax. So do I."

"Then please consider my request to come back to your medical facility and carry out further inspections. Consider why I might be asking you to let me do this. Consider why I have to ask you for proof. Why I can't just be satisfied with your word. Please try to put yourself in my place."

"I'll try. And I'll get back to you in due course."

The comm channel closed. "She's right about Alden," Bowers said.

You're just saying that because he snubbed you, Dax thought in irritation—then caught herself. *I'm seeing base motives everywhere. Even Sam—loyal, dependable Sam.*

"I'm afraid you may be right," she replied.

Twenty-three skyturns before her extraction was due to occur, Neta Efheny boarded a water shuttle bound for a set of well-known coral caverns that lay forty skims to the north of the city. They were a popular destination for Ata workers who had been granted time away to restore their bodies and thus apply themselves better to their functions when they returned. The caverns also happened to be close to Efheny's pickup point, chosen precisely because she could reasonably find a reason to be traveling that way but far enough from the cities to lie outside the main cover of the planetary security nets.

The journey to the caverns took a quarter of a skyturn. For most of the voyage the shuttle had to travel

across the open water of a large lagoon. The other Tzenkethi on the shuttle hid beneath the canopies covering
the decks designated for their use, chatting with their
companions. Most of them were Ata-Es who worked in
maintenance units like Efheny's, some of them in the
same building complex. The whole of the Department
of the Outside was now off-limits to anyone below
an Ata-B grade. The Ata-EEs had been redeployed to
other tasks, but everyone else had been granted restorative leave for the duration of the closure. Although
the break from work was a gift to Efheny, allowing her
a legitimate reason to travel to her pickup point, it also
unfortunately meant that when Còrazame asked if she
could accompany her to the caverns, Efheny couldn't
think of a good reason to say no. Still, Efheny didn't
doubt that it would be easy enough, when the time
came, to slip away from her friend and go off on her
own. And in the meantime, she would take these few
days to rest, like her workmates.

Near the end of their journey, the shuttle left the
lagoon and entered a narrow passageway that eventually came out into a complex of tiny roofed caverns. The
mood of the voyagers changed, becoming more cheerful and unrestrained. As the shuttle meandered through
the maze, the canopies were thrown back, and the holiday makers oohed and aahed at the intricate beauty of
the caves through which they were passing. The walls
were set with mosaics of stone and coral, and the daylight, entering through filters in the roof, refracted into
countless colors on the stonework and the ripples of the

water. In various discreet corners, they could glimpse Ata-EEs hard at work, reminding the travelers that they, at least, were free from their tasks for a while and reaffirming their sense of the order of things.

Efheny, sitting beside Corazame and trying hard not to think about what the next few days might bring, watched her fellow travelers with mixed feelings. *Do they not even wonder why they've been allowed this holiday? Or is that too much for them even to consider? Do they have to tell themselves all the time not to concern themselves with the business of superior grades, or is it purely instinct? Surely some of them must sense that there's something going on. That their whole diplomatic corps is in an uproar. Their empire could be at war for all they know. Even now, fleets could be massing at their borders, getting ready to invade, or their Rej could be making the decision that would send his own fleets out to invade someone else's territory . . .* But then, she reflected, most of them didn't even know that there were worlds beyond the Tzenkethi system. That information was reserved for grades higher than these Ata-E followers. Most of them knew only what they were told in their E-grade lessons and bulletins, what they needed to know in order to be able to perform their life tasks. But surely *some* of them must wonder if there was more.

Efheny knew that this puzzle lay at the heart of her fascination with the Tzenkethi. It was why she could happily sit and watch them forever. On the surface, everyone behaved as they were supposed to behave: said the right words in the right order, used the appropriate dialects, tempered the natural glows of their bodies to the appropriate hues and levels. But she never knew for sure whether they had entirely internalized these beliefs. It was a matter of endless speculation for her. If your function as a Tzenkethi didn't require much thought, did you then train yourself not to think? She knew that sometimes hours went by when all she had thought about was her deck work, whether she was wasting time or gel or nutrients, whether Karenzen or Hertome would be satisfied with her efforts, whether she would be praised or chastised. Did you forget to think? Or did you just pretend? Was everyone here pretending as much as she was?

Beside her, Corazame was singing softly to herself. Away from superiors, Corazame's skin was a beautiful radiant golden color that she was rarely able to reveal in her day-to-day life. *Even Cory, who on the surface seems a model Ata-E, has her secrets,* Efheny thought. *Even she carved a small space for herself that the screening and the tests and the enforcers couldn't find. And even after her love ended, the memory sustains her in some way.* She glanced around the deck. *But what about the rest of them? Do they have their secrets too?* Tired, worried, anxious about what the coming days might hold, Efheny suddenly felt envious of these happy, singing people. *I wish I could be like them. I wish I could switch myself off entirely, give myself over fully to this life. No more worries. Only do what I was told, day after day, never have to think again because I know someone is thinking* for *me . . .*

She realized that Corazame was no longer singing.

"Maymi," she murmured. "Look who's here."

Efheny looked up, then quickly dropped her gaze. Hertome Ter Ata-C was standing there, looking down at them both in amusement.

"Mayazan Ret Ata-E," he said. "And Corazame Ret Ata-E." At their names, they both gestured their thankfulness for his attention and then, when he signaled to them to remain seated, indicated their gratitude to be recipients of his consideration.

"Well," he said dryly, "what a *pleasant* surprise. I hope that you're both benefiting from this period of restoration that you've been granted? I hope you will return to your functions restored?"

"Very much, Ap-Rej," said Corazame, who had dimmed her skin again to her customary deferential hue. "This one offers her Ap-Rej thanks for his kind interest and assures him of her desire to use her time here to the best of her ability."

"This one too," said Efheny, "offers her Ap-Rej gratitude for his interest. She gives assurances of benefiting from the time she has been granted here."

There was a pause. Corazame sat with her hands folded and her eyes down, and Efheny did the same. "Ret Mayazan," said Hertome at last, adopting a form of words that reaffirmed his status and implied a forthcoming admonishment, "you must come with me."

Obediently, Efheny rose and followed him at a respectful distance, her head bowed and her hands tucked behind her back. She heard some of the other travelers murmur at the sight of them, perhaps wondering what the Ret had been doing to attract the attention of a Ter. Glancing back briefly over her shoulder, she saw Corazame give her an agonized look, and she made her skin emit a soothing pulse. *Hush, Cory. Don't worry about me.*

Hertome led her to a quieter part of the boat. When they were out of earshot, Efheny gestured her submission and her willingness to please. "How might this one assist her Ap-Rej?"

"Will you drop this crap?" Hertome said roughly. "We don't have time for these games anymore. There's something going on. Something big. Something serious. You're leaving, aren't you?"

Efheny did not reply. She hung her head and stared at the floor, hoping that any observer would see an unsatisfactory Ret receiving correction and instruction from an Ap-Rej.

"One of my colleagues has been arrested," Hertome said. "I think the Tzenkethi are going to close our embassy. They've expelled four diplomats already, and I think they're going to expel everyone. I can't get through to anyone. And if I can't get through to anyone soon, I'll be stuck here for who knows how long. I can't stay here much longer, Mayazan. It's driving me mad!"

He cut himself off quickly. Efheny said nothing, only wished that she could close her ears to everything that he was saying. What if she was taken? The only defense was to know nothing. She fixed her eyes on a rivet in the floor of the boat.

"You're leaving, aren't you?" he said again. "That's why you've come up here. You've got to take me with you. If they've got one of us, there's a chance the whole network will be rolled up, and it won't be long before my cover's blown." He paused. When he spoke again, his voice was low and stripped of the dry humor that had hitherto laced all his exchanges with her. "I'm desperate, Mayazan."

The walls and roof of the cavern now felt uncomfortably close. Efheny stared down at the ground. If she didn't listen, she wouldn't know what he was saying. She wouldn't have to *think* about what he was saying.

"But I can see that doesn't matter to you, does it?" he said. "You'll play by the book and do your duty and damn the consequences for anyone else. You know, I'm amazed you want to leave here. You've got no more initiative than that stupid little floor scrubber who's always dangling at your elbow. You fit right into this damned place! But you have to understand that the choice isn't really yours." He gripped her wrist. She shuddered. "Make no mistake about it, Mayazan, you *are* going to take me with you. Because if I go down, you're going down with me."

He took hold of her chin and, deliberately, lifted her face so that she could not help but look straight at him, at his too alien eyes. He gave her a small, sour smile. "Let's face it," he said, "isn't that what being allies is all about?"

8

FROM:
Civilian Freighter *Inzitran,* flagship, Merchant Fleet 9

TO:
Ementar Vik Tov-A, senior designated speaker,
Active Affairs, Department of the Outside

STATUS:
Estimated time to border: 20 skyturns
Estimated time to destination: 25 skyturns

Instruments indicate continued program of long-range scans.

FROM:
Captain Ezri Dax, *U.S.S. Aventine*

TO:
Admiral Leonard Akaar, Starfleet Command

STATUS OF TZENKETHI FLEET:
ETA at Venetan border: 10 days
ETA at Outpost V-4: 12 days

Beverly Crusher drew back the blinds and looked across the Venetan capital. It was night. The sky was an inky blue, dotted with unfamiliar constellations, and she could see no moon. Did this world even have a moon? She was ashamed that she did not know. There was so little, really, that she knew about the Venetans. So little any of them knew. She had come on this mission believing that they could soon bring the Venetans back to their former friendship with the Federation, partly because she believed in Jean-Luc's skill in forging bonds with other cultures, and partly because she believed that they would soon be persuaded of the reasonableness of the Federation's requests. But at every turn, they had misspoken and miscommunicated, and now were barely speaking at all. Was this some Tzenkethi influence that she had been unable to detect? Or had they completely misunderstood the Venetans?

Take this city, although "city" was not the right word for it at all. No skyscrapers, no great roads cutting through, no bustle of nighttime traffic or the sudden scream of sirens. Instead, skeins of lamps running along the hillsides lit thoroughfares curving through quiet leafy districts. There was the gentle whisper of the river that wound through the valley and, distantly, the faint echo of a late-night tram rattling toward its terminus. Otherwise, everyone slept. But the calm was illusory—or, at the very least, fragile.

Except here, Crusher thought, hearing her husband and Jeyn in quiet conversation behind her. Here, in this room, time was running out. Here, two Starfleet officers and a Federation ambassador struggled to find a way to keep everyone talking before the chance to talk was lost for good.

Crusher drew the blind. There were no answers out there, only more puzzles. With a sigh, she walked back across the room and stood watching the gentle play of the fountain.

"You've been deep in thought, Beverly," Picard said. "Have you come to any conclusions?"

"Here's the problem as I see it," she said. "The Venetans, for whatever cultural reasons, simply hadn't considered the possibility that we might all be spying on each other. Put that way, it does seem crazy, but it's what happens, and it's what they're taking exception to. I don't know why it never occurred to them before, but it seems it didn't."

"They're a quiet and neighborly society," Jeyn said. "A society built on continuity and stability, and fairly isolationist for much of their history. Long-lived too. I bet there aren't many secrets here. If you and your neighbors know each other well, why spy on each other?"

"Then there's their somewhat disconcerting tendency toward complete frankness in their interpersonal relationships," Picard added. "Truth telling might lead to an open society, but it does make diplomacy surprisingly difficult." He gave a short bark of laughter. "You think they'd like Detrek rather more than they do."

Crusher sat on the arm of the couch next to him. "Ah, but they think Detrek is blustering," she said. "They think all the noise is covering over something."

"Who knows?" said Jeyn. "It might well be. I'm at a loss to make sense of her aggression otherwise. One cannot—one *should* not—say that it's simply how Cardassians are. For one thing, it's not true. I've dealt with many subtle individuals from their worlds."

"And yet despite our own desire for friendship," said Crusher, "we have somehow managed to convince the Venetans that we are hypocritical liars paranoid enough to spy on the Tzenkethi and ally ourselves with another set of paranoiacs who have been spying on them in turn."

"Put that way," Jeyn said, "it's hardly surprising the Venetans haven't warmed to us. But you hit upon the heart of the problem, Beverly: the Tzenkethi. Now that, surely, *is* a suspicious culture. Mistrustful of anything beyond its borders. It's late enough and I am frustrated enough that I would even go so far as to call them xenophobic."

Picard frowned. "Certainly they are hostile. But we know relatively little of the Tzenkethi as a whole."

"We know that they are prepared to feign outrage at the presence of Federation spies on their homeworld," said Jeyn.

"Unfortunately, I believe we would also be guilty

of that if it suited our purposes," said Picard. "However, it's sufficient to make the Venetans pull down the shutters and refuse to speak to any of us."

Jeyn sighed. "Beverly, what of your own mission? Can you shed any light on this uncharacteristic hostility?"

"No," Crusher said. "And, if I'm being frank, I'm increasingly at a loss to understand why the admiral insisted I came on this mission. How exactly can I test for biochemical influences in any meaningful way? The usual checks on food and water have thrown up nothing. So what am I supposed to do? I can hardly stop people in the street and ask them to submit to a medical exam. And before you say anything," she raised a finger to stop Jeyn speaking, "I won't scan in secret. For one thing, it's unethical. For another, if I was caught, it would only reinforce the Venetans' belief that we're duplicitous liars." She shook her head in frustration. "I don't understand why Akaar sent me here."

"And we're beginning to run out of time," Jeyn said. "Those ships are on their way to Outpost V-4, and we still have no real idea what's on them. We need to get the Venetans talking again. To us and to the Cardassians. Because, given their current antagonistic stance, my feeling is that should the Cardassians detect any Tzenkethi merchant ships moving toward the Venetan base on *their* borders, they're not going to wait to find out whether they're carrying medical supplies or candy or enough biomimetic gel to kill every

Cardassian on Prime. They're going to scream into Venetan space. And then . . ."

"And then we're at war," Crusher said softly. "Again." *And with biogenic weapons.* She stood up and paced the room, trying to suppress her revulsion at the thought.

The room fell silent. At last, Jeyn spoke. "We need to get the Cardassians and the Venetans talking again. But how can this be achieved? I can't see either Rusht or Vitig being willing to talk to Detrek."

"What about Dygan?" Crusher said. "He's the link between us all. He's worked alongside us on the *Enterprise,* which associates him with us as much as with Detrek, whom he barely knows. Yes, I know we're not exactly flavor of the month with the Venetans, but at least we haven't been spying on them." She raised her eyes upward. "Well, they haven't discovered any Federation spies here," she said. "I'm not even going to speculate what might happen if they did. But if they won't speak to Detrek, they might speak to Dygan."

Picard said, "And as long as they're speaking to someone, there's still a chance that we can find a way through all of this."

Dygan arrived at the door of their suite within minutes of receiving the message from the captain. He looked doubtful when Picard explained how they hoped he would be able to help, but he immediately offered his services.

"Of course if you think I can help, Captain, then

I'll most certainly try," he said. "But I'm not sure a Cardassian face is what the Venetans want to see right now—"

"We have to try, Dygan," said Picard. "Somehow, we have to keep on talking to each other." He turned to Crusher. "Beverly, I want you to go with him."

"Me? Jean-Luc, I think this needs someone more experienced at negotiations—"

"No. If Jeyn or I go, it will appear by sending our front-line negotiators that we are backing down. But sending you—a senior Starfleet officer—will make clear to the Venetans that we are taking this meeting very seriously." He squeezed her hand quickly. "You'll be fine. Keep it simple. Remember that you're there as a diplomat, not as a doctor. All you need to communicate is that we want peace, but we also need proof that Outpost V-4 is not about to become a threat to us."

Crusher was not entirely convinced that the nuances of Federation diplomatic hierarchy meant much to the Venetans, but it seemed simple enough when he said it. So when she and Dygan arrived at the atrium, she was dismayed to see that Vitig had brought Alizome Vik Tov-A.

"I thought this was to be a private meeting," Crusher said warily.

"The Tzenkethi are our friends," Vitig said, sounding exactly like a parent becoming impatient with a willful child. "We have no secrets from them. I would tell Alizome everything that happens here. Why then should she simply not attend the meeting herself?"

Crusher was appalled. *Nothing gets past Alizome.*

"Besides, her people have been offended by you as much as we have been offended by the Cardassians."

"You speak truly as ever, my friend Vitig," Alizome said quietly and graciously.

"But come, Ravel Dygan," said Vitig. "You wished to speak to me."

Dygan nervously cleared his throat and stepped forward. He lifted his hand, palm forward, in the traditional Cardassian manner, a friendly and respectful gesture. Vitig, to Crusher's surprise, responded correctly, pressing her palm against his. She seemed amused by Dygan but not in an unkindly fashion. Again, Crusher was left with the impression of someone very old watching children at play.

"Dygan," said Vitig, "you find yourself in a difficult position, do you not? You're caught between friendship to your Starfleet colleagues and loyalties to your homeworld's representatives. None of us would care to find ourselves in such a predicament. But the way that you have conducted yourself during your time on this world has impressed us greatly. We are prepared to hear what you have to say."

Dygan blinked. Crusher too was surprised. The Venetans had shown no sign of paying much attention to the junior members of the various deputations. How did they know so much about Dygan? They couldn't be *spying* on them, could they?

Crusher shook herself. That was impossible. For the Venetans to engage in such a degree of underhandedness while managing a seemingly genuine display of horror at the thought of Cardassian spies walking among them would imply a degree of psychosis that she didn't want to contemplate. And Crusher was as sure as she could be that with the Venetans, what you saw was what you got. There would be nothing more behind Vitig's knowledge of Dygan than the fact that the Venetans paid equal attention to everyone, regardless of title or function. It was to their credit, rather than something to arouse suspicion. *But suspicion is too easily aroused at the moment . . .*

Dygan again cleared his throat. Vitig gave him an encouraging smile.

"I'll try not to waste your time, Vitig," Dygan said. "I'm from a culture that enjoys word games and wordplay, and that likes to leave meaning in the gaps between words, but I don't think that will go down well here."

Vitig nodded, and Dygan seemed to gain a little confidence.

"What I want to say is that it seems to me that we've misjudged you at every turn, Vitig, and it's my belief—I'm speaking for myself, you understand," he said hastily, "not my government—that we've represented ourselves in the worst possible light. We're a people with a troubled past. I'm sure that you know this." Vitig nodded again. "Not too long ago, we brought ourselves to the brink of destruction, and since then we've been learning to do things differently. We're still learning, and sometimes we make mistakes.

But our hearts"—he gave a small smile and tapped his chest—"are in the right place."

Vitig smiled back at him. "And what about the leader of your mission? Is it your opinion that her heart is in the right place?"

Crusher watched Dygan turn a slightly paler gray. "I'm afraid I don't know the negotiator very well."

Vitig's smile deepened and her eyes were warmed by the slight amusement Crusher had seen before. "Your people chose strangely when they delegated her to speak for them here. They'd have been wiser to choose you."

"Me?" Dygan looked genuinely startled. "I'm just a glinn—"

Vitig fell back in her chair. "Oh, these titles that you give each other and take upon yourselves! It's as if you *believe* in them. Believe that they define you, rather than define a function that you perform. Whatever a 'glinn' might be supposed to do," she said, "Ravel Dygan, I think, speaks truthfully and honestly, and with the desire to do good rather than harm. Yes, your government chose the wrong negotiator."

She favored Dygan with a full smile. Dygan ducked his head. Crusher, sitting quietly next to him, bit her lip and hoped . . .

"Yet his government makes many such strange choices," Alizome said suddenly, from her corner. Crusher saw the fur on Vitig's arms rise ever so slightly.

"What do you mean by that?" she said.

Alizome stepped forward. She moved like liquid,

Crusher thought, every step flowing as if her whole body was in motion, and her skin shimmered silvery-blue like moonlight on the water of a lagoon. "I can think of many unfortunate appointments made by the Cardassian government, even in recent years, when, according to Glinn Dygan, his people have been trying to make amends for their former crimes."

"Such as?" Vitig frowned. "You must be specific, Alizome. Implication and insinuation serve none of us, and do us no credit either."

"Such as the Cardassian ambassador to Earth."

A pause. *Hell,* thought Crusher.

"Go on," Vitig said quietly.

"The Cardassian ambassador to Earth was once a member of the Obsidian Order," said Alizome. "I know that your convention has kept itself distanced from the affairs of the wider quadrant, Vitig, but I believe *that* name is familiar to you."

Vitig rose from her chair. She took a few paces around the atrium, which was quiet and empty this late at night. "Yes," she said after a while. "Yes, it is. And the Federation has seen fit to welcome such a person as a suitable ambassador to their world. Crusher, do you deny this?"

"No," Crusher said simply. "I don't. I can't. But I would say that everyone deserves a second chance." *That was weak,* she thought as she said it, and she saw Alizome's skin glitter ever so slightly. *Amusement, Alizome? Or triumph?*

"How do you know that Ambassador Garak was

once a member of the Obsidian Order?" asked Crusher, more out of curiosity than in challenge. "That was a very secretive organization, after all."

Alizome gave her a pitying look. "We know the ambassador of old, Doctor Crusher."

Vitig turned back but did not return to her chair. "I think that you should leave now," she said. "I have nothing else to say to you tonight, Beverly Crusher." She glanced at Dygan. "Ravel Dygan, I hope that you will take no sense of personal failure from how this meeting has ended. But I would advise you to reflect upon whether the people you choose to serve deserve your service. Please," she said again, "leave now."

Silently, Crusher and Dygan left the atrium. Dygan looked stunned. "I'm . . . not sure I quite understand what just happened then, Doctor," he said, when the door to the room closed behind them.

They walked slowly along the corridor. *What happened was that we were stitched up,* Crusher thought angrily. *We skipped in there like a couple of amateurs and Alizome sent us packing. This wouldn't have happened to Jean-Luc, or Jeyn—or Chen. Why am I here?*

"We were outclassed," she said shortly and, seeing Dygan's glum expression, she patted his arm. "Not your fault. I wasn't expecting Alizome to be there." But, Crusher thought, she *should* have expected Alizome to be there. It was clear to her that Alizome was the one controlling events, and she, Jeyn, and Picard combined seemed unable to find a way to counter her moves. Tzenkethi plans for Venette had been laid long ago, Crusher suspected. The Federation and its allies had been invited along only to participate in the endgame.

They came to the door of Dygan's quarters. He hesitated before going inside. "I hope you'll pass on my sincere apologies to Captain Picard," he said quietly.

"What? Dygan, you have *nothing* to apologize for. If anything, I should apologize to you. I wasn't prepared, and I took you in there with me—"

"Nevertheless," said Dygan.

"What I'll tell Captain Picard," Crusher said, "is that you behaved impeccably, and that you're a credit to your uniform and your people."

That seemed to cheer him up a little. "Thank you, Doctor Crusher. Good night."

He went into his quarters. Crusher hurried back to their suite. Both Jeyn and Picard looked up at her hopefully.

"No good," she said flatly.

Jeyn's shoulders slumped. "Then what now? They won't talk to the Cardassians, they'll barely talk to us. Who else is there?"

"There's still someone," said Picard, "someone with whom you've made a particular connection these past few days, Beverly."

"Of course." Crusher snapped her fingers. "Ilka!"

Heldon at last got back in touch. Dax took the message in her ready room. She left Bowers on the bridge. She was increasingly uneasy about having another present and unacknowledged during these encounters with Heldon, as if she was violating some trust. Besides, the whole conversation was being recorded.

"Heldon," she said. "Can we come and inspect your medical facility again?"

"I am prepared for you and one other—your doctor, perhaps—to come across again, Dax. But I have one condition."

"Fire ahead," said Dax with a slight sense of foreboding.

"The Tzenkethi medical team must be present throughout."

"I'm sorry, Heldon," Dax replied, "but that's not acceptable. This is between you and me, between the Venetans and the Federation. I'm not here to deal with the Tzenkethi, and I'm not empowered to deal with the Tzenkethi." That last wasn't entirely true, Dax thought guiltily, as she was fairly sure that any action she took that prevented any navithium resin from arriving on Outpost V-4 would eventually be forgiven by her superiors. *Any action within reason. I doubt they'd want me running amok shooting every Tzenkethi within range . . .* But it was a helpful fiction if she was going to be able to deal with Heldon without the Tzenkethi always nearby. "I don't have the authority to deal with them."

"Authority?" said Heldon, baffled. *"Aren't you a citizen of the Federation? Is that not sufficient to give you authority?"* She shook her head. *"Your customs and your systems are very strange to me, Dax. But if that's how it*

*has to be, then I must decline. You have to understand
that when you show suspicion toward the Tzenkethi, you
slight us, their hosts. They are our* friends."

"That might be the case, Heldon, but they are most
emphatically not *ours.*"

And so their conversation ended at an impasse
again. Dax checked on the arrival of the Tzenkethi
ships. They were a little under ten days away from the
border. A little under ten days, or two hundred hours,
and counting down.

"Think, Dax," she muttered to herself. "You have
to prove to Heldon that what's coming on those ships
really is the serious threat that we believe it is. So how
do you do that?"

First of all, she decided, by going back to her
briefing documents and, in particular, the reports
from Leishman and Helkara of the scans they had
conducted of Outpost V-4. After two hours with her
head down (*one hundred ninety-eight hours to go*), she
realized she was coming back again and again to the
solvents. The P96 solvents already on the base, which
were used to stabilize a variety of compounds including navithium resin. If they had a sample, perhaps they
could narrow down which solvent it was, and so which
compounds it was going to be used for.

But Heldon wasn't simply going to hand them
over.

Dax stood up, stretched, and rubbed the back of
her neck. Then she took a deep breath and opened a
comm channel.

"Susan," she said. "Will you come to my ready room, please?"

Susan Hyatt, hearing what Dax had in mind, nearly started bouncing off the bulkheads.

"No, Ezri, I *won't* tell you that it will be fine. It's a *terrible* idea. It would expose Peter Alden to exactly the kinds of triggers that could do him enormous harm. A tired man in a stressful situation, the possibility of capture by Tzenkethi—he should be resting, not running around on undercover missions on a Tzenkethi-held base!"

Guiltily, Dax thought of her conversation with Heldon in which the Venetan woman had said much the same thing.

"Send someone else with Kedair. Send Sam. He's been desperate to get off the ship—"

"It has to be Alden," Dax replied. "Only he is even remotely equipped to deal with the Tzenkethi technology in that medical facility. Susan, he's my friend. I don't want him to come to any harm—"

"Then don't put him in harm's way."

"But I *have* to know whether those Tzenkethi ships are bringing navithium resin here. I've asked nicely, again and again, and I'm getting nowhere."

"But there's no guarantee that getting a sample would even answer that question. It might not tell you that the ships are definitely bringing the resin. It might only tell you *perhaps*."

"Even then, it would be a much less qualified 'perhaps.' Besides, it will be a bargaining chip. And I need something, because right now I don't have anything. The Tzenkethi might be *days* away from putting bio-weapons within strike range of Federation space, and there isn't a damn thing I've been able to do about it! Well, now I think I can. They've been outmaneuvering us at every step. It's time we started to outmaneuver *them*."

"You're the captain," Hyatt said. "But if this comes at the cost of Peter Alden's sanity, I don't think you'll forgive yourself, Ezri."

Alden, summoned in his turn to Dax's ready room, sat and listened to her speak, then leaned back in his chair. "You want me to go back to Outpost V-4," he said.

"Yes."

"With Lieutenant Kedair."

"Yes."

"In secret."

"Yes."

"And acquire from its medical facility a sample of the P96 solvents stored there."

Dax too leaned back. "You're sharp as nails tonight, Peter."

"And this is a request."

"Yes, and haven't I asked nicely?"

"Why don't you just order me over there, Ezri? After all," he said bitterly, "you all but ordered me to leave."

"Peter, whatever you think of me right now, you know in your heart that I am your friend and that I'm concerned for you. You went too far earlier, and you know it. You also know that your behavior could have jeopardized this entire mission and taken us some way toward outright hostilities with these people."

He stared at her for a while, and then he began to laugh, full and very genuine laughter.

"What?" Dax said. "What's so funny?"

"You've got some nerve, that's what. In one breath you're asking me to go on a dangerous mission and in the next you're insisting that you're concerned for my welfare!"

"Yes, well, captain's prerogative. Will you go?"

"What? Oh, of course I'll go. A chance to get one past the Tzenkethi? I'm not going to turn that down." He rose from his seat. "I should find Kedair. We have a mission to plan." He stopped by the door. "I won't let you down, Ezri."

"I know that, Peter. I won't let you down either."

Ilka invited Crusher to her suite as soon as she received her request for a meeting. "I must apologize if I've woken you," Crusher said on entering the room. The lighting had been lowered and Ilka had a faint air of dishevelment about her. Her usual meticulous dress and careful adornment were nowhere in sight.

"No, you haven't woken me," Ilka said, pointing toward her desk, where padds and other data files were piled up. "I wonder, are any of us sleeping tonight? I've been in near-constant communication with my government, and I'm sure that's been the same for you and your colleagues too." She gestured to Crusher to sit down, and, with an instruction to the computer, the lamps came gently to a slightly brighter level, like woodland in the late afternoon. "But how can I help you, Beverly? I know it's been a difficult day for your team. Is there anything that I can do to help?"

"I hope so. We're stuck, Ilka," Crusher said frankly. "I went with Dygan to speak to Vitig, but Alizome was there, and she prevented any meaningful dialogue from taking place. No, actually, let me be scrupulously accurate about what happened: Alizome sabotaged the meeting." *And I was an easy target.*

Ilka clicked her tongue. "A malign influence, that one."

"You said it. Anyway, there's no way now that any of our senior representatives will get anywhere near the Venetans, and in fact I doubt they'd willingly see any of our junior members again, myself included." Crusher leaned forward, her hands falling open on her knees in a gesture that was half hopeless, half supplicatory. "Ilka, you're the only remaining lead negotiator who has anything remotely like a channel open to the Venetans. You're the only senior representative here from a Khitomer power who isn't implicated in this whole spying farce. The Venetans are angry with the Cardassians for spying on them, and angry with us for spying on their friends. But I haven't seen any accusations flying around about *your* government yet."

"So you want me to speak to the Venetans on your behalf?"

"If you think you're able to do that."

Ilka sat back in her chair. She tugged thoughtfully at one earlobe. "If I *do* meet with Rusht and Vitig, what do you want me to say?"

"Try to persuade them that they have to reopen formal negotiations. If 'formal' is the right word for what's been going on. But it's better than all *this*." Crusher held up her hands helplessly.

"This?"

"Talking through back channels. Sending messages through each other. You have children, don't you, Ilka?"

"Yes, I do. Four."

"Then you know what children's games can be like. That's what I feel we're trapped in now."

Ilka smiled, and Crusher knew she understood. Pressing her advantage, she went on, "It's only adding to the hostility and the suspicion that we're all feeling. If Rusht and Vitig would only listen, we and the Cardassians are ready to talk. Apologize if necessary. After all, we're all smart, experienced people. I'm *sure* we can come up with a way of apologizing that doesn't make us feel like we're down on bended knee pleading for favors. What do you say, Ilka? Will you go and speak to the Venetans for us?"

To Crusher's dismay, a frown crossed Ilka's face.

"Should I be preparing myself for a no?"

Ilka stood up and started pacing the room. At first,

Crusher thought it was simply evasiveness or nervousness, and then realized that Ilka was checking for recording devices. *But surely the Venetans would not do that? And Ilka must have taken precautions already in case the Tzenkethi were listening?* When the Ferengi woman finished her circuit of her office, she sat back down next to Crusher and spoke in a low, conspiratorial voice.

"I've already hinted to you that there are divisions within my mission, Beverly," she said quietly.

Ah. Not her opponents. Her own people.

"We may be showing a united front to the outside world, but we are not as one among ourselves. Several of my juniors"—she bared her teeth briefly, and Crusher suspected she would prefer to give them a different, less anodyne description—"are pushing me to take a more independent line. They believe that our association with Detrek is an embarrassment for the Ferengi Alliance and that our interests would best be served by putting some distance between us—"

"But Detrek *is* our ally. For all the damage she's done, that still counts for something." A cold feeling ran through Crusher's veins. Without Ilka, and with the Cardassians ejected from the room, the Federation would be on its own. "You're not leaning that way, are you, Ilka?"

"No, no!" Ilka said quickly. "As you say, for all her faults, we have signed a treaty with the government that Detrek represents, and so we have obligations to her and her people. My position is clear—we must back up our allies, particularly the Federation. But although I am head of this mission, I am not the only power within it . . ." She held out her hands.

Crusher understood how awkward Ilka's position was. There were plenty on Ferenginar who did not think a female was suited for high office and were looking for any failure on her part to prove that no female could be trusted with such responsibilities. Any misstep or wrong decision on Ilka's part would not only end her own career but also might do irreparable damage to the many females following her. Agreeing to speak to the Venetans on behalf of the Federation and the Cardassians would be deliberately going against an opinion held by many on her team, and no doubt they would not forgive her.

Crusher opened her mouth to take back her request, but Ilka spoke first.

"I'll go," she said quietly. "If I don't do this now, they'll only find some other way to undermine me. If my own people are set on destroying me, I might as well go down for my principles as for anything else. I'll contact Vitig immediately and ask her to meet me within the hour."

Crusher felt a weight lift off her. She knew she could trust this clever, gifted woman. She offered her hand, which Ilka clasped.

"Thank you," Crusher said.

"It is my pleasure, Beverly. I only hope that somehow the quiet voices of reason can keep going long enough to outlast noisier and less tolerant tones."

"Keep an eye on Alizome," Crusher advised. "It'll be best if she's not at the meeting, but if you can't prevent that, then make sure she doesn't get a chance to intervene. She'll try to slander you—and your government. So keep watch."

Madame Ilka bared her small white teeth. "Oh, I'll be ready for Alizome," she said. "I hope she's ready for me."

9

FROM:
Civilian Freighter *Inzitran*, flagship, Merchant Fleet 9

TO:
Ementar Vik Tov-A, senior designated speaker, Active Affairs, Department of the Outside

STATUS:
Estimated time to border: 17 skyturns
Estimated time to destination: 22 skyturns

- - - - - - - - -

FROM:
Captain Ezri Dax, *U.S.S. Aventine*

TO:
Admiral Leonard Akaar, Starfleet Command

STATUS OF TZENKETHI FLEET:
ETA at Venetan border: 9 days
ETA at Outpost V-4: 11 days

It's not the hours that get to you, thought Ezri Dax, as she waited on the bridge of the *Aventine* for news of Alden and Kedair, *it's the minutes. The too-slow, lengthening minutes . . .*

There was a great deal that Dax loved about command, but this, she thought, was by far its worst aspect: the long dark wait watching the clock while colleagues put themselves in danger on your orders. Bad enough under normal circumstances, but worse when you weren't one hundred percent satisfied that one of them was fit for the task you'd set him, and you knew exactly how high the stakes were.

Dax glanced again at the time. Alden and Kedair had been gone for thirteen and a half minutes. They were under a communications blackout, of course, but if everything was going according to the plan, then within the next two minutes they would be approaching the medical facility through the service tunnels, whereupon Alden's knowledge of Tzenkethi security systems would come to the fore. Dax agonized again over her decision to send him on this mission. *Maybe this will be too much for him. What if he's suddenly confronted by Tzenkethi? What if it seems like they're going to attack him? Will he break? Will he crack?*

Dax consulted the latest reports from Venette. It didn't take her long to see how badly the situation there was unraveling. But rather than making her even more anxious, the news from Venette strengthened her resolve. *This is going to be worth it,* she told herself firmly. *Diplomacy has been getting us nowhere. The Tzenkethi are trying to insinuate themselves into position on our borders so they can point biological weapons at us, and I won't allow it.*

A tap on her shoulder startled her out of her reverie.

It was Bowers. "It'll be worth it, Ezri," he said, quietly, guessing her thoughts as always. "And don't worry. Kedair's switched on for the both of them."

"Thanks, Sam. I hope so."

There followed another half hour of make-work, clock-watching, and nail-biting before the bridge heard from the transporter room that Alden and Kedair were back from Outpost V-4—and with the samples they'd been sent to get. Relief flooded through Dax as she hurried to meet them in the sickbay.

She met Hyatt in the turbolift, also on the way there.

"Well, Captain," Hyatt said, "seems you got away with it. I'm glad about that. But let's hope that Peter Alden doesn't end up paying a high price for what you've just put him through."

Alden, when Dax saw him, didn't seem to be any worse for the experience. He was cheerful and bright-eyed (*a little too bright-eyed?* Dax fretted), and greeted her enthusiastically.

"Job done," Alden said. "Hope we've got what we need now to prove to Heldon exactly what those bastards are up to."

Helkara and Tarses were standing by to take the

solvent samples and carry out their tests on them. Alden left to get some sleep.

Dax grilled Kedair. "How was he?"

"Fine," said Kedair. "More than fine. Couldn't have done it without him. He knew his way around those Tzenkethi security systems like a Ferengi knows the Rules of Acquisition. Anyone might think his life once depended on it."

When Kedair had left, Dax asked Hyatt for her opinion. "What did you think? Did he seem okay?"

"Adrenaline alone will keep him going for a while yet," Hyatt said. "It might be years before we see if there's been any lasting damage. Hopefully he won't be mid-mission."

Another four agonizing hours passed before Dax got word from Tarses that their tests were complete. She headed back down to the sickbay, clean, white, and orderly. Tarses and Helkara had mixed news for her.

"The samples we've got are informative," Helkara said, "but not definitive. Not all P96 solvents can stabilize navithium resin. But these particular samples can."

"So what does that tell us?" Dax asked with a sinking heart. Surely the nerve-racking past few hours hadn't been for nothing? "Anything new?"

"Nothing particularly new," said Tarses. "We have not, of course, proved that the Tzenkethi ships must be carrying navithium resins. We have only demonstrated that the solvents stored on Outpost V-4 *could* be used to stabilize navithium resins."

"Leaving us slightly more sure than we were before that they will be—but not certain," Dax said. She slammed her hand against the worktop, sending a tray of medical instruments rattling. "Damn it!"

"And I'm not sure this is the kind of evidence that we could present to Heldon, Captain," Helkara said. "For one thing, she might want to know how we acquired our samples."

"In addition," Tarses said, setting the instruments straight, "there are many other resins with which these solvents can be used, which serve the emollient function needed by the Tzenkethi and which are entirely benign as far as humans are concerned . . ." His brows creased as if something had suddenly struck him.

"What is it, Simon?" Dax urged. "What are you thinking?"

"Allow me a moment to think this through." Tarses, deep in thought, continued making minor adjustments to the tray imperceptible to Dax's eye. "The Tzenkethi claim that the air on Outpost V-4 is made unpleasantly arid by the compounds added to the atmosphere by the Venetans. Is that correct?"

"Well, that's what they *say*," said Dax.

"And, as a result, they need particular kinds of skin emollients in order to be able to live and work on the base. But if this is true," Tarses continued, "then any emollient sufficient to the task would be suitable. And certainly Starfleet has many such substances at its disposal . . ."

Dax saw where he was going. "So why don't *we*

supply it to them? Could we do that, Simon? Could we really do that?"

"If we knew what kind of emollients were required, I could replicate enough for our immediate purposes. And Starbase 261 would have the resources to offer a larger, perhaps even permanent, supply."

"And in the meantime we'd be able to make the offer," Dax said. "An offer that Heldon would hopefully not be able to refuse."

"The chief medical officer on Starbase 261 is an acquaintance of mine, Captain," Tarses said. "I could have an answer from her very quickly."

Dax contemplated the full implications of his idea. "It would seem like a friendly overture on our part," she said. "And if the Tzenkethi refused, it would look suspiciously like they wanted to make sure that their own resins were on Outpost V-4." She laughed. The whole plan was starting to look very attractive. The Federation would seem not only eager to find a peaceful solution but magnanimous too.

"There's another reason the Tzenkethi might refuse," Helkara said.

"Oh, yes?"

"Not to sound paranoid, but they might be afraid we were trying to poison them." Helkara looked embarrassed. "I know it sounds bad, but I'm just trying to think through all the possible responses, Captain. They might accuse us of it, even if they don't believe it to be true."

"Which I assume it wouldn't be," Dax said. "At

least, I *hope* the Federation hasn't yet resorted to waging covert biological warfare on our enemies. But here's another thought. If Heldon thought the Tzenkethi were implying that we *might,* it could lower her estimation of them." Dax gave a decisive nod. "Get on to it, Simon. Find out exactly what we need to offer and how quickly we could produce it. We've got nothing to lose from this and a great deal to gain."

Neta Efheny sat alone in a quiet corner of the boat, her hands resting on her lap, trying to steady her thoughts. The point where she would have to slip away was drawing ever closer, but Hertome Ter Ata-C had been keeping her under near-permanent surveillance. Only at night, when the Rets went off to their cabins, and the Ters to theirs, was she out of his sight.

Efheny knew too that she had attracted a great deal of notice from the other Ret Ata-Es traveling on the boat. Most of them were keeping their distance, uneasy about one of their number who was attracting such pointed attention from an Ap-Rej. Efheny knew their reasoning: whatever misdemeanors the Ret Mayazan was committing, they did not want to be implicated in any fashion. Only Corazame came near her, sitting down with her to eat at every meal, talking to her friend in a bright, overloud voice. And, of course, Hertome was keeping watch.

Efheny sighed and looked out from under the canopy down at the bright water of the channel along which they were passing. Perhaps this time alone

was for the good, allowing her to clear her mind and
run through her plans for her imminent pickup. She
reached down and ran her hand through the sapphire
water. And allow her time to savor this beautiful world
before she left for good . . .

"Maymi?"

Efheny looked up. It was Corazame, of course, her
staunch ally.

"Can I sit down?"

Efheny moved along the bench to make space. "Of
course, Cory."

Corazame sat and then looked around quickly and
anxiously.

"The Ap-Rej is eating," she said in a low voice.
It was wise, when you were outside, to assume that
someone might overhear and report an inappropri-
ately phrased statement. "Maymi, I have to speak to
you. There's no way I can speak to our Ap-Rej directly,
but I have to offer you advice, and through you offer
advice to him." Her hand went instinctively up to her
mouth, as if to cover over the outrageous implication
that someone like her might be in a position to offer
advice to a superior. "You must have seen that the situation between you has been noticed. You are taking
terrible risks." She seized her friend's hand. "I am sure
that one of the enforcers is watching you. I don't know
whether she noticed of her own accord, or whether one
of the others alerted her—but, Maymi, you must take
care!" Corazame pressed her hand. "I don't want you
to be sent for reconditioning. I've seen people after-

ward. They're *emptied*! There's nothing there. Yes, they sing and they work, but that's all that's left. I don't want that to happen to you."

Efheny dropped her head and squeezed out a few fake tears.

"Cory, I'm so afraid," she whispered. "But this isn't my doing. I told our Ap-Rej before we left that our meetings couldn't continue. But he insists! He's the one who followed me here. How do I refuse a superior? How are any of us to refuse?" She dropped her voice. "And I'm afraid that if I *do* refuse, he'll approach the enforcers and tell them I'm disobedient, that I've refused to follow his legitimate requests . . . Cory, what am I supposed to do? I'm so frightened. I was flattered at first, to think that such a one would even notice one like me. But I've been a fool. What am I to do? What are any of us to do?"

Efheny wiped at her leaking eyes, hoping that she had made the story convincing and that she had said enough to plant the right idea in Cory's mind. Beside her, Corazame sat deep in thought for a while. When she spoke again, her voice was quiet, but firm. "I think you already know what we have to do, Maymi."

"If I knew I'd do it."

"Hush. Everything will be fine. But we're going to have to be brave. You said he might approach the enforcers . . ." She dropped her voice. "So we must approach them first."

The previous skyturn, two Mak enforcers had come aboard, traveling on the route for a while on business of their own. They had of course disappeared into the part of the boat reserved for the senior echelons, but the Ata quarters had been busy with the news of their arrival: Who were they here for? Was someone in trouble? A few eyes had fallen on Efheny. Neither enforcer had yet put in an appearance, but the Atas' fascination with them would continue for some skyturns yet.

Efheny, who had been pondering their possible utility since their arrival, made her jaw drop at Corazame's suggestion.

"*Approach* them? Cory, is that *possible*? One of them is graded BB! I'm not sure they even have any dialects in common with us."

"If they're graded so highly, they'll be permitted to learn our dialect," Corazame said doggedly. "They'll certainly have the ability. I know it's a risk—"

"But won't it make us stand out? That's not appropriate for Atas of our grade. We might end up censured—"

"But they are the only people here who have an Ap-Rej's authority over Hertome. We're not *slaves*, Maymi. And we are most certainly not Hertome's slaves! You and I, all of us, we serve our beloved Rej. But because he can't always be with us, he lets others speak and act on his behalf so that we are all under his protection, even those of us who bring so little to our world. Yes," Corazame said, her mind made up, "we must approach the enforcers. We'll beg permission to speak, and we'll hope in the name of our most beloved and exalted Rej that they grant us permission and see us."

Corazame stood and pulled Efheny up after her.

And Neta Efheny, who had intended this outcome all along, obediently followed.

Tarses quickly got back to Dax with the information that she needed. When Dax entered the sickbay, she saw six large containers on the nearest worktop.

"Is this what we need?" she said. Tarses nodded. "Simon, you're a marvel!"

"I carried out some research into what kinds of skin emollients would be suitable for the Tzenkethi," he told her. "Based also on what I learned from the solvents acquired from Outpost V-4, I've prepared samples of six different possible options. I have been in touch with Doctor Bishop at Starbase 261, and she confirms that she could supply us immediately with excellent stocks of three of these and produce the rest quickly. If the Tzenkethi are willing, then we can supply them with everything they need, and perhaps this crisis can be defused."

"And if they're not willing," Dax said, "we can only hope that to Venetan eyes that will seem hostile or evasive."

"Certainly accepting our offer is the most reasonable decision to make, given the alternatives," Tarses said. "Assuming, of course, that the Tzenkethi do indeed wish to avoid war."

Big assumption, thought Dax, and one that Peter Alden most likely wouldn't make. Thought of Alden put another idea into her head, one Dax didn't like much but nevertheless felt duty bound to explore.

"Where did you get your information about Tzen-kethi physiology, Simon?" she said casually, running a fingertip around the seal of one of the containers. "Did you speak to Alden?"

"The commander is still off duty," Tarses said. "But there was sufficient information in the Starfleet Medical database." He frowned. "Why? Should I have spoken to Commander Alden? I'm aware that he is an expert on Tzenkethi political affairs, but does he also have expertise on Tzenkethi physiology?"

"No, not that I know of," Dax said quickly. "And better not to wake him."

She'd learned what she needed to know. Now she didn't have to worry that Alden had suggested to Tarses options that were in some way inimical to Tzenkethi health. *And how low have I come, to think that about a friend?* she thought. *Can I even think of myself as his friend any longer, when I suspect things like that about him?* But she had to check. She had to be certain.

"Thanks, Simon. I'm very pleased with all this. I'll get on to Heldon right away."

Dax returned to her ready room and got in touch with Heldon, who received the offer with a combination of surprise and unconcealed relief. *"This is very generous of the Federation, Dax. And you're right that it could well be the way out of this impasse that we've all been looking for. I will of course have to consult with my Tzenkethi colleagues—"*

"Of course," said Dax, keen to appear accommodating.

"But I can't see any reason why they would refuse. Thank you. I take this as a sign of good faith." Heldon gave a bright smile. *"I'm glad that at last we are finding the grounds upon which trust can be built."*

Dax cut the comm and fell back into her chair, relieved that things seemed finally to be turning the corner. While she waited to hear from Heldon, Dax read the updated reports from Venette, which sunk her spirits for a while, until she reminded herself that she would soon be able to cut through all the diplomatic wheeling and dealing with a solution of her own. She checked in with Hyatt, and the counselor told her that Alden was still off shift and in his quarters, presumably sleeping. No signs, yet, that he was suffering any adverse effects from the mission. When Bowers eventually persuaded Dax to get some sleep herself, she went off to her quarters in a positive frame of mind: *I think I've got away with it. I really think we've cracked it. It was worth it.*

Her hopes were dashed two hours later. The captain was awakened by an incoming communication from Heldon. The Venetan's face, usually so warm, so friendly, was stern again, and very angry. Dax steeled herself. Was it possible that Heldon had somehow found out about their raid on the medical facility? They were all sunk if she had . . .

"Dax," said Heldon, *"a grave situation has arisen here and, as a result, I need to speak to Peter Alden. I must ask you to send him to Outpost V-4 at once."*

She knows, thought Dax. *Hell!* But then she stopped herself. *Why only Alden? Why not Kedair too?*

"That's a most unusual request," Dax replied calmly. "If you wish to speak to the commander, I can certainly ask him to come to my ready room, and you—and I mean you, Heldon, nobody else—are welcome to ask him whatever you like. Will that be sufficient?"

"No. Unfortunately that will not be sufficient."

"May I ask why not?"

The screen went suddenly dark. "Heldon?" Dax said quickly, leaning in toward the comm. "Heldon, are you still there?"

The screen filled with a pale blue glow, and the Tzenkethi medical officer, Entrigar Ter Yai-A, came into view.

"Captain Dax," Entrigar said. *"Our friend Heldon has made a request of you. Are you going to comply?"*

"No, I'm not," Dax replied firmly. "Not without a very good reason. Ter Entrigar, the last time I checked, Outpost V-4 was still a Venetan base and not yet a Tzenkethi one. If you don't mind, I'll speak to Heldon or I'll speak to nobody."

Heldon's voice came from slightly beyond Entrigar. *"I've made my request,"* she said. *"I can't force you to hand over Peter Alden, nor do I wish to do so. But I'll take it as a sign of good faith if he is here on Outpost V-4 within the hour."*

Dax, her stomach twisting with fear and incipient panic, tried to keep her voice calm. "I've already offered a sign of good faith, Heldon. I've offered a resolution to this whole crisis. How about we discuss if your Tzenkethi friends are prepared to let you accept our offer of whatever supplies they need? Because it strikes me as very convenient that the moment I make an offer that could end this affair in a matter of days, I'm asked to surrender one of my senior officers without being given any good reason why."

There was no reply.

"Heldon," Dax said insistently. "Have your friends said whether or not our offer is going to be accepted? If not, have they said why?"

Still silence from the other end. What was going on down there?

"Well," said Dax, "until I hear back from you as to whether or not our offer is going to be accepted, think about what's on the table, Heldon. And when you see your way to responding to it, I'll take that as a sign of good faith."

Dax cut the comm channel and swore creatively for the best part of the next two minutes. And when Bowers alerted her that a coded transmission had been sent from Outpost V-4 to the Venetan homeworld, Dax knew she wasn't getting any more sleep that night. Shortly, she was going to have a whole lot of explaining to do. And she would very much like a few explanations herself.

10

FROM:
Civilian Freighter *Inzitran,* flagship, Merchant Fleet 9

TO:
Ementar Vik Tov-A, senior designated speaker,
Active Affairs, Department of the Outside

STATUS:
Estimated time to border: 15 skyturns
Estimated time to destination: 20 skyturns

- - - - - - - - -

FROM:
Captain Ezri Dax, *U.S.S. Aventine*

TO:
Admiral Leonard Akaar, Starfleet Command

STATUS OF TZENKETHI FLEET:
ETA at Venetan border: 7 days
ETA at Outpost V-4: 9 days

Dax eventually got her explanations from Picard. He appeared on the viewscreen in her ready room looking tired, fretful, and about a minute away from explosively losing his temper.

"*Dax, what the hell has been going on over there? What's all this about a bomb?*"

Dax nearly dropped her coffee cup. "A *what?*"

"*A bomb, Captain Dax, found on Outpost V-4. The Tzenkethi representative here, Alizome, just graced Ambassador Jeyn and myself with her presence. She had two pieces of news, neither of them good: first, Rusht is unlikely to speak to us again, and, second, this is because the base coordinator at your end contacted her to say that a bomb had been found on Outpost V-4. What's going on? Is Heldon lying?*"

That explained the coded transmission to Venette, Dax thought. "No, Heldon's not a liar."

"*So you think they really* have *found a bomb on the base? Well, whether or not they have, the situation here has become critical. The only reason we haven't been banished from Venette immediately is that the Ferengi negotiator has agreed to speak to the Venetans for us. That, and they happen to like Glinn Dygan . . . Dax, what is happening over there? Is this another Tzenkethi sideshow? Or is there something in it?*"

Dax had hardly heard a word he'd said. Her head was spinning and the blood was thumping furiously in her ears. *Susan warned me,* she thought. *Preemptive action, she said . . .*

"Dax?"

Quickly, Dax gathered herself. She cleared her throat. "Have they said where this bomb was found exactly?"

"In the medical facility." Picard's eyes sharpened. *"Captain, is that particular detail significant in some way?"*

Slowly, Dax rubbed a fingertip beneath one eye and then tugged at the lid. Surely this had to be a Tzenkethi ploy? Surely he wouldn't have . . . Or would he? Hyatt had warned her. And Heldon had seen it too.

"Dax?"

She leaned forward in her chair. "Captain, we need to make sure this channel is very secure."

They carried out the usual precautions, and then Picard, his face grim, said, *"I think you'd better speak freely, Captain Dax. What exactly do you think is going on?"*

Dax took a deep, shuddering breath. "Before I tell you that, you need to know that the night before last we mounted a covert operation to Outpost V-4. I sent my security chief, Kedair, and Commander Peter Alden of Starfleet Intelligence over to get ahold of samples of the P96 solvents that are being stored there."

Picard closed his eyes, very briefly, then opened them. *"Your reasoning, presumably,"* he said very tightly, *"was that you needed a sample in order to ascertain whether the solvents are indeed needed for navithium resin, or to stabilize another substance entirely."*

"That was my reasoning."

"Then I admire your audacity, Captain, while reserving judgment about the wisdom of such a potentially provocative move."

Provocative? Explosive, more like.

Picard's voice went very dry. *"Let us not dwell for the moment upon its legality. Did you at least learn something useful?"*

"We learned enough to be able to offer to supply the Tzenkethi with a number of alternatives to the resins they are bringing on those ships. Human-friendly alternatives."

"I see. I assume that Alden and Kedair acquired these samples from the sickbay of Outpost V-4?"

"That's right."

There was a pause before Picard spoke again. *"Captain Dax, in my wildest dreams, I never imagined having to put a question like this to a fellow Starfleet officer. Did Starfleet Intelligence issue you orders to sabotage the medical facility on Outpost V-4?"*

"No," Dax said promptly. "But I don't know if they issued orders to anyone else."

"Explain."

"Commander Alden may have a different agenda."

"Ah."

"I know he's received communications through . . . separate channels. I can't shake the feeling that he might be under orders. But there's another question mark in my mind, Captain."

"Go ahead."

"He might have been acting on his own initiative."

"What? Planting a bomb?"

"I told you what my senior counselor said—"

"Yes, stress, exhaustion, and the possibility of a deeper malaise . . ." Picard's eyes widened. *"You sent him on this mission without being certain of his mental state?"*

"I did," said Dax. "He was the only one with the expertise to get through any Tzenkethi security systems that were in place. I made a judgment call, and I sent him. My senior counselor, to her credit, nearly hit the roof when I told her."

"I can imagine." Picard pressed his fingertips against the bridge of his nose. *"So. We are left with the possibility that a Starfleet officer is indeed responsible for this attempted sabotage. But we do not know if this was under orders, or whether he was acting on his own initiative."*

"Naturally, Starfleet Intelligence will deny all knowledge."

Picard grunted his agreement. *"Dax, you know Alden."*

"I knew him a long time ago. He's not the man he was."

"Still . . . Do you think he did this?"

Dax sighed. "I think it's possible, but I think it's possible that the Tzenkethi are planning to put bioweapons within strike range of our borders. Senseless and irrational, but *possible*. I just don't know for sure. For what it's worth, I'll also point out that this didn't happen until I offered the Venetans an alternative to the navithium resin. I make that offer and, lo and behold, a bomb's discovered on the base."

"You think the Tzenkethi might be behind this? That Commander Alden, whether acting alone or under instructions, has nothing to do with it?"

Dax threw up her hands. "Yes. The problem is that I can't know for sure. But this is how they seem to operate, isn't it? One shock revelation after another. First the Federation spy on their homeworld, now this. So that we're always left reeling, always kept off balance. Alden might have planted a bomb on Outpost V-4. But the Tzenkethi there might well have done it themselves. I just don't know for certain either way. That's been our problem all along, hasn't it? We don't know anything for sure, and when we make accusations, they sound like delusions."

"Quite." Picard rubbed his brow. *"You describe my difficulty as well. There is practically no form of words I could use to say any of this to the Venetans. Even if they were willing to speak to us. They're already indignant we've implied their Tzenkethi friends intend to arm the base with bioweapons. Now I have to hint that the Tzenkethi have planted a bomb on a Venetan base and have been attempting to make Starfleet officers look like the perpetrators."*

"I don't envy you that conversation."

"And I don't envy the conversation that you will soon be having with Commander Alden."

No, that wasn't the kind of conversation anyone would look forward to. Dax pushed aside her *raktajino,* her taste for it gone.

"I suggest you try to find out whether indeed Alden

did do something unwise while on that base. I also suggest that you put him under lock and key. And . . ." Picard sighed, deeply. *"I shall attempt to communicate with Rusht and Vitig through whatever channels remain open to me. Ideally without Tzenkethi oversight. I'll leave you with this less-than-consoling thought, Dax—all that's standing between us and war right now are the Ferengi."*

The glittering coral caverns surrounding the travelers had been forgotten. Instead, they had turned inward to their own affairs. The whole boat was humming with the news that the Rets Mayazan and Corazame had begged permission to speak to the enforcers. Conjecture was rife, but almost everyone agreed that it must have something to do with the Ter Hertome and the unusual nature of his interest in the Ret Mayazan.

Apart from this single point of agreement, there was a great deal of dissension among the other Ata-Es on the boat about Mayazan's decision to approach the enforcers. Efheny told herself that as a xenoanthropologist she had a unique opportunity to observe such a social minefield, but she was uncomfortable being at the center of it. True, some of the other Atas were on her side, many of them having quietly suffered at the hands of bullying superiors. But many more dismissed her as an attention seeker. There was always a Ret, they said, who thought she was better than the rest. Some even thought a little reconditioning wouldn't do the Ret Mayazan any harm and might remind her of her purpose. A couple went out of their way to signal their displeasure; one even spat at Efheny as she walked past.

"Ignore them," Corazame said boldly. This whole business had given Corazame a new air of confidence. "They think you've broken rank, reporting an Ata to a higher grade. But if they're not careful, they'll be summoned before the enforcers too."

"Why?"

"*Why?* Sometimes you ask the strangest questions, Maymi. Why do you think? Because putting loyalty toward other members of one's grade first isn't right. First we must be loyal to every Ap-Rej, and through them loyal to our beloved Rej himself. They speak for him, after all." At that thought, Corazame shivered. "I hope we've done the right thing. But I'm sure," she lowered her voice before saying the almost unspeakable, "I'm *sure* that Hertome is in the wrong."

After two skyturns, Efheny and Corazame received a response from the enforcers, conveyed through hand signals via an Ata-EE who served their part of the ship. They were instructed to come to the front of the boat and present themselves to their superior. As they passed through the locked doors that separated the Ata quarters from those of their superiors, Efheny saw that Corazame was trembling with barely suppressed fear. She herself had conflicting emotions. There was the constant fear of discovery and the particular anxiety arising from exposing herself to the direct scrutiny of an enforcer. She had not come close to one before. What if they were equipped or trained to see straight through her cover? At the same time, Efheny was excited by the prospect of the unusual encounter in which she was about to participate. It would be a test not only of her expertise as a field anthropologist in correctly gauging the interaction but also of her nerve as an operative. It would give her confidence for the coming few days, and if all went according to plan, it would rid her of the problem of Hertome for good.

The Ata-EE server directed them to the enforcer's room. They entered and knelt at once, dropping their heads respectfully and gesturing their submission and desire to please. From the sound of movement above, Efheny knew that someone was standing on the anterior deck closest to them. As demonstrations of superiority went, it was fairly obvious, but nonetheless effective. Between the enforcer's display and the instinctive physical responses bred into her, Corazame was almost weeping. Efheny instructed her own bio-engineering to give a similar impression.

"I am Inzegil Ter Mak-B," the person above said. She had a low voice with unusual intonation, presumably as a result of speaking to them in a dialect that was not her own. "You may raise your heads and look at me."

Efheny, bending her neck to an uncomfortable position, looked up along the anterior deck. Looming over them was a tall woman with steely silver skin, wearing the dark uniform that all Tzenkethi knew and feared.

"Which of you is the Ret Mayazan?" said Inzegil.

Efheny, not yet granted permission to speak, signaled that was her name and status.

"Ret Mayazan," said Inzegil, "you and your friend must understand that you have made a serious accusation. If I decide that your accusation is unfounded, this could result not only in your reconditioning but also in your declassification to null. This is your last chance to withdraw your charge against an Ap-Rej. Do you wish to do that?"

Corazame stifled a tiny cry. But neither of them spoke. Inzegil made an imperious gesture. "Then say what you must, Ret Mayazan."

"Ap-Rej," Efheny murmured, hoping that she was keeping her voice sufficiently low, "this one humbly offers gratitude for the leave given her to speak. This one offers her loyalty to her Ap-Rej and through her to her most beloved and exalted Rej . . ."

"I'm quite sure of your loyalty. Tell me your complaint."

In quiet, carefully phrased words, Efheny told Inzegil the same story she had told Corazame: that Hertome was making demands on her that she believed were not permitted and consequently she begged her superior's protection from him. She finished by acknowledging that the situation was not within her abilities to judge, and that was why she had asked permission to speak today. Her tale finished, she fell silent and waited for Inzegil to reply.

Throughout, the Mak enforcer's demeanor had been austere and serious. When Efheny finished speaking, Inzegil sighed and paced along the anterior wall toward them. The steely glitter of her skin was almost dazzling this close. Efheny's eyes began to water.

"My colleague and I had already observed the Ter Hertome's odd behavior toward you," Inzegil said. "We've been waiting for you to approach us. After two more skyturns, you would have been summoned before us and asked to account for why you had not called upon our superior judgment in this matter."

Coming closer, Inzegil put her hand first upon Corazame's head and then upon Efheny's. It was a kindly gesture, like an adult to a child, although Inzegil could not have been much older than either of the Atas before her. Some biological process must have been at work, because Corazame was immediately comforted. Her sobs subsided. But Efheny also felt oddly reassured by Inzegil's touch.

"You and the Ret Corazame have behaved appropriately," Inzegil said gently. "Your plea has been heard. I shall summon Hertome Ter Ata-C before me to answer my questions."

She dismissed them both, and they backed out of the room with their heads lowered. Once they were past the dividing door and safely back in the Ata quarters, Corazame began to cry. Efheny put her arm around her. *Not long now, Hertome,* Efheny thought as she shakily soothed her terrified friend. *Not long now and you'll be troubling me no more.*

Crusher, Picard, and Jeyn waited silently in their suite for Madame Ilka to come to see them. There was little that could be said. They all knew how much was riding on Ilka's meeting with Vitig. If Ilka couldn't persuade Vitig to speak to them, they knew they would be leaving Venette very soon. And then what? Crusher shifted uneasily in her seat. And then starships heading toward the border. Starships from at least three powers within the Khitomer Accords. These ships would be met by Tzenkethi ships, no doubt, sent to help the Venetans in their plight. This would almost certainly bring out the Klingon fleet. (Bacco was surely speaking to the Klingon ambassador right now to remind him of his government's treaty obligations.) And that would surely provoke the other Typhon Pact members to action . . .

Crusher rested her head on one hand. *Three small systems, but they just happen to be in exactly the wrong place. And that makes them enough to take us all to war.* She sighed and checked the time. *Our last chance for some kind of diplomatic solution. Our last chance to talk it out. But how did it ever get to this? How did we get from nearly bringing the Venetans into the Federation to quarrels over solvents and resins and the long dreadful night before war? What went wrong?*

The chime on the door rang. Jeyn jumped up to respond. Ilka entered, her expression somber. None of the three Federation representatives looked at each other.

"I do have *some* good news," Ilka said, taking the seat offered by Jeyn, "but you won't like the rest of what I have to say."

"If there's any good news," said Jeyn, "we'll take it. We'll take anything right now."

Ilka folded her hands in front of her on the table-top. "I saw Rusht and Vitig. Alizome was there too, I'm sorry to say. We'd barely begun to talk when news of this bomb on Outpost V-4 emerged. The three of them disappeared for several hours." Ilka glanced around at the three of them, unable to mask her annoyance. "Not the best start to our conversation, from my per-spective. I *assume* the thing wasn't yours?"

"If it was," said Picard, equally testily, "it wasn't authorized."

"Or not officially authorized, at least," Ilka retorted.

"Ilka, please," Crusher said softly. The Ferengi woman, turning her way, gave Crusher a sad smile.

"Well," she said, "having got off to that dreadful start, when we reconvened I was rather at a disadvan-tage. Even more so when Rusht announced immedi-ately that she intended to speak to you all tomorrow morning—"

"But that's excellent news!" Jeyn cried. "Madame Ilka, I'm not sure we can thank you enough—"

"Don't start thanking me yet," Ilka said bluntly. "I haven't finished. That's the good news, although what exactly Rusht has to say to you, and whether or not you'll be given the opportunity to reply, I don't know." She sighed and closed her eyes briefly.

Here it comes, thought Crusher. *The bad news.*

"My government," Ilka said, "was extremely con-cerned to hear about the bomb on Outpost V-4."

"In fact we have no proof that such a thing exists," Picard said. "Only a report from Heldon—"

"Her word is good enough for me, Captain Picard," Ilka said softly. "And certainly good enough for my government. Which, as I say, was most concerned to hear about it, and most eager to disassociate itself from it—"

"Naturally," said Picard, "anyone would. President Bacco has already issued a statement conveying her shock at the news and assuring the Venetans of her desire to discover the guilty parties, whoever they may be. I don't doubt she's ready to give the same assurances to your ambassador."

"Unfortunately, those assurances would be coming too late. My government, on realizing that its direct channel to the Tzenkethi and the Venetans was still open despite this news"—Ilka touched her chest—"instructed me to make an agreement with the Venetans that secures Ferengi interests. This I have done. The removal of our people from Venette has already begun, and we are in the process of coming to an agreement over the lease of the Venetan base on our border, particularly on the matter of there being permanent Ferengi observers in place. Both Rusht and Alizome were eager to discuss possible concessions—"

"Well, of course they were," said Jeyn angrily. "You've done a deal at our expense!"

"Ambassador Jeyn," said Ilka quietly, "I've done what my government instructed. You would have done exactly the same."

Not at the expense of our allies, Crusher thought. She felt bitter, angry . . . betrayed, even. And foolish. She thought she'd made a connection with Ilka. It seemed she'd been badly mistaken. When Ilka gave her an apologetic look, Crusher turned away.

"Does your government understand, Ilka," Picard said, "that this is not a guarantee of protection for Ferenginar if war does indeed break out? The Typhon Pact will not distinguish between those members of the accords that stood firm and those that did not. More likely you have presented yourselves to them as weak."

"Maybe," said Ilka, "and maybe not. That is a risk my government is apparently willing to take. *Tsch!* None of us wants war, Captain. I believe that even of the Tzenkethi. Yet nobody seems prepared to say 'Stop!' Perhaps this will serve as the wake-up call we all need."

"I hope so, Madame Ilka." Picard rose from his seat. "We should not keep you any longer. No doubt you have a great deal to do. Thank you for your efforts on our behalf."

Ilka, with a rather shaky sigh, stood up. Picard offered his hand freely. Jeyn, reluctantly, did the same.

"Well, my friends," Ilka said, "I know that this is hardly the news you were hoping to hear, and it is a matter of very deep regret to me that I have to be the one to bring it. I'll be joining our people at our embassy now and leaving with them tomorrow." She glanced at Crusher, who had remained seated. "I sincerely hope that the Great River brings you all in time to a safe haven."

Ilka turned and headed toward the door. After a moment, Crusher followed her out.

"Ilka," she called after her. "Wait a moment."

Ilka turned. "Beverly," she said with a small sad smile.

Crusher was about to say something angry but then stopped. Was that fair? Ilka was a diplomat, a representative of her government—and, more than that, she was a Ferengi female, who was going to have to prove herself again and again for the whole of her life. Ilka was always going to be the first one through. She was always going to be the one people would watch, and if she ever made a mistake, they would say: *See? We knew females could not cope. We knew they were not smart or clever or able enough. We should not let more of them through. This one was enough.*

Crusher stretched out her hand. Ilka hesitated for a moment, then smiled and took it.

"I wanted to say that you're going with my warmest wishes," Crusher said. "Best of luck for the future."

"Thank you, Doctor. I'm glad that you of all people are able to understand." Ilka grasped Crusher's hand between both of hers. "Go safely."

She gave her brilliant smile and left. Crusher, returning to Jeyn's suite, thought, *I do understand why you had to do this, Ilka. But how could you bring yourself to argue a case that you didn't believe?*

Picard said softly, "It's a doctor's privilege to serve a higher purpose. Soldiers and diplomats—we serve imperfect masters of imperfect worlds. But we strive toward the good. Don't judge us too harshly, Beverly."

11

FROM:
Civilian Freighter *Inzitran,* flagship, Merchant Fleet 9

TO:
Ementar Vik Tov-A, senior designated speaker, Active Affairs, Department of the Outside

STATUS:
Estimated time to border: 12 skyturns
Estimated time to destination: 17 skyturns

- - - - - - - - -

FROM:
Captain Ezri Dax, *U.S.S. Aventine*

TO:
Admiral Leonard Akaar, Starfleet Command

STATUS OF TZENKETHI FLEET:
ETA at Venetan border: 6 days
ETA at Outpost V-4: 8 days

If the voyagers had been enthralled at the news that two lowly Ret-Es had sought an audience with the Mak enforcers, it was nothing compared to the news that the Ter Hertome had been called to answer to an Ap-Rej for charges made by his inferiors. Again, Efheny found herself uncomfortably at the center of attention. Any operative balked at being the object of so much interest, and she could only hope that this brief period in the limelight would be over before she had to make her getaway.

Barely a quarter of a skyturn had passed since she and Corazame had seen Inzegil. Now they made their way again through the dividing doors and were brought to the enforcer's room. Entering, their heads bowed and making appropriate gestures, Efheny was startled to see that Inzegil was standing on the inferior deck rather than positioned above their heads as on the previous occasion. She was still taller than them both, and her shimmering skin, her dark uniform, and the sleek weapon at her hip reinforced her authority over them. Over Hertome too, Efheny hoped.

"Enter," said Inzegil. "Do not kneel." She gestured to one side of the room. "You may sit there. You are granted permission to listen to the conversation between two superiors that will soon be happening in this room."

They went over to the corner that Inzegil had indicated and curled up their legs beneath them. Inzegil strode across the room and up to the anterior deck, taking her position there once again.

"Bring in Hertome Ter Ata-C," she ordered an unseen server.

The door opened, and Hertome entered. As another Ter, empowered to give orders, he was not required to kneel in Inzegil's presence. Instead, he signaled his inferiority in functional echelon and genetic grading from his stance and his dimmed skin tones. He stood with his head bowed and his hands clasped behind his back. Efheny had never seen him so humble. She wondered how long the erratic human behind Hertome's face could keep this up.

At Inzegil's command, Hertome gave his version of the story: that the Ret Mayazan had been the one to approach him, and that he had repeatedly tried to regulate her behavior and guide her back to a proper course. He regretted his failure in this respect and offered his humble apologies to Inzegil.

When he was done, Inzegil walked a few steps toward him along the anterior deck. Efheny held her breath. Both stories were a pack of lies, of course, but which of them was the enforcer going to believe?

"I have listened to all your accounts with interest," Inzegil said. "And, of course, I consulted psychometric test scores and work assessments for all three of you." She gestured but did not look at Efheny and Corazame in their corner. "Both the Rets have performed their assigned tasks in exemplary fashion," she said, "no more and no less. They show a clear understanding of the nature and limits of their function. But in your file, Hertome, I see occasional but worrying notes from your superiors about your overassertiveness. You will not be aware that on one occasion you were very close to being recalibrated down a grade."

This came as no surprise to Efheny. *Humans,* she thought. *Unreliable. Not suited for this kind of work.*

"Only the efficiency of your unit prevented this happening," Inzegil said. "You may show them gratitude for their loyalty."

Hertome obeyed, giving Efheny a cold stare as he did so.

"Even if your story were true, Hertome," Inzegil continued, "then at the first approach from the Ret Mayazan, you should have recommended her for monitoring and perhaps even reconditioning. At the very least, you should have ensured her redeployment from your unit, to prevent her coming into daily contact with you and allowing her childish fantasies to flourish." She moved farther around the anterior deck until she loomed over him. "And if you were uncertain as to whether you were within your authority to instruct her, you should have consulted a superior. That is why you have superiors. You are not equipped to make such decisions alone, and you are not expected to make such decisions alone."

She altered her stance to something more formal. She was about to give judgment.

"I am not inclined to believe your story, Hertome," she said. "That concerns me deeply, since it means that you have lied to me. If I could prove this, I would be empowered to decommission you immediately. Here and now." She touched the weapon at her hip. "But since your files show that you have been a hard worker and so in your own way have served our Rej, I will give you the benefit of the doubt. Here are your instructions, Hertome Ter Ata-Ċ. At the next stop, you will leave this voyage. You will be met and escorted from there to commence fifty skyturns of reconditioning. That should be sufficient to remind you of the limits of your authority and the proper nature of your functions. I will not recommend any recalibration, but you should bear in mind that your C grade now carries a query alongside it. What do you have to say?"

Hertome, his voice very low, said, "This one must thank his Ap-Rej for reminding him of his functions and providing him with an opportunity to correct his faults. May he assure his Ap-Rej of his eagerness to begin the work necessary to improve him?"

"I hope so. You may go, Hertome. Return to your cabin and remain there until we reach our next port of call." Inzegil turned away and walked to the superior deck, where she sat at her desk, high above her three inferiors.

Hertome, turning to leave the room, caught Efheny's eye. "You've killed me," he called across to her from the safety of his audio-disruption field. "I hope you're happy."

Efheny looked away from him, down at the floor of the inferior deck. When Hertome was gone, Inzegil's voice floated down to Efheny and Corazame. "You too may go now. Turn your attention back to your immediate duty of restoration. You should not think about this matter again."

Gesturing their gratitude, the two Rets fled the room and back to their side of the ship. Partway there, Corazame gave a small scream. "Oh, Maymi! We've made a terrible mistake."

For a moment Efheny thought that she meant something really serious, and then Corazame said, "Now we have to answer to Karenzen!"

The relief that she didn't mean anything else, and of having avoided exposure, not to mention having defeated Hertome . . . suddenly Efheny burst out laughing. Corazame, also clearly relieved at having escaped the room, began to giggle too. They hurried back to the Ata quarters. Hertome was out of the way, and now all Efheny had to do was get past Corazame and make her way to the pickup point. And then . . .

And then to Cardassia.

Cardassia. That dry world, with dry work waiting for her, so far away from this dazzling, mesmerizing, generous planet. She tried not to think about it. Instead she played her part as Mayazan and ran giggling back with Cory to their quarters, putting all thought of her imminent departure from Ab-Tzenketh out of her head.

When the Rets had gone, Inzegil Ter Mak-B turned her attention to the paperwork arising from the case. Opening her portable comm to file her report, she spoke quickly, informing her colleagues back in the city that the case had been resolved and there was a dysfunctional Ata in need of collection. Her information was noted and logged, and two colleagues were assigned to his pickup. Next she put the necessary wheels in motion to ensure his subsequent reconditioning. Checking the logs at the various Re-Co camps on the north side of the city, she looked for one able to take an Ata of that one's grade for fifty skyturns, and at such short notice. It wasn't a lengthy period by any means, but it was of sufficient duration that she had to look slightly farther afield than usual to find a camp that could accommodate him and provide the necessary program. When this was secured, she closed the comm and reflected on the case.

Sweet girls, those two Rets, she thought, but silly. Ideal targets for an Ata Ter with grand ideas about himself, such as Hertome turned out to be. What a mess they'd got themselves into! At least the smaller one (What was her name again? Corinzame?) had the sense to get her little friend to appeal to her superiors. Inzegil had been serious when she'd told the Ret girls they'd been in danger of reconditioning themselves if they'd not presented themselves to her. Maintenance Unit 17 had been under observation for potential behavioral irregularities for some time.

The lead had come from an Ata-EE attached to the Department of the Outside who had been deployed for the past two and a half twin-months to provide ancillary support to the maintenance units there.

Ata-EEs, always on watch for instruction, saw and heard everything, and consequently were implanted with data-recording devices equipped with intelligent monitoring software that tracked the behavior of those around them and alerted the appropriate local enforcers of any irregularities. It was an entirely automated system: the Ata-EEs didn't know they had these implants and the data was automatically transferred to the relevant enforcer divisions. Besides, it wasn't their function to make such judgments about what was and was not relevant. There were software systems designed to do that far beyond any Ata-EE's ability. Sometimes the irregularities turned out to be coincidence. Sometimes there was a more serious malaise. Hertome Ter Ata-C had been flagged a while ago, although it was his first meeting with the Ret Mayazan that had moved the status of his case from "under observation" to "potential intervention."

At the thought of Hertome, Inzegil felt a rising sense of disgust. There were always some like that one, she thought, who used their power to prey upon their charges. It was an absolute betrayal of their function, of the trust placed in them as an Ap-Rej. Some of the Rets were very vulnerable. Take those two girls: their heads were no doubt full of E-grade songs and holo-romances, making them too easily persuaded that a superior was interested in them. They should have more sense than to imagine such a thing was possible. But that was the problem: Atas of that type *weren't* always sensible. That was why they had superiors, and that was why an enforcer division such as Inzegil's existed: to monitor the behavior of these grades and to intervene to protect them from themselves when necessary.

The door below her opened, and her colleague, Artamer Ter Mak-B, came in. Inzegil came down from the superior deck to join him. Artamer was much older than Inzegil and had performed this function for much longer. He had observed the meeting with the Atas from the next room and then had followed the Ata-EE taking Hertome back to his cabin.

"Well," he said, "he's back in his cabin and the doors are sealed. All seems pretty straightforward to me. Case closed. Can we go back to the city now?" He glanced over at the window. Artamer was unusually sensitive to being outside. Not even shutters and canopies always helped him persuade himself that he was safe. "I *hate* it when the job brings us out of town."

Inzegil, crossing the room to close the blinds, said automatically, "Our purpose is to serve."

"I know, Inzy, I know. Have we served yet?"

"I think so . . ."

Artamer gave her a narrow look. "Don't tell me you think there's more to this than the obvious? Big Man Ter tells a daft little girl that she's the only one for him, and then when he makes the inevitable move on her, she realizes it's not all love's young dream and comes running to us to sort out the mess. How often have we seen that?"

It was true—this was a standard irregularity and

one they were often called on to resolve. But Inzegil's instincts were very good, and today her instincts were telling her that the case was not over yet.

Artamer too, the Autarch bless him, knew and trusted his colleague's instincts. "Come on, Inz," he said with resignation. "Tell me what's on your mind."

"It's Hertome," she said. "There's something about him I don't like."

"He's a predatory creep," Artamer said bluntly. "What's to like?"

"I don't know. There was something about his responses to me that didn't ring true."

"Sounded perfectly contrite from where I was sitting. And what does it matter? Even if he *was* concealing his true feelings, reconditioning will sort that out for him."

"If he gets as far as reconditioning."

"What?" Artamer looked at her in disbelief. "You think he might try to go on the run? That would be mad! Where would he go? Outside, he'll soon start to panic. Back to the city, and the EE-network will pick him up." He shrugged. "Let him go on the run if he wants to. That's his problem. There'll be a nice warm cot waiting for him in Re-Co when he realizes that he doesn't like the great outdoors very much after all."

"Oh, I'm not worried about Hertome Ter Ata-C," said Inzegil. "He can drag himself all the way down to decommissioning as far as I'm concerned. What *does* concern me is what he might do to those two Rets in the meantime."

Now Artamer really sat up and paid attention. "You think he might try to harm them?"

"If he's the kind that doesn't understand that the fault lies with him, then he'll externalize that fault, and he'll put the blame on the people who reported him to the enforcers." She glanced at Artamer, who was listening with keen interest. "I might be misjudging him. He might be sitting quietly in his cabin waiting for his pickup and reflecting upon his errors."

"If he has any sense, he'll be doing just that. What do you want to do? We can stop the boat now and take him back if you want."

"Mmm . . ." Inzegil considered that. "I'm not sure it would be best. If he understands his fault and is simply waiting to be collected, stopping will cause a serious disruption and might distress some of the Atas. And those two girls wouldn't be very popular. They shouldn't be punished any more. Agonizing over what we might do to them was punishment enough. But if we wait, he might find a way to get to them." She paused. "Our chief responsibility is to the Rets. We're here to protect them from Hertome as much as from themselves."

"Then let's stick around. Hand Hertome over to his collectors, then see the two of them back to the city." Artamer sighed. "Oh, well, not *too* long now till the boat turns for home."

"I think that's probably for the best," Inzegil said. She gestured an apology. "Sorry, Art. I know you're keen to get back."

"That's all right, Inzy. It *is* our function. But sometimes I find my function very hard."

Dax sat in her quarters with Bowers and Hyatt and watched the recording of Alden's interview. Alden was running rings around her first officer and counselor. Partway through, she switched off.

"I know," said Bowers apologetically. "What can we do? He's trained to withstand torturers."

"Susan," Dax said. "Any suggestions?"

Hyatt sighed. "Perhaps Sam and Lonnoc could eventually get him to make a mistake," she said. "But it would take time—"

"We don't have time," Dax said. "We're on the brink of war." She tapped her knuckles against her cheek. "What if I talked to him? What effect might that have on him? Would he trust me?"

"Ezri," Hyatt said, "you're one of the *last* people he trusts right now, with the possible exception of whoever ordered him to do this—if such a person exists. Speaking as a counselor, and with Alden's well-being in mind, I'd say leave it to Sam and Lonnoc. Lonnoc's demonstrated her reliability on the mission with him, and as for Sam . . . well, everyone trusts Sam. He just gives off that vibe."

Bowers shook his head. "I know when I'm out of my league, Susan."

Dax pondered her options. "If he was ordered to do this, he won't say a word to them. He might to me."

"I don't think he would," Hyatt said. "The only

way that Peter Alden is going to confess to this is if he was acting on his own initiative. Eventually, the strain of the secret will become too much and he'll have to tell. But he wouldn't tell you. He won't risk breaking down in front of *you*. It needs someone close to you, but not you. If there *are* answers to be had, then Sam and Lonnoc will get them. But it's going to take careful handling, and it's going to take *time*."

"We don't *have* time," Dax said again.

Hyatt and Bowers looked at her sadly. "Decision's yours, Captain," Bowers said, with a rueful smile.

Decision's mine.

A somber mood lay upon the hall when the Federation representatives went to meet Rusht, Vitig, the people of the Venette Convention, and Alizome Vik Tov-A.

The hall was packed. The seats vacated by the Ferengi and Cardassian diplomatic teams were filled by Venetans who did not want to miss seeing this pivotal moment in the history of their worlds. Only around the Federation contingent was there a suggestion of space, as if the people of Venette wanted to signify the distance between them and their difficult visitors. Crusher keenly felt the absence of the other parties. It was as if Alizome had picked them off, one by one. Now only the Federation remained to represent the Khitomer Accords, and to prevent the militarization of the Venetan border.

But what cards do we have to play? Crusher thought desperately, looking around the hostile room. *There's*

still the offer to deliver whatever medical supplies the
Tzenkethi require, but will we get a chance to make that
offer again? Surely this whole business with the bomb is
going to stop us even mentioning it.

Rusht, her expression grim, asked her fellow Venetans for quiet. Once the room had settled, she passed
around padds showing images and readings that gave
information about the explosive device found on Outpost V-4. The data was displayed on screens around
the room and, Crusher assumed, could be seen in
every Venetan dwelling.

"I have learned from all our prior conversations,"
Rusht said to the Federation team, "that simply assert-
ing the truth—that an attempt was made to sabotage
Outpost V-4—will be insufficient for you." She gestured to the padds and the screens. "Here is as much
evidence as I am able to give you from this distance.
You could now claim that these images have been
falsified, and that Dax should be given permission to
inspect Outpost V-4 again. However, you have my
word. Doubly. You have my word that these images are
not forgeries. And you have my word that no Starfleet
officer will ever again set foot on a Venetan base."

The room gave its strong approval.

"Rusht," said Jeyn, "we do not doubt your word.
But you do us a great disservice. And you give us no
proof that this bomb was planted by a Starfleet officer—"

"Who else would it be?" Rusht said. "One of us,
forgetting herself and her principles entirely? From

what I hear from Heldon, the most likely candidate in that respect is your own Peter Alden. Or do you mean to imply that it is the Tzenkethi on the base who are responsible?" Her expression became even more severe. "Again and again, I've told you that we do not look favorably upon your attempts to slander our friends. But you do not *listen* to what we say!"

"But Rusht," Picard replied quietly, "you slander us in turn when you suggest that one of our officers must be responsible and yet offer no proof that is the case. It goes against *everything* this uniform stands for."

Rusht frowned. An uncertain ripple crossed the room. When it died down, Rusht nodded. "You're right, Picard. That was unjust of me, and unworthy of us all. But there is a simple way to resolve this and to demonstrate your good faith: send Peter Alden to Heldon on Outpost V-4. She is sympathetic, intelligent, and reasonable. She will soon determine whether or not he is responsible."

Picard shook his head. "No."

"Why not?" asked Rusht.

The room wanted to know that too.

"Do you think that we'll *harm* him?" Rusht said. "We're more likely to discover whether he's suffering from some emotional distress that your own doctors have either failed to see or else have willfully ignored. Again, I must ask that he speak to Heldon. I understand that he is a friend of Captain Dax, and that perhaps her loyalty to him prevents her from issuing whatever order would make him go back to Outpost

V-4. That's certainly commendable on her part, but unwise. But *you* can order Dax, can you not? That is how your system works? And she would obey that order, wouldn't she?"

"Yes," Picard said. "But I will not order her to do so. And no, Rusht, I do not believe that you would harm him. Not you." He looked meaningfully along the table toward Alizome.

Crusher drew in a silent breath. *You're taking a risk, Jean-Luc. I hope it pays off.* But, really, what other option was available to them? Either they somehow separated the Venetans from the Tzenkethi, or they left now and prepared for war.

Rusht, baffled, followed Picard's gaze. And recoiled. "You believe that our *Tzenkethi* friends would be the ones to harm him?"

"I believe it's possible."

Alizome leaned forward to speak, but Picard continued his offensive.

"Rusht, has it crossed your mind that even though *you* are scrupulously telling the truth, your allies might be lying? And that they might be lying to *you*?"

Deep disapproval sounded from around the room. Picard lifted his voice to keep pace, but he did not sound aggressive. He merely sounded authoritative.

"There is no proof," he said, "that this bomb was planted by anyone from Starfleet during their visit to your base. It's possible, yes, but it's also possible that it was planted by your so-called allies to prevent you from accepting our offer of alternative medical supplies."

Again, he had to raise his voice to be heard over the noisy consensus surrounding him. "Our officers were on your base for a few hours at the most, and they were accompanied throughout. Your 'allies' certainly had much more opportunity to plant the bomb—and motive."

Now he turned to address the whole room and, through the recording devices, the whole Venette Convention. He swung his hand out toward Alizome, and, with the gesture, implicated her government and her Autarch.

"Isn't it possible," he said, "that they're *lying* to you? That they were lying to you before we arrived, that they've been lying to you throughout these talks, and that they will continue lying to you until their bio-weapons are placed on your base and your three beautiful systems are put into the front line of a bitter war among the major powers? Isn't it *possible*?"

The room fell terribly, frighteningly silent. Crusher gripped her hands around her knees. *I know they've said they prefer plain speaking,* she thought, *but does anyone want to be spoken to so plainly?*

Alizome unraveled from her seat. "This is slander! Captain Picard, how often will you harass my people? Not content with attacking our ships, now you attempt to destroy our friendships—"

"Speaker Alizome," Picard replied, "I am not here to talk to you. I am here to talk to those delegated by the Venette Convention to speak on their behalf. You claim to support their right to self-determination and yet you prove that to be a lie every time you speak on their behalf."

That, Crusher saw, had hit its mark. The consensus around the room collapsed as quickly as it had formed, and every single Venetan seemed to want to make his or her opinion known. Alizome raised her voice in an attempt to be heard over the noise. A mistake, Crusher thought. She was only proving what Jean-Luc had said.

"Such an accusation cannot be allowed to stand!" Alizome cried. "Unless you withdraw it at once, I shall advise the Autarch to close your embassy on Tzenketh and expel all your diplomats."

"Be quiet!" said Rusht, banging the palm of her hand against the table.

Everyone fell silent. Resting her hands flat upon the table, Rusht addressed Picard. "Will you withdraw your accusation?"

"No, I will not."

"And will you order Captain Dax to send Peter Alden to Outpost V-4 and speak to Heldon—and Heldon alone!—to answer her questions?"

"No, I will not. But I have some questions for *you,* Rusht. Will you accept our offer, made in good faith, of alternative medical supplies? Will you ask your friends to turn their ships around?"

Rusht hesitated. Crusher, holding her breath, leaned forward in her seat. She could see the doubt in Rusht's mind. She watched her look around the room, trying to determine whether there was any consensus to be found in the faces around her. Crusher could not tell what that consensus might be, but Rusht seemed to know.

"No," Rusht said, "I will not."

There were some aghast cries around the hall, but more, Crusher thought, there was a strong sense of approval. Rusht, whatever her personal misgivings, had done what they wanted her to do.

"Then regretfully," said Picard, and again he seemed to be addressing the whole Venette Convention, "I must tell you that the militarization of Outpost V-4 will not be permitted. I have consulted Negotiator Detrek, and she has confirmed with her superiors, as I have with mine, that neither of our governments can allow those Tzenkethi ships to enter Venetan space. If the ships try to cross the border, they will be stopped, boarded, and their crews taken prisoner. Is this clear, Rusht?"

"It's clearly an act of war," said Alizome.

"It's clear, Captain," said Rusht. She looked very old now, Crusher thought, and bewildered, as if all the rungs on the ladder of her understanding of the world had suddenly collapsed.

"We'll leave now, Rusht," Picard said. "With your permission, I will take all Federation and Starfleet personnel with me on board the *Enterprise.*"

Rusht nodded her consent.

The Federation contingent departed, surrendering the room to Alizome.

12

FROM:
Civilian Freighter *Inzitran,* flagship, Merchant Fleet 9

TO:
Ementar Vik Tov-A, senior designated speaker, Active Affairs, Department of the Outside

STATUS:
Estimated time to border: 9 skyturns
Estimated time to destination: 14 skyturns

FROM:
Captain Ezri Dax, *U.S.S. Aventine*

TO:
Admiral Leonard Akaar, Starfleet Command

STATUS OF TZENKETHI FLEET:
ETA at Venetan border: 5 days
ETA at Outpost V-4: 7 days

Dax went down to the brig and stood beyond the force field looking in. Alden pulled himself up into a seating position. They stared at each other across the barrier between them.

"So," Alden said. "Made up your mind yet what you're going to do?"

"No."

"Ah." He gave her a chilly smile. "So you still think I'm a potential saboteur?"

"You've not said anything to convince me otherwise."

He stood up and slowly made his way toward her. Soon they were standing only a couple of feet apart. "In that case, you should hand me over."

"It would prevent a war," she pointed out.

"For the moment, anyway." He licked his lips. "It won't be the Venetans who interrogate me, you know. Whatever they say. The Tzenkethi will persuade them to hand me over. Trust me. They're very persuasive."

She waited for him to continue.

"Do you know how they treat enemy agents, Ezri? I do. I've seen the effects. They've no respect for anyone who is not Tzenkethi. We're impure, sources of potential contamination." He laughed. "How do you respect a virus? You can admire its complexity, you admire how well it works to achieve its ends, but even then you study it only to find out ways to defeat it. No, they don't respect us. The higher echelons barely respect their lower grades." He placed his hand upon the force wall and stared directly at her. "Did you know that there's a caste of Tzenkethi bred not to speak? Can you believe that? The scientists decided that they didn't need to speak in order to perform their functions. They're the sick ones. It's a sick society, a wrong society, a *bad* society. We're right to oppose them and we're right to hate them."

Dax drew closer. They were face to face. "You are making a mistake," she said, "if you're still thinking of me as Ezri Tigan. I am Dax. I'm the sum of many parts. I've been a mother, a father, and the lover of both men and women. I've been a diplomat, a legislator, a pilot—yes, and a killer. I've seen countless friends die. I've outlived thousands of them—and still died eight times myself. I'm older than you think—and I'm much less patient than ever. If I can stop a war by handing you over, Peter Alden, you'd better believe I'd do it."

He blinked. Suddenly he seemed very young—and very vulnerable. His face was pale and clammy. He turned away from her quickly, and sat down again, deflated. He folded his arms and closed his eyes. "Then go ahead and do it. It's only what I expected would happen one day."

She left and strode toward her ready room. She was sure that Heldon wouldn't harm him, but she could not be certain that was true of the Tzenkethi. And while she trusted Heldon—trusted her more than she did Alden, whom she'd known for years—how long would Heldon be able to resist Tzenkethi pressure?

Heldon had said that she was afraid. And that fear would be fertile ground for the Tzenkethi to work on, to persuade her to hand Alden over to them. *That sickness,* Dax thought. *None of us are immune. Not even those of us old enough to know better.*

Bowers came to find her.

"We're done here, Ezri," he said. "The talking's over. A blockade of the Venetan system is about to begin. We've received orders to rendezvous with the *Enterprise* on the border." He looked at her sympathetically. "You have to make a decision about Alden."

"I know."

They walked back slowly to the bridge. "As well as our ships," Bowers said, "Cardassian ships are being dispatched to provide support. The Tzenkethi fleet is moving in response. As I say, you need to make a decision about Alden."

They reached the bridge, where Dax gave the orders to set a course to rendezvous with the *Enterprise.*

"Commander Alden?" Bowers asked quietly.

On balance, Dax thought, Alden had probably planted that bomb. But she wasn't going to leave it to the Tzenkethi to get the truth out of him. Besides, she had made him a promise before sending him on the mission to the starbase.

I won't let you down, Peter.

"Commander Alden stays where he is," Dax replied. "I'm not handing over a fellow officer."

Bowers exhaled slowly. "An executive decision, Ezri?"

"Yes."

"I'm glad I wasn't the one having to make it."

"I think that's what the extra pip is for, Sam."

The Federation was leaving Venette. Glinn Dygan, uncertain of his immediate duty, stood by a wall in the atrium of the Hall of Assembly and tried to look inconspicuous. Not easy for a Cardassian in this place, particularly one of Dygan's size and, worse, in uniform. The stream of people exiting the meeting hall and coalescing in gangs of two and three to dissect events shot him angry—even poisonous— looks as they went past.

It was a relief to see Doctor Crusher on the far side of the atrium. She waved in greeting and slowly pushed her way through the crowd toward him.

"Dygan," she said, "the Captain asked me to find you. You're with us."

Dygan slowly exhaled. "Thank you, Doctor," he said. "I'm not sure I could—" He left his sentence unfinished, but Crusher nodded her understanding. He could not serve Detrek. "Well," he said. "We tried."

"*Some* of us tried."

His face paled and he dropped his head. She touched his arm.

"Hey, it's not your fault."

"Thank you, Doctor, but I can't help feeling responsible for what my people have done here—"

"You can't be responsible for that. Only for yourself. And you've acquitted yourself admirably. The problem was that some people came here wanting a fight. Not just Detrek. Alizome too. That's all it takes."

He nodded slowly and looked around the atrium. "I suppose we should leave. I doubt we're welcome here."

"I suppose so." Crusher reached up to tap her combadge, but her hand stopped partway there. She was looking across the room. Dygan, following her gaze, saw Rusht.

Rusht was very frail. She walked slowly, leaning on Vitig for support. As she passed through the crowd, the Venetans fell back, opening up a pathway for her to pass through unhindered, murmuring their thanks and respect. Dygan dropped his eyes. He felt ashamed looking at her, as if he was in part responsible for her sudden decline.

"Dygan," Crusher said. "Come with me. One last chance."

She pushed her way purposefully toward Rusht. Dygan followed as quickly as he could. When they reached the two Venetans, Crusher said, "Rusht. Please. May I speak to you?"

Vitig glared at her. "Have you and your people not done enough damage already?"

"The damage so far is nothing compared to what we'll see if we don't stop this," Crusher replied. "Rusht, I'm a doctor. I took an oath to cause no harm. I don't know what your people know about war, but it's *terrible*. Whatever horrors you've imagined, it's a hundred—a thousand—times worse." She was speaking very quickly. "I've sat by friends and been unable to do anything to save them. I've told other friends that their loved ones have died. Your worlds are beautiful, Rusht. Your people are gracious and wise—but in this respect you are innocents. I don't want you and your people to see all that I've seen since I last came to your world."

"Then go away and leave us in peace!" Vitig snapped. "Take your ships away from our borders. Let us be friends with whoever we choose—"

"Your friends mean us harm, Vitig," Crusher said. "And if these medical supplies are indeed as innocent as they claim, then the secrecy and threat in which they've been cloaked sickens me. Do you know what navithium resins do to human flesh? I do. I've seen what the burns are like. I've seen the state of human lungs that have breathed in air thick with navithium. If you had seen that, you'd understand why we react with such horror even to the suggestion of such weapons close to us. My oath as a doctor—to do no harm—means I cannot simply go away and leave you in peace. Because the same courtesy is not being extended to me."

The atrium had fallen silent. Dygan held his breath. Rusth, who had been listening quietly, but with attention, looked around. "Where is Alizome?" Her voice was weak and trembling. "Our friend should have the chance to reply to this."

"Not Alizome," Crusher said firmly. "These are *your* worlds, Rusht—"

Too late. Alizome, passing through the crowd like

a streak of lightning, reached Rusht's side. She grasped the old woman's other arm. "Are they distressing you?" she murmured. "They should have left by now."

"Alizome." Desperation had crept into Crusher's voice. "You can stop this. Please, stop it!"

"That is up to you, Doctor." Her eye fell on Dygan. "You may wish to begin by curbing your Cardassian friends. This latest threat is surely beyond even that bloodthirsty people."

"What threat?" said Dygan.

Alizome turned her cold gaze on him. "To attack Outpost V-15 if the blockade there is broken."

"But that's not a military base," Dygan said. "Those people are civilians—"

"You should take that up with your castellan, Glinn Dygan," Alizome replied.

"I don't believe you," Crusher said flatly. Vitig's hackles rose.

"You're accusing her of *lying*?"

"Yes," Crusher said. "I am. I wonder if she'll deny it. I wonder if she can."

Alizome merely smiled. Then Crusher's communicator chirped. Alizome, tightening her grip on Rusht's arm, drew the old woman away. "You should take that message, Doctor. Better still, you and your allies should leave."

The time had come. Neta Efheny listened to the soft sounds of sleeping that were coming from the bunk above her, and then, carefully, she eased first one foot out of the bed and then the other. Overhead, Corazame shifted. Efheny froze, but Corazame did not wake.

Subvocalizing instructions to her bioengineering, Efheny switched on her night vision to make the little room clear to her. She instructed her audio-disruption devices to come on, to mask any sound that she might make leaving the room. Then, carefully, she levered herself up from the bed. Movement was what would give her away. Fortunately Corazame, who had been in a state of high excitement since their meeting with Inzegil, seemed to have worn herself out recounting the tale to their fellow travelers, and she was fast asleep.

Efheny slipped across the room and out into the narrow corridor that ran between the Ata cabins. There was nobody in sight. She stole along the corridor toward the door that led out onto the deck. Shivering from the night chill, she hurried across to the bench where, for the past few skyturns, she had been concealing supplies. A small amount of food. A knife. A medkit. Everything else she carried with her. The map to lead her to the location was part of her visual display. The beacon built into her bioengineering would automatically send the signal for her pickup and would switch on shortly before she was due to be transported out.

Really, her superiors had thought of everything. All Efheny had to do was walk up into the hills and sit at the pickup location until her transport arrived. Once her extraction was complete, they would remove the small data recorder embedded above her left eye and take the data away to analyze. She would be given back her old body and her old life.

Efheny shivered again and quickly stashed her gear, then looked out from the boat. The previous evening they had come out of the winding passages between the coral caverns and docked against the small island that marked the midpoint of their voyage. Tomorrow, the boat would turn around and return to the city, taking its passengers back to their functions. But it would leave without Efheny on board. She was making her way inland, up into the hills. Her priority now was to put as much distance between her and the boat as she possibly could before she was missed.

An access ladder ran down one side of the boat. Efheny climbed down this and then—slowly, carefully—stretched out one leg so that her foot was touching the shore. For a moment, she hung in unsteady limbo, then she gathered her nerves together and made the jump ashore.

She landed with a thump and rolled flat onto the ground. Her breath came short and rapid. She listened hard but could hear nothing other than the gentle lap of the water, the creak of the old boat. After a few minutes like this, she was satisfied that nobody had heard her leave.

Time to go. Efheny stood up and looked ahead. Her superiors had chosen her exit point wisely: a few paces in front of her, a small wood of *keteki* trees would provide good cover for the first stage of her walk inland. She oriented herself with the pointer on her visual display and moved quickly and silently toward the trees. They were well spaced, *keteki* trees of this height needing room and moisture, allowing her to make good progress. Soon the boat was far behind her.

As she walked, and the adrenaline rush that had brought her this far began to fade, she reflected upon how easily she had slipped back into her role as an operative. How quickly the training kicked in, almost as if it was instinct, something you were born to. Even after so long undercover, you never forgot it, not really. It was etched into you—they made sure of that—like deep scores across your psyche. And yet the work itself . . . Efheny suppressed a sudden surge of laughter. It was like her cover job. Long hours of tedium followed by moments of gut-wrenching terror and high anxiety, when you thought you were about to be exposed, or when Karenzen Ter Ata-D was yelling your name. Thought of Karenzen made her think of Corazame, and Efheny felt a rare stab of guilt that, in arranging for Hertome's reconditioning, she had condemned Corazame to Karenzen's care. Poor Cory was in for a miserable time.

But that was not Efheny's problem, not any longer, and she could not afford to let her mind stray back to the life she had been leading until recently. She turned her attention instead to her immediate task of getting as far as she could before morning. Cory was an early riser, and Efheny reckoned she had no more than a quarter skyturn before she was missed. So she set a good pace, and she did not let her mind drift back to everything she was leaving behind. She focused instead on her surroundings: the tall trees with their purplish bark and silvery leaves, the ever more distant whisper of the lagoon, the occasional bark of a night animal on the hunt. She listened for any sound that her absence had been noted, any alarm or hue and cry from the water's edge. Nothing came, but the fact that she was listening was what counted. It meant that, within the space of about an hour, Neta Efheny knew without a doubt that she was being followed, that she too was being hunted.

"Commander Alden remains on board the Aventine,*"* said Picard. *"Has Admiral Akaar made his opinion on this known yet?"*

"With respect to the admiral, if he wanted Alden handed over to the Tzenkethi, he needed to issue some instructions to that effect." Dax ran her hand through her hair. The conspicuous lack of orders about Alden's fate prior to the departure of the *Aventine* from Outpost V-4 troubled her, adding substance to her fears that Starfleet Intelligence might have been behind the attempted bombing of the base.

"What do you intend to do with him?"

"For now, he's confined to the brig. But I guess I'll be handing him over to Starfleet Command, as soon as—"

Picard gave a wry smile. *"As soon as all this is over, do you mean? That could be some time, Dax."*

"Then he'd better get comfortable," she said bitterly. Wearily she contemplated the paperwork piling up on her desk: new shift rosters, crew rotations, all the necessary rearrangement to put the ship back on high alert. This was just the lull before the storm. "What happened? What went wrong?"

"On Venette? Simple enough. The Cardassians came spoiling for a fight, and the Tzenkethi were willing to give it to them."

"But you've been in situations like this before. Why has this one spiraled so badly out of control? Surely nobody really *wants* a war? Not now, not after so much death . . ."

"One would hope not."

"So why were people so ready to let it happen? Where were all the good guys when we needed them?"

"The best lacked all conviction," suggested Picard.

"Yes, yes, and the worst were full of passionate intensity. But that's not true, is it? I don't lack conviction. And neither do you. What I lack is any real sense of who my allies are, and I don't mean people with whom my government has signed an agreement. I don't even necessarily mean people wearing the same uniform. Look at Peter Alden!"

"Who do you mean, then?"

"I mean . . . people who share the same values as us. People who are prepared to risk trusting each other. People who greet strangers with an open mind and an open hand, hoping for friendship. People who, when faced with something new, something different, are

curious rather than mistrustful. I remember when . . ."
Dax trailed off.

"We'll get there again," Picard said.

"Will we? Rushing from crisis to crisis, we're changing. And what will we become? Will there be any room for those of us who want to understand other civilizations? Am I overreacting?"

Picard sighed deeply. *"Do I think we are losing sight of one of our primary purposes? Yes, I do. But what else is there to be done? A child . . ."* He frowned, and she wondered if he was thinking of his own son now. *"A child needs security in order to be able to explore in safety."*

"There's only one problem with that analogy."

"Yes?"

"We're not children."

"So we fondly imagine." He smiled. *"Get some sleep, Dax. We'll speak again tomorrow in person."*

They cut the comm, but Dax remained at her desk for a little while longer and ran through the events of the past week, trying to see the steps that had led them here. What was it they said about the road to hell?

Velentur Island was remote, and the pier stuck out some way into the open water of the lagoon, so Inzegil went up to meet her colleagues from the city, while Artamer went to get Hertome. Inzegil was no more comfortable outside than most Tzenkethi, but her desire to perform her function effectively generally overrode this.

The enforcer air car lowered itself almost soundlessly onto the water, slipping into position next to the pier. The Atas were temporarily confined to their decks on the other side of the boat and would not hear or be troubled by Hertome's removal. Seeing the familiar face of her colleagues Getiger and Zedenzik, Inzegil waved. They raised their hands in greeting in their turn.

"Arty shivering downstairs, is he?" Zedenzik said, once they were aboard.

"Performing his function to the best of his capabilities," Inzegil said, mock-virtuously. Her colleagues laughed.

"So we have an Ata-C who thinks too much of himself," said Getiger. "What about the Rets? Are we taking them too?"

Inzegil shook her head. "I think they've learned their lesson."

Getiger whistled. "Hope you didn't come on too strong with them, Inz. We want them still functional."

"Let's say they're unlikely to forget the encounter, which I think is all to the good. Artamer and I are going to travel back with them and make sure they return safely to their tasks. Has the Department of the Outside reopened yet?"

"As closed as an A-bulletin," Getiger said. "Whatever's happening up there, these ones might get a few more days' restoration out of it yet."

"I'm sure we can arrange redeployment for them," Inzegil said thoughtfully. "Too much restoration time can make Atas fretful and unsettled. It's not good for them. I'll get onto it once we're under way. Some new tenements are about to open near mine, and the building work's nearing completion. The place is a mess. A few freshly restored maintenance units would come in useful."

"You're a tough one, Inzy," Zedenzik said with a smile.

"It's in their best interests," she said. "And it would be irresponsible of us to give them the opportunity to be unhappy."

Zedenzik nodded around the boat. "Are you really planning to travel all the way back on this thing?" His skin glittered. "Poor Art. What's he done to deserve you?"

"He's honored to perform his function to the best of his capabilities," Inzegil said, getting another laugh. She checked the time. "Where is he? It shouldn't take this long to bring an Ata-C up from his cabin."

She turned back to the boat and was met by one of the Ata-EE servers, who gestured to her that she was wanted down below by the other Ap-Rej. Leaving her colleagues, Inzegil went quickly down to the Ata section. Artamer was standing by Hertome's cabin, a grim expression on his face. Inzegil knew what she would see before she looked.

Hertome Ter Ata-C's cabin was empty.

"He's gone," said Artamer tersely. "Don't know when and don't know how. That door was sealed tight."

"Have you checked on the Rets?"

"Sent a server. Didn't want to go marching in there."

Inzegil nodded her agreement with his decision.

This case had caused enough disruption to this voyage already. Now that there had been a serious new development, it was imperative that none of the Atas got wind of it.

The server soon returned. With the quick hand signals that her kind were trained to offer their superiors (efficiency being more important from them than obeisance, which was taken for granted), she reported that Corazame and Mayazan were not to be found in their cabin, or anywhere in the Ata section, or anywhere beyond. Inzegil's heart sank. This was exactly what she feared might happen: that Hertome would run away and take the Rets with him. But whether they had gone willingly, or whether Hertome had forced them, Inzegil did not yet know.

Nan Bacco checked the mirror. She looked sharp, despite forty hours without sleep, thanks to an ocean of coffee, a cold shower, and a stylist-on-call. She needed to be sharp. Sharp as a scalpel. The Cardassian Ambassador to the United Federation of Planets was about to pay her a call.

The door swung open. Garak entered, polished as a much-used weapon. At Bacco's signal, he took the seat opposite. "Well, Madame President," he said, with a smile. "The best laid schemes of mice and men—and allies—gang aft agley."

Garak's knowledge of human literature would put a professor to shame. Usually Bacco enjoyed batting epigrams his way, but she wasn't in the mood for literary banter this morning. Instead, she got down to business. "Don't make me order Starfleet to fire on your ships, Ambassador."

Garak's smile broadened. "You won't do that."

"You want to bet?"

"You need us as much as we need you."

"I'll send ships to defend that base—"

Garak opened his palm. "By all means, do. But try to remember that we are your ally. Not your enemy—and certainly not your satellite."

Bacco leaned forward in her chair. "Damn it, Garak! What's Garan playing at?"

Garak pursed his lips. "Believe me when I say that I too find the castellan very tiresome on occasion. But it plays well in public."

She looked at him. He looked unblinkingly back. Then he turned and looked out of the window. *Ah*, thought Bacco. *So that's it. A little posturing from the castellan to make sure we don't take her for granted.* Her eyes narrowed as she studied Garak, still absorbed in whatever the hell was going on outside. Suddenly, he turned to look at her directly. He was smiling, as if to say: *Have you caught up yet?*

I wonder, Bacco thought, *what exactly Garan asked him to say.*

"Sometimes," said the Cardassian Ambassador to the United Federation of Planets, "I think I've spent too much time among humans. Too long away from Cardassia." His smile slipped. "As yet, the question of our attacking the unhappy Venetans is, I am glad to say, for the future. In the meantime we should, I believe, maintain a united front." His eyes went icy. "Still, it won't do the Venetans any harm to believe that they're in danger."

You cold-blooded, coldhearted bastard.

"Madame President, before we move on I simply must say—that particular shade of emerald is a *triumph* on you. Now—what's next on our agenda?"

FROM:
Nanietta Bacco, President, United Federation of Planets
Rakena Garan, Castellan, Cardassian Union

TO:
The people gathered under the Venette Convention
Alizome Vik Tov-A, designated speaker for Korzenten Rej Tov-AA, Autarch of the Tzenkethi Coalition

We repeat our request that the twelve ships en route to the Venetan System halt in their approach. We restate the warnings given by our representatives on Venette: none of these ships will be allowed to enter Venetan space. We urge you to seek a peaceful settlement to this crisis.

FROM:
Inzegil Ter Mak-B, Senior Enforcer, Area 9,
Subsection 56

TO:
Her most excellent Ap-Rej Mertikor Ter-Mak-A[?],
acting head of Unit 9, Department of Behavioral
Supervision

MESSAGE:
One certified and two potential Ata runaways at loose
on Velentur Island (within jurisdiction Subsection
72). Possibility of hostage situation. Requesting
immediate air support from Subsection 72.

In the name of our most beloved and exalted
Autarch Korzenten Rej Tov-AA, and in defense
of the integrity of his order, I serve and salute
you!

- - - - - - - - -

FROM:
Admiral Leonard Akaar, Starfleet Command

TO:
Captain Ezri Dax, *U.S.S. Aventine*

PRIORITY MESSAGE, SECURITY CODE ALPHA-2:
Do not proceed on your rendezvous with the force currently deployed on the Venetan border. New coordinates to follow.

In addition, Commander Peter Alden is to be restored immediately to active duty. Be aware that this order comes directly from the office of the president of the Federation.

Week 3

Resolutions

13

4 DAYS TO WAR . . .

FROM:
A syndic formed to consider evacuation
procedures

TO:
The people gathered under the Venette Convention

MESSAGE:
Do you need to evacuate your dwelling? These
guidelines will help you decide and help you to
evacuate.

You do not need to evacuate if you live in a 60+%
green area. Any attack will be targeted on so-
called "urban areas." So-called "rural areas"
should be safe. You may wish to consider whether
you can help with evacuees. Consult the syndic
formed to consider evacuee care.

You are advised not to evacuate if you cannot easily reach transport. This may be because your transportation is unreliable, or because you are too young, old, or unwell. Consult the syndic formed to create shelters. A sub-syndic will exist in your area that can assist in building shelters.

You are asked to consider not evacuating if you have expertise that can be drawn on: medical, firefighting, communications. Sub-syndics are being formed in your area to coordinate your skills.

All others: consider evacuating. This syndic has created a checklist of what you should take with you and the steps you should follow. This checklist follows . . .

CAPTAIN JEAN-LUC PICARD
CAPTAIN'S LOG
The twelve Tzenkethi ships remain en route for Outpost V-4 and our listening posts along the border report fleet activity. The Cardassians too are building up their fleet along their border with the Venette Convention near Outpost V-15 and there remains the possibility that they might not only fire on Venetan ships but also go on the offensive. This would of course put a strain on our relations with the Cardassians and I can only hope

that we do not find ourselves in the impossible position of trying to protect the Venetans on one border while blockading them on another.

One last ship had been permitted entry into the Venetan system. Reaching the bridge of the *Enterprise* just in time, Crusher watched as the Ferengi vessel *Zek*, bearing Madame Ilka and the staff from the Ferengi embassy on Venette, crossed out of Venetan space and went into warp. As far as the Federation and Starfleet were concerned, the border was now closed.

"That's the last," Worf said.

"Thank you, Commander Worf," Picard said. Leaving the bridge to his first officer, he went into his ready room. Crusher followed.

They listened for a while to transmissions coming from the Venetan broadcasters, as they offered advice to the people of the three systems on how to organize themselves in the event of a Cardassian attack and any subsequent Tzenkethi reprisals. Crusher nearly cried to hear their dogged bravery. She listened to instructions for evacuation procedures, how to build quick shelters, how to give emergency medical aid. Eventually, Picard cut the comm. "It won't come to that, Beverly. I promise."

"Isn't there *some* kind of pressure you could be putting on Detrek?"

"I'm pressing as hard as I dare. You'll recall the admiral's instructions to keep the Cardassians sweet."

"But that was before this threat to Outpost V-15. The Venetans have no military to speak of. The Cardassians would be firing on civilians. Can't you speak to Detrek again?"

"Beverly, there'll be back-channel discussions going on that we know nothing about. I can't simply blunder in and demand that Detrek does something. What can she do? She's as powerless as I am."

"So we do nothing?"

"We do what we can. We carry out our orders to maintain the blockade—and we await new orders."

"And if the Cardassians open fire on civilians?"

The lines on his face hardened. "Then we'll do what we must."

The enforcers from Subsection 72 greeted Inzegil and Artamer cautiously but with some quiet excitement. They were junior to them both, hence the rural rather than the urban beat, and trouble rarely came this far out.

"We have one confirmed runaway and two potentials," Inzegil explained. "I'm concerned about the welfare of those two. The confirmed runaway may be unbalanced and may become desperate."

Trekitor Ter Mak-C said, "Whatever you need, Ter Inzegil. We can put air cars at your disposal, heat detectors—"

"All of it," Inzegil said. She glanced at her colleague, standing by. "Well, Arty? Do you want to go back with the others to the city? Getiger said he'd stay if you preferred."

Artamer sighed. "I'll stay to the bitter end, Inz. But wait till I get my hands on Hertome Ter Ata-C. He'll be begging for Re-Co by the time I've finished with him."

After a skyturn, Efheny abandoned her attempts to shake off her pursuer. She was having no success, and the meandering path forced on her as a result was in danger of making her late for the pickup. There would be only a small window of opportunity for the ship sent to collect her to come this deep into Tzenkethi space and make a safe exit. She would have to force her pursuer into the open.

She stopped to take stock of her surroundings. The *keteki* trees provided her with cover, but they did the same for him. Still, she was fairly sure which direction he was coming from. Scouring the immediate area, she picked up a thick branch that had fallen from one of the upper boughs. She tested its weight. Good. Solid. Hardly a disruptor, but it would do. Sitting down with her back against the twin trunk of one of the trees, she held up her makeshift weapon so that it was clearly visible and waited for her shadow to reveal himself.

She assumed it was Hertome. It was certainly someone who knew what he was doing, but enforcers would have air cars and trackers at their disposal, and would surely have made swifter progress. This was somebody who wanted to follow rather than capture her. No doubt he'd been watching to see when she left the boat and then sneaked out of his cabin and trailed her ever since. But he would be missed as soon as the enforcers arrived from the city to collect him.

Efheny cursed him under her breath. It would be just her luck if the enforcers sent to track the runaway Hertome stumbled over her instead. She gripped her branch. As long as he was following, he would be bringing enforcers after her.

She heard a crack of twigs nearby. She knew he could have prevented her from hearing that, so he must want her to know that he was close. She rolled her weapon around in her hands.

"Hey, Hertome! Weren't you meant to be going for reconditioning? Your escort will be here by now. You'll be missed. You'll be bringing people after us." *You crazy liability of a human,* she added to herself.

"One more reason for you to take me with you, Mayazan!" he called back. Now she knew exactly where he was. "Tell you what, why don't we just hurry to your pickup point? Then nobody gets caught and everybody's happy."

"Are you armed, Hertome?"

"Alex," he called. "My name is Alex."

"I don't want to know your name!"

"Easier to kill someone then, isn't it? I know all the tricks of the trade, remember? You're not getting away with my murder that easily, Mayazan. I'm Alex Gardner, I'm twenty-seven years old, and my old mother thinks I'm on a humanitarian mission to one of your worlds. You know, on account of us being allies? Remember that? Allies? I'm Alex Gardner, your ally, and you're going to know the name of the man you're killing."

She cursed him. Then: "What do you want?"

"You know what I want. Take me with you!"

"I'm not authorized to do that—"

"*Authorized?* Mayazan, this is life or death. We're supposed to be *allies*."

"You're the one who chose to break cover. You kept following me. If you'd just kept your head down, you'd be safe in the city right now!"

"I wouldn't! I told you, our network's being rolled up. They'll have my colleagues by now, and they'll be coming for me soon." His voice became desperate. "I can't let that happen, Mayazan. I can't let them take me. Surely you understand that?"

But Efheny didn't understand. Again, she found herself bewildered at the decision his superiors had made to send him here. Did he not understand that there were certain risks you took upon yourself when you chose this line of work? You accepted them and you got on with the job. Tormenting yourself with the prospect of capture and interrogation only destabilized you. You put it out of your mind, or else, if it became inevitable, you did not struggle. Struggling only meant it would hurt more. *Don't think of capture unless it happens,* her instructors had said. *Then accept your fate.* If Alex Gardner—*no*, she told herself firmly, *Hertome Ter Ata-C*—could not bear the thought of being in Tzenkethi hands, then he should not be on Ab-Tzenketh, and the people who had sent him here were the ones murdering him, not her. *Humans,* she thought again, bitterly. *They are a menace!* But she was stuck with one, and he wasn't going away, and he was bringing enforcers closer all the time. She needed to get moving again, and quickly.

Deliberately, Efheny put down the branch. With her back still against the tree trunk, she stood up. She raised her hands to show she was now unarmed.

"Come out," she said. "We'll talk."

There was a pause, and then he emerged from behind a nearby tree. He still looked like Hertome, which would help. He walked toward her, slowly and uncertainly. When he was close, but not within range, he stopped.

"Thanks," he said.

"You're welcome," she replied. Then she shot forward, ramming the side of her hand into his neck, launching herself onto him, and struggling to get both her hands around his neck. She very nearly had him, but he was a professional too and, in a split second, her advantage was lost.

They fought fiercely, bitterly, both knowing that her advantage was that he didn't dare kill her; both knowing that her disadvantage was that much more delay would cost them both the opportunity to leave. She had speed, but he had strength, with which he grappled himself around on top of her. Just as she thought she was going to lose, she heard someone cry her name. He was pulled away from her.

Taking her chance, Efheny scrambled backward

and up onto her haunches. She started in dismay at the sight of her deliverer, who was now ineffectually beating Hertome on the back with both fists.

It was Corazame.

Dax received the *Aventine*'s new instructions directly from Admiral Akaar. She set a new course for Cardassian space, where she was to rendezvous with a Cardassian ship, the *Aklaren*. With Akaar still on the line, Dax raised her concerns about this vague new mission.

"May I ask why the *Aventine* is being sent?"

"It will become clear when you rendezvous with the Aklaren. *In the meantime, best possible speed."*

"Wouldn't it be better if we assisted the *Enterprise*? We're the closest ship, we're the fastest ship. And it's not going to be much of a blockade while there's only the *Enterprise* there—"

"They've got plenty of support coming, Starfleet and Cardassian. But the Aventine? *We're going to need your speed elsewhere."* Akaar frowned. *"It'll make sense in time, Captain."*

"I have one more question, sir."

Akaar glared at her. *"Proceed, Captain."*

"Peter Alden."

"Yes, I thought you'd want to ask about him."

"Is it wise to put him back on active duty?"

"I assume you're not seriously going to accuse an officer of Alden's caliber of such a hasty and ill-judged act?"

Still deeply uncertain about the truth of what had

happened on Outpost V-4 and the extent to which Starfleet Intelligence might be implicated, Dax forbore pressing further. To do so might imply that the admiral was also party to . . . what had he called it? A "hasty and ill-judged act."

"There's also the question mark hanging over his state of mind. Are we sure it's in Alden's best interests to expose him to further stress?"

"We're all stressed. We're in the middle of a crisis. We need every hand on deck—"

"Have you read the report of my ship's counselor?"

"I have. But seriously, Dax—has she spoken to Alden at any length?"

"Not at length, no, sir."

While Alden had been in the brig, Hyatt had taken the opportunity to speak to him, but even a counselor as experienced as Susan Hyatt would need a considerable length of time to work with a man like Alden. Trained interrogators were among the most difficult patients, as Ezri Dax had cause to know, and all Alden had to do was sit there and say nothing. Susan Hyatt was probably canny enough to get through eventually, but certainly not without time—and they were running out of time.

The fact that he wasn't talking troubled Dax. *Was Peter under orders?* That thought troubled Dax even more. Heldon's rebuke that Alden's active status spoke badly of Starfleet's concern for its people weighed heavily in her mind. Was it simply that he was indispensable for this new mission? What would Peter Alden say if somebody ordered him to talk?

"Well," Akaar said, *"when your counselor has spoken to him at length, I'll read that report with interest. In the meantime, you have an experienced officer at your disposal. You'll be needing him over the next few days. Akaar out."*

Let's hope he's fit for duty, then, Dax thought. *Or as fit as the rest of us.* But "needing him"? Dax didn't like the sound of that. Not given what she suspected of Peter Alden's particular areas of expertise.

"Cory!" Efheny said in horror. "What are you *doing* here?"

Hertome swung around and grasped Corazame by her wrists. She struggled against him for a while, until he ordered sharply, "Ret Corazame! Stop this at once!"

Her conditioning ran deep. She stopped, and hung her head, and gestured an apology as best she could with her trapped hands. Efheny, moving carefully around Hertome, came closer.

"Cory, why are you here? You shouldn't be here."

Corazame looked up at her with big, fearful eyes. "I'm here to look after you, of course."

From within the cover of the audio disruptors, Efheny heard Hertome laugh. She hated him more than ever.

"I woke in the night," Corazame said. "You'd gone. I was worried that he . . . the Ap-Rej . . . I was worried he'd done something to hurt you, so I slipped out and saw you leaving the boat. Then I understood." She looked at Efheny with reproachful eyes. "Oh, Maymi! You shouldn't have lied to me. You know I would have understood. I knew you'd be meeting him, so I followed you. Maymi, listen to me, please! I don't know what he's said to you, but it isn't true. You can't get away. There's nowhere to go. Where would you go? You can't live beyond the cities. Nobody can live out . . . out here, in the wild."

"Cory, it's not like that—"

"I know he's said he loves you, but he's lying! Maymi, you have to stop this before it goes too far and you're lost for good. They'll decommission you. You'll be null! It's not worth that. And you don't have to do what he tells you—"

"Cory, we're not lovers. We were never lovers."

Corazame looked at her in confusion. "Then why did you say you were?" She glanced uncertainly back at Hertome. "What's happening? What's going on?"

From within the audio-disruption field, Hertome said, "Are you going to tell her? Or shall I?"

Efheny didn't answer. She walked over to where she'd left her branch on the ground. Picking it up, she went to the *keteki* tree under which she'd waited for Hertome. Then, in a sudden frenzy of rage and frustration, she beat at it, hard, with the branch, screaming and cursing. When she was done, she turned back around.

Hertome was watching her in fascination. Corazame, however, was sitting on the ground, weeping, with both arms wrapped around her head, as if that meant that somehow she couldn't be seen. Stupid, stupid little Cory.

"Finished?" Hertome said.

Efheny blinked. *Yes.*

"We'll travel together from here on, Mayazan. Otherwise, you know what I'll do. I'll go back to the boat, and this one"—he gestured down to Corazame—"this one will be coming with me. When the enforcers take me, they'll take her too."

"You're not going to put one finger on her," Efheny said, stepping toward him.

She stopped. High above them, but coming closer, was the clear *chik-chik-chik* of an air car.

"Enforcers!" Hertome hissed. He dived for cover, pulling Corazame with him, and Efheny flattened herself against the tree. The air car came close enough overhead to set the leaves of the *keteki* tree shaking but swept past and away across the island. When they were sure it had gone, Hertome came back out, dragging Corazame along with him. Slowly, Efheny went toward him. She did not meet Corazame's frightened and questioning eyes.

"I imagine," Hertome said, "that you're following a visual display toward the pickup point. So we'll follow you. What happens when you get there?"

"There's a portable transporter hidden up there," Efheny said. "I have to activate it by a certain time to ensure the pickup takes place."

"Where's it hidden?"

"Farther up the hill." She nodded at Corazame.

"Look, Hertome. Alex. You've got what you want. You can let her go. Send her back to the boat. She'll probably get in trouble for going off alone, but she won't face more than a few extra work shifts and Karenzen will make it bad enough for her. She's suffered enough. Let her go."

"She'll tell the enforcers where we are. She won't be able to help herself."

"Not if I ask her not to. Come on, Alex. This is between us. Besides, you know what she's like. She's a little fool. One night outside and I bet she starts screaming loud enough to bring half the Tzenkethi secret service down on us."

She thought for a moment she had him, but he shook his head and pushed Corazame forward. "No. This one is my insurance policy. You try anything, I'll hurt her. You try to hand me over to the enforcers again, and she comes with me. She can go home when I'm on my way home." He gave a grim smile. "Lead on, Mayazan."

14

3 DAYS TO WAR . . .

GLINN RAVEL DYGAN, PERSONAL LOG
I've never been ashamed to be Cardassian—until today. Sure, it's not as if we're the most peaceful people in the Alpha Quadrant, but those of my generation weren't responsible for that aggression and we've been doing our best to stop that from ever happening again. But what do you do when your elders seem to be heading down that same path? How do you stop them? Detrek said to trust her. I'm not sure I trust myself anymore.

Nearly six hours from the border between Cardassian and Tzenkethi space, the *Aventine* rendezvoused with a slick, small Cardassian cruiser heading their way. Once communications were established, an operative from the Cardassian Intelligence Bureau who offered the name Hogue Nekelen asked permission to come aboard. Dax was watching as her transporter chief, Spon, activated the controls.

Nekelen, when he materialized, turned out to be small and slick, not in uniform but impeccably dressed in the rich dark colors that Cardassians favored. His black hair was trimmed short, in the new fashion that had taken hold since the Dominion War (the regulation longer, military style had for some reason fallen out of favor). He did not delay in briefing Dax on their mission.

"We have an undercover agent in urgent need of extraction," Nekelen explained, as Dax led him to the nearest conference room. "But time is of the essence in this mission, and at the request of our ambassador to your world, your president has kindly offered the fastest ship at her disposal in order to assist us in completing the extraction in time."

"An undercover *spy*?" Dax couldn't quite believe what she was hearing. A blockade of the Venetan system was under way with ships from three fleets massing on the border and preparing for open war, and *Aventine* was being sent on a fetch-and-carry run? Or had Ambassador Garak not quite forgiven Ensign Dax for her clumsy attempt to cure his claustrophobia all those years ago? "Well, Nekelen, does the ambassador know that Starfleet is on a war footing?"

Nekelen's icy smile didn't reach his eyes. "With the greatest respect, Captain Dax, we are not yet at war. There are three days, are there not, before the Tzenkethi ships reach the Venetan border?"

"Yes—"

"—which gives us *ample* time to our destination and back so that you might participate in the latest brouhaha besetting our already bedeviled alliances."

Brouhaha? *Bedeviled?* Were all Cardassian spies sent on a special course so they could sound like Garak? Wasn't the Obsidian Order supposed to be defunct? Or did they model themselves after Garak as a matter of course? Fair enough if they did, Dax acknowledged. If anyone could be called the winner of the deadly game played by the Obsidian Order, it was surely her ever-smiling, never-shabby former client and current ambassador to the Federation, Elim Garak. No doubt his legend and mystique would endure. And no doubt he was delighted that this was the case.

"May I at least ask," said Dax, "where exactly this agent is right now?"

Nekelen looked almost pained to be asked such an obvious question. "Why, Captain! Ab-Tzenketh, of course. Surely you didn't think we'd pull you away from the blockade for anything less?"

"Oh, no, of course not. Where else would I be? I'm just glad it's not anywhere heavily defended or currently on high alert. Otherwise we might *really* be in trouble."

Nekelen beamed at her. "Well, generally speaking, these things are simply a matter of planning and expertise. Which reminds me, I really must speak to Commander Alden as soon as he's available. We'll be

needing him, I suspect, if we're going to get into Tzenkethi space and out alive."

A red light pulsed brightly in the corner of Neta
Efheny's eye and then cut out. They'd reached the
pickup point.

She stopped to look around. They were about two-
thirds of the way up a hill, and there was little in the
way of cover. Corazame, stopping behind her, said,
"Maymi, I don't like it here."

Of course she didn't. There was nothing to dis-
tract her from the open sky, the slope behind them,
and the view out to the lagoon. Efheny thought it was
beautiful, but Tzenkethi preferred to observe the natural wonders of their own world through holoscreens.
"Don't worry, Cory," she said. "We'll find somewhere
to shelter. You won't be out here for long."

"Mayazan," said Hertome from within the disruption field, "is this the place? Is this the pickup point?"
He too surveyed the area, but with more professional
expertise than Corazame could bring. "Are you sure
this is where we're supposed to be? It's not the place
I would have chosen. We're far too exposed. Anyone
coming this way by air would easily spot us."

"I'm sure," Efheny said. She pointed ahead. "Look,
there are *cezik* bushes over there. They might offer
some cover."

At least, she hoped they would offer cover. The previous night had been grim: the three of them huddled
together under a makeshift roof that Efheny and Her-

tome had pulled together from leafy *keteki* branches. They'd all sat under it, sleepless, listening for air cars. Hertome and Efheny had combined their heat reflectors in the hope that they would cover Corazame too. It seemed to work. But in the early hours of morning, Corazame began to weep, silently but uncontrollably. Efheny had dosed her with calmers from the medkit. She'd been dozy and docile all day as a result, letting Efheny pull her and Hertome push her wherever they wanted her to be.

They walked in single file around the contours of the hill: Efheny in the lead, Hertome at the rear, and Corazame sandwiched between them. The bushes, when they reached them, turned out to be clumped around a wide hollow in the hillside.

Efheny slid down into the hollow and took its measure. It was not quite the height of the average person, but it was certainly wide enough to fit the three of them. And it wouldn't be for long, of course. She tugged at the branches of the bushes. "We can make some cover with this," she said. "Come on, Cory. I'll show you what to do."

As they worked, Cory seemed to wake up a little. She turned her back to Hertome and whispered to Efheny, "Why are we doing this, Maymi? We shouldn't be hiding. They're only going to find us. We should go back before that happens. Plead our case, plead for forgiveness. I know . . ." She glanced back over her shoulder. "I know that whatever you said before, Hertome must have forced you to come out here."

"Cory," Efheny said firmly, "nobody forced me to come out here. The sooner you get that idea out of your head, the better. We're not going back. We're stuck here for now, and we have to make the best of it. And right now that means building a shelter from these wretched *cezik* leaves."

Once the task was done, they were all exhausted. They pulled their temporary canopy over the hollow, and Hertome and Efheny appraised their efforts.

"Well, it's hardly the best camouflage I've ever seen," Hertome said. "But it's going to have to do."

Efheny sat on the edge of the hollow and then jumped easily down. "Cory, come down. Come backward," she said, seeing Corazame falter on the edge. "Kneel down and swing your legs around. Hertome will have your back until you're sure I have you."

Carefully, they helped Corazame. Hertome followed, needing no assistance. Silently but efficiently, almost as if they were partners, he helped her arrange the branches over them.

They sat squashed together in silence. The canopy of leaves shifted in the breeze, dappling the ground and their bodies with light and shade. Corazame laid her head down on her arms. Efheny checked her chronometer. Three and a half skyturns before her pickup. What was she going to do? It wouldn't be long, surely, before Hertome realized that she had lied about the portable transporter. There was no such device. The ship that was collecting her would follow the signal coming from the data-recording implant embedded above her left eye. She'd led Hertome into the middle of nowhere, with enforcers on his case and no means of escape. How long before he guessed?

"Mayazan," he said quietly, "where's the transporter?"

"I've got the coordinates," she said. "I'll go and find it as soon as it gets dark."

He nodded slowly. "But you're sure this is the place—"

She lifted her hand to silence him. "Listen!"

Corazame too had heard the noise. Craning her neck back, she stared up through the thin cover of leaves. "Enforcers," she whispered, once the *chik* of an air car could be clearly heard. She put her head back down on her arms. "Oh, somebody help me! My beloved Autarch, forgive me!"

Hertome put his hand on her shoulder, but that made her trembling worse. "Don't worry, Corazame," he said. "I'm sure the Ret Mayazan knows what she's doing."

Efheny didn't respond. She twisted her neck to follow the sound of the air car, relaxing only when she was sure it had passed them by and was heading out toward the lagoon.

They sat in silence for a while. *How did I get here?* Efheny wondered. *How did I find myself here, in this wilderness, with a dangerous human and a terrified girl? All I wanted to do was observe. All I wanted to do was live among the Tzenkethi, and serve Cardassia as I did . . .*

"Do you have any water?" Hertome asked. "We've walked a long way today."

Efheny gestured toward the bag she'd brought from the ship. "Don't drink it all at once. We've three skyturns to get through. We might not be able to find more."

He nodded and took one sip, rolling it around his mouth before swallowing. He tapped Corazame on the arm and handed her the water bottle.

"Drink," he ordered her. "Only a little, mind. I don't think Mayazan planned for us all to come along on her little field trip."

Fearfully, Corazame followed his example, taking one small sip and rolling it around her mouth. When she handed the bottle to Efheny, she gave her friend a gentle, pleading look. *Tell me what is happening?* Efheny turned away from that unintended but unbearable accusation. She huddled back against the wall of the hollow, closing her eyes. What in the name of the Blind Moon was she going to do about Corazame?

Hertome was his own problem. He'd taken his chances when he'd chosen to come along with Efheny. It was his own tough luck that he was going to be disappointed. But Corazame . . . Once Efheny was gone, she'd be on her own. It was only a matter of time before the enforcers searching the area caught up with her, and when that happened, Cory would find herself facing her worst nightmare.

Efheny shifted uneasily. You picked up bits and pieces here and there about reconditioning, mostly the whispers and gossip of the utterly uninformed. Pelenten in the unit said that he'd heard it didn't hurt, not unless you tried to resist. So the secret was not to resist. *Corazame . . . Corazame.* The real secret was not to require Re-Co in the first place. But poor Corazame wasn't going to have that option. They'd find her and they'd take her away—this poor, gentle, loyal girl— and it would be Efheny's fault. If Neta Efheny had never come into Corazame Ret Ata-E's life, she would have lived in peace as the model Tzenkethi, hardwork- ing and humble and happy with her station, with the memory of a fleeting love to carry her through when the days seemed too dreary, too tiring. Efheny could pretend to herself as much as she liked that Corazame wouldn't get hurt. But it wasn't true. Corazame was going to be destroyed.

The sun passed overhead. The afternoon dwindled and night came. Corazame fell asleep. Hertome fought sleep but eventually succumbed. But Efheny didn't sleep. She watched her friend, and a great anger washed over her: not with Cory but with Hertome for putting her in this position. As quickly as the anger descended on her, it passed and weariness overcame her. In a few more hours, she would be on her way back to Cardas- sia. But Neta Efheny was so very tired. She wanted to lie back and sleep forever. Not in a few hours. Now.

As the air car swept over Velentur Island once more, Inzegil glanced at Artamer and frowned. The blinds on the air car's side windows were shut, but he looked as glum as an EE server at the start of its shift. She should take him home.

Frustrated, she gripped the car's controls. How long could it take for two Mak enforcers to find three Atas? Earlier, Inzegil was sure they'd found them. They'd picked up the trail of one of them, but then it suddenly disappeared, as if that person had acquired knowledge of how to move around unseen. But how would Atas have learned to do that? What else did Hertome Ter Ata-C know? How much of a danger was he to those two girls? With a sigh, Inzegil turned the air car around for one last sweep. Artamer groaned.

"Last one for tonight, Arty," she promised. "We'll start again in the morning."

Watching Alden and Nekelen standing before a holodisplay in the observation lounge, making their plans to steal into Tzenkethi space, Dax understood why Alden had been restored to active duty. The knowledge of how to get them across the border, through to Ab-Tzenketh, and out again. How often must he have done this? When he'd gone undercover himself, or else collecting agents that he'd placed there . . .

"I assume we'll be modifying the warp field to present the *Aventine* as a Tzenkethi vessel?" Alden said to Nekelen.

"I suggest we appear as a Venetan freighter, Commander, if it's all the same to you," Nekelen countered.

Alden pondered the suggestion and nodded. "I can see the sense in that."

Dax asked, "Why Venetan? Why not Tzenkethi?"

Alden put his hands up on the table. "Under normal circumstances, I'd say Tzenkethi, but their border patrols will be on high alert. All shipping will be under close scrutiny, and they know their ships too well. But if we appear Venetan, any inconsistencies in their sensor readings can be put down to us being a ship type that they're not entirely familiar with."

"Besides," said Nekelen, "it's remarkably easy to lay one's hands on information about Venetan spacecraft." He pointed to one end of the holodisplay, where ship specifications were scrolling past, and sighed overdramatically. "One hardly knows what to do with such an embarrassment of information. What a strange little culture they are. One barely needs to spy on them at all."

"Perhaps if we all did the same as the Venetans," Dax said mischievously, "all this subterfuge would become unnecessary. Imagine it, Nekelen! No secrets, everything out in the open—"

Nekelen looked appalled. Alden merely smiled. "It's a pleasant fantasy, Ezri, but there'll always be someone with something to hide."

"And long may that continue!" said Nekelen. "I'm far too old to think about embarking upon a new career."

Alden laughed. It was fascinating to watch the two men together, Dax thought. How easily they'd fallen into conversation, gotten onto the same wavelength. It was almost as if Alden's profession gave him more in common with this sly, dry little operative than with the people who wore the same uniform as he did. And if Hogue Nekelen played the part of a CIB agent to perfection, surely Peter Alden's performance was no less accomplished. Less crowd-pleasing, perhaps (Garak always did play to the balcony), but still polished. The intelligent, self-contained, solitary man on the verge of middle age, with a quiet charm that had certainly worked on Dax when he'd arrived on the *Aventine*—was it all presentation? Was it all a matter of self-control?

Where was the real Peter Alden? Dax wondered. Did he ever get the chance to exist? Or had he been left behind at the academy, when a ready-made role presented itself, like Ezri Tigan had almost disappeared under the influence of Dax? *But Ezri's here,* Dax thought. *The fast talking, the curiosity about the world and others, the eye for the big picture rather than the detail* . . . That was all Ezri. Dax had just provided the foundation for her to thrive. Perhaps that had happened to Peter Alden too. Dax hoped so.

They crossed the border into the Tzenkethi system within the hour, on Red Alert and with the engine modifications in place. Alden came over to Dax, sitting in her bridge chair, and leaned over to speak to her. He kept his voice low so that nobody else could hear.

"I know you don't trust my word any longer, Ezri, but I want to say that I understand why. I didn't for a while. But I do now."

"*Really?*" she gently rebuked him.

"And I want you to know that you can trust my experience, and you can trust my expertise."

"Peter," she gestured around the bridge, "I'm trusting you with my ship and my crew."

"Most of all," he said, "you can trust me when I say that I want to stop the Tzenkethi more than I want anything in this life."

Yes, thought Dax sadly, as he turned away. *That's what I'm most afraid of.*

Crusher watched on the viewscreen in her office as six Venetan ships inched toward the border, testing the waters and whether the Federation really would make good their outrageous, unbelievable threat. *They look so tiny. Like little pieces of handicraft, or children's toys.*

Whereas, in comparison, even the smallest of the ships sent to support the *Enterprise* looked huge: mass-machined and heavily weaponized. *We must seem monstrous,* Crusher thought. *Giants swatting at flies, using a sledgehammer to drive in a nail.* There was little to feel proud about in all this. *There's nothing the Venetans can do to stop us.* But there was the problem: this wasn't about the Venetans. This was about the Tzenkethi and, behind them, the powers that comprised the Typhon Pact.

The pilots of the six Venetan ships seemed to be coming to the same conclusion as Crusher about their chances. They halted at a safe distance from the border. She listened to Picard reminding them that, for the moment, no ships could be permitted to pass in or out of Venetan space. The six ships lingered awhile and then turned back.

For now, Crusher thought sourly, watching the already tiny ships grow smaller. It had been the same all day and, from the reports they'd received, the same along the part of the border being policed by the Cardassians: a few ships would turn up to take the lay of the land, would see the gunships on their borders, and would slink away. If the Venetans had been lukewarm toward the Federation before, they were now set on the path of permanent enmity.

And all this was simply the warm-up. Once the Tzenkethi ships arrived, there would be a pitched battle. Perhaps a couple would get away, fleeing into Venetan space. They would of course be pursued; their cargo could not be allowed anywhere near Outpost V-4. The Tzenkethi would express outrage at the violation of Venetan borders, and more Tzenkethi ships would be sent. That would bring out more ships from the Khitomer Accords in response, and more from the Tzenkethi in response to that . . . and when Crusher followed her line of thought through to the inevitable conclusion, she found she could not bear the horrors that her head was holding.

Her comm channel chimed. *"Bridge to Crusher,"* said Picard. *"I have a message for you from Alizome Vik Tov-A."*

Crusher nearly fell off her chair. "Excuse me?"

"She asked for you by name. 'I'll speak to Doctor

Crusher, and Doctor Crusher alone,' she said. 'I will only speak to the ship's doctor.'"

"The *doctor*? Is she sick? No, don't answer that."

"It might simply be that speaking to either me or Jeyn would be too humiliating. Especially given the trouble I've caused their ships in the past."

"But to use that word. *Doctor . . .*" Beverly shrugged. "I guess there's only one thing for it. I'll have to talk to her. Isn't that what we've been trying to do all along?"

"My ready room is at your disposal, of course."

"No," Crusher said, after a moment's thought. "I'll speak to her here. On my own turf."

"Very good. I'll be with you shortly."

So Crusher spruced up her uniform, brushed her hair, and sat before the companel trying to think statesmanlike thoughts. She thought of Bacco, razor sharp, ready for anything, and of Ilka, who said little and heard a great deal, and of Rusht, dignified and responsible. But her thoughts inevitably settled on Alizome, the mastermind behind all this, perfectly indecipherable and brilliantly controlled—and who had outmaneuvered her twice already.

You can do this, she told herself. *You have the advantage here. She has come to you. So stay calm. Let her do the talking. Tell her nothing. Stay silent if you have to. Don't let her make you feel you have to fill in the gaps.*

Simple.

Picard entered her office and positioned himself out of sight.

The comm chimed. Picard gave a brisk nod. "Put

her through," Crusher said, and the UFP logo dissolved to show the beautiful, impassive face of Alizome Vik Tov-A.

Even at range, and through a screen, Alizome's physical presence was remarkable. A shimmering haze of golden light seemed to surround her, like the halo in the icon of a Byzantine saint, accentuating her superiority and authority. Crusher found herself wondering what the effect must be on other Tzenkethi. Did they become used to these glittering displays? Or could they never forget the powers in their lives? Were they dazzled each and every time, like peasants in the fields looking up to see the lord of the manor on his fine horse in his fine clothes riding by on his way to his fine house?

"Doctor Crusher," Alizome said in her melodious voice, *"thank you for agreeing to speak to me."*

"You're welcome."

There was a pause. Looking past Alizome's glow, Crusher could see the distinctive curves and natural colors with which the Venetans decorated their rooms. It was to Alizome's credit that she had chosen to remain on Venette throughout the crisis, Crusher thought, although, of course, fleeing the planet at the first sign of danger was hardly the best way to signify support to your allies. She waited for the other woman to speak.

Alizome licked her lips. *How the hell do I interpret that?* Crusher wondered. Did Alizome know that to human eyes that would make her seem predatory? Or was it involuntary? Was she nervous? Crusher knew so little about the complexities of Tzenkethi body language. She might be missing all kinds of signals that she was supposed to see. How was the Federation—how was *she*—meant to find common ground with the Tzenkethi when so little was understood about something so basic?

I can't tell. So there's no point in trying to guess. But she can still speak first.

"*How much do you know about my people, Doctor?*"

First hurdle passed. "Very little," Crusher admitted. "You're the first representative of your people that I've met at any length." She risked a smile. "I'd like to know more."

"*Yes, I'm sure you would.*"

Crusher didn't rise to the bait. From the corner of her eye, she saw Picard give her an approving nod.

"*Matters have come to an unfortunate pass here,*" Alizome said eventually.

I'll say, thought Crusher, *and then some!*

"*It's unfortunate that your government has proved so untrusting and intractable.*"

"I agree that lack of trust is unfortunate."

"*And I'm glad that we agree. I am also glad, therefore, to be in a position to make a gesture of friendship toward you. I hope you'll accept it in the spirit in which it is offered.*"

"What gesture, Alizome?"

"*I have just been honored to speak to our Autarch, our most exalted and beneficent Rej, Korzenten Rej Tov-AA—*"

For a brief moment, Crusher teetered on the verge of bursting out laughing at the string of honorifics. She imagined she was supposed to be impressed by them, but it seemed the Venetans' influence was rubbing off on her. The Autarch's titles struck her as overblown. *Korzenten may be the Autarch, but I wonder who's Lord High Everything Else.* She was struck, too, at how the long list couldn't help but undermine Alizome's authority, reminding Crusher that Alizome was ultimately answerable to someone else, in the way that Crusher was answerable to Starfleet Command. *I wonder how pleased the Autarch is at this unfortunate pass in which we find ourselves. I wonder how pleased he is right now with Alizome.* Hope rose cautiously in her heart. *I think we may just have her on the run at last . . .*

"*Our Autarch has most generously offered to send a deputation to Starbase 261 to inspect the medical supplies that your government has offered.*"

Suppressing her delight, Crusher said, "That's a most interesting and generous offer, Alizome."

"*Thank you, Doctor,*" Alizome said. She too knew that she was backing down. "*However, I do wonder if you understand the* full *nature of its generosity.*"

That put Crusher back on the alert. This wasn't simply the ritualized language that all diplomats used to talk up the case they were making. This, she sensed, was an invitation to understand something important about the Tzenkethi. If she could only work out what it was.

Think, Beverly. Think about everything you've read. Think why she asked for you, for the doctor . . .

If the Tzenkethi came to Starbase 261 to talk about medical supplies, she reasoned, they would not be able to leave without giving away *some* information about their physiology. Yet all the specialists' reports that Crusher had read emphasized again and again their psychological fears about bodily integrity.

Now the significance of this gesture made sense. Inviting Federation doctors to discover more about Tzenkethi biology was offering the Federation access to something sacred, something very protected. It might also avert a war . . .

A war that nobody wanted, and which, Crusher was increasingly coming to believe, the Tzenkethi were not particularly keen to have either. *This might be the first truly nonhostile gesture we've ever received from them. I'd even go so far as to say that they're signaling that they're willing to trust us.*

"*Do you understand, Doctor Crusher?*"

"Yes," said Crusher firmly. "Yes, I believe I do. You're right, Alizome. This is a remarkably generous offer. I'll present it to the president immediately." Making sure she didn't lose sight of the immediate crisis, she added, "But what about your ships? Will they halt their approach to Outpost V-4 while we discuss this offer?"

Alizome smiled and shook her head, as if to say that she wasn't prepared to give up everything. "*Not yet, Doctor. Our people on Outpost V-4 are still in need of those emollients. We would be remiss to withhold them. For the sake of their health. You are a doctor. You understand."*

"I understand. I hope to speak with you again, Alizome," she said, and cut the comm.

Crusher felt like an electric charge had been put through her. She drew a deep breath. "So that's the deal," she said. "We stand down our ships, they reveal a little of their physiology, and in return there'll be no war." She glanced at her husband. "I think it's a good deal."

He grunted. "Let's see if Admiral Akaar agrees."

15

2 DAYS TO WAR . . .

FROM:
A syndic formed to consider rationing

TO:
The people gathered under the Venette Convention

MESSAGE:
Water rationing: Find as many containers as you can and store water. We do not know how long water supplies will remain drinkable. Fill as many containers as possible with drinking water and seal them.

Local sub-syndics for water supply can provide you with vacuum sealers that will help to keep the water clean and fresh. Water sterilization tablets are also available from these sub-syndics.

If a sub-syndic for supplying water has not been formed in your area, please consider forming one with your nearest neighbors. Advice on what to consider follows . . .

- - - - - - - - -

COMMANDER BEVERLY CRUSHER
CHIEF MEDICAL OFFICER'S LOG

Whatever I expected from this mission, it was not that I would end up playing diplomat in perhaps the most sensitive meeting that we've had so far. And play the part solo. But that's where I am. And I can't help this feeling of dread. Everything about this mission so far has been a failure. My own small attempts to observe any physiological changes in the Venetans. Jean-Luc's and Jeyn's attempts to keep Detrek under control. Then the Ferengi leaving, and now a return to the old belligerent ways by the Cardassians. It's hard not to feel this mission is jinxed in some way. But this time, any failure on my part could have disastrous consequences.

Picard asked Jeyn to join him and Crusher in the observation lounge. "Frankly, it's a bewildering offer," Picard said, when Jeyn arrived. "Anything that we give to them obviously couldn't be used to make bioweapons."

"So why would they make such a deal out of coming to inspect it?" said Jeyn. "Surely they haven't gone through this whole charade simply to gain access to Starbase 261? Their information networks must be giving them excellent data on our starbase specifications—"

"I don't think we should be thinking of this offer in those terms," Crusher said. "My instinct tells me that there's genuine fear behind this. I think the Tzenkethi are afraid that we're hurtling toward a war that they don't want either—"

"Yet this situation is entirely of their own making," Picard said. "Think of the opportunities Alizome has had over the past week to call a halt—"

"But there came a point when we'd all come too far," Crusher said. "Jean-Luc, you and I both know that we've been standing here thinking: *How did this happen? How did we get to this?* I think the Tzenkethi have been wondering the same but until now we haven't been able to think of a way to back down without losing face. Is it *really* so difficult for us to believe that the Tzenkethi are as horrified at the prospect of war as we are? All this time, we've been obsessing about them manipulating events, but I think they have as little control of what's been happening as we do."

"They've certainly manipulated the Venetans," Jeyn said.

"Yes, you're right on that score, Ambassador, but I also think the Tzenkethi didn't expect us to issue an ultimatum. I believe their entire plan here was based on sending the Ferengi packing as soon as possible so that we'd be isolated and have to back down. I think they thought it would demoralize us. I know that when Ilka left, I was certainly demoralized!"

"There's a great deal in what you say," Picard said slowly. "We have only recently emerged from a devastating war. Perhaps they were relying on us not to have the stomach even to contemplate another war so soon."

Jeyn gave a short, sharp laugh. "Detrek's presence may have been a blessing in disguise after all!"

"She certainly was a most memorable colleague," Picard muttered.

"But perhaps not just for us," Jeyn said. "If the doctor is right, the unexpected presence of the Cardassians might have thrown the Tzenkethi plans into disarray too and driven them farther than they'd planned to go. And now they're looking for a way out."

"A complication of Cardassians," Crusher said with a smile. "We weren't the only ones thrown by Detrek."

"They were right about one thing," Picard said, drumming his fingers along the arm of his chair. "I *don't* have much stomach for another war. Still," he went on, levering himself up from his chair, "if they're willing to make this offer, it seems they don't have much stomach for it either. But why push us so close to the brink?"

"Think about what Alizome was hinting in her offer," Crusher said. "Think of their fear of bodily disintegration as a symbol for their borders. That way that net of weapons around the Venetan border isn't so much offensive as defensive. Like putting on a mask to protect yourself from an infection."

"And about as effective." Picard smiled. "I can see why they wanted to speak to a doctor."

"Yes, well, it all counts for nothing if the Federation Council won't have it."

Picard went over to the comm. "I'll certainly be advising Starfleet Command to accept Alizome's offer," he said. "But ultimately, it's the Council's decision."

The sky over Ab-Tzenketh was cloudless, and the lights from the Autarch's palace on the Royal Moon were clearer than ever. Through a gap in the roof of leaves, Efheny stared at the moon shamelessly, picking out whatever features she could. Were those windows? Or perhaps those? A thrill passed through her. Could the Autarch himself be standing at one of them, looking down upon her?

A low moan interrupted her train of thought. Turning, Efheny saw Corazame sitting with her hand in front of her face, as if to shield herself from her Autarch's reproachful gaze. She looked cold. Her skin was mottled with dark patches and her glow very dull. She was shivering too. Efheny took off her jacket and placed it around Cory's shoulders.

"When are you going to get the transporter, Mayazan?" Hertome said.

"Later. When the moons have set."

"I know you're talking to each other," Corazame said suddenly. "I don't know how you do it, but I know you can. But there's something *I* want to say. Something I want to say to both of you."

"And what makes you think you can speak without my permission, Ret Corazame?" Hertome said roughly.

"With respect," Corazame replied, to Efheny's amazement, "I do not believe that you are my Ap-Rej."

"I've not been reconditioned yet."

"No," Cory said politely but doggedly. "What I mean is that I do not believe you are an Ap-Rej at all."

"Why do you say that, Cory?" Efheny said in surprise.

"Oh, Maymi." Efheny was stunned to hear the gentle reproach in Corazame's voice. "It's obvious that you're not an Ata-E. It was obvious to all of us. All those odd questions and silly mistakes. Do you know how often we've had to cover for you? Pelenten thought that you were an EE that had been recalibrated and was struggling to understand your new function. We felt sorry for you, so we tried to protect you. We wanted to keep you with us rather than have you sent back down. Who wants to be an Ata-EE? But do you know how often we've made sure your errors weren't seen by Hertome and Karenzen?" Corazame smiled. "You didn't know, did you?"

No, Efheny thought, in shock, she had not known any of this. She had thought she'd been doing so well. Hertome's laughter, hidden from Cory, rang in her ears.

He shut up as soon as Corazame continued. "And then there was you, Hertome. You were another puzzle. Oh, don't misunderstand me. We thought you were a good person to have as Ter, but we were sure you wouldn't remain in that position for long. If anyone was heading for recalibration, it was you. Karenzen has been counting the skyturns until you were gone." She shivered. "I suppose he'll be happy now. Unbearable, but happy." She gave a shuddering sigh. "Not that I'm going back there. But I do worry about the others. Poor Pelenten! Poor Nemeyan! He's got them where he wants them now."

Neither Efheny nor Hertome replied.

"Anyway," Corazame said, collecting herself, "it's not simply that you're oddities. So what else could it be?" Her voice suddenly dropped. "I know my aptitude scores mean I'm only able to understand the E-bulletins, and I know my knowledge is limited to what's needful and my superiors are best placed to judge what that means. So I apologize if what I'm about to say sounds like the usual foolishness of an Ata-E. But . . . I've heard that there are other worlds beyond these under the protection of our beloved Rej. I've heard that on these worlds, there are people who are not like us, who look different and do things differently. I know that no world can be as blessed as those in the care of our Rej, but . . . I've heard there are places where people are free to be whoever they want to be, where they can love whoever they want to love. I think that you might be from one of these places, Hertome. And"—she looked up, directly at Efheny— "I think you might be too, Maymi."

A night bird flapped past. Efheny stared up

through the *keteki* leaves at the glimmer of the Royal Moon.

"Well, Ret Mayazan," said Hertome openly. "What do you have to say to that?"

Efheny looked down at the ground. "Cory, you should put such things out of your mind."

"But are they true, Maymi?" Corazame asked softly, urgently. "Do you know? Do you know for sure?"

"It doesn't matter whether they're true or not!" Efheny burst out. "That's not our business. If it was needful for us to know such things, our bulletins would tell us. But they don't. So we should put such questions out of our minds and perform our function to the best of our ability, for the sake of our Autarch who loves and protects us!"

"You bloody hypocrite," Hertome said in wonder. "She comes all this way to look after you, and you feed her a pack of lies. What are you going to do about her? Are you just going to leave her when you go? You know what they'll do to her when they find her. She'll never have a thought like that again—"

"Shut up!" hissed Efheny. "Shut up!"

"At last, the glimmer of a soul."

"I said shut up!"

Corazame said, "You're talking to each other again. Not letting me listen. As if I'm a child."

You are *a child, Cory!* Efheny thought fiercely. *You're a child who's well out of her depth and who's going to be punished by relentless adults.*

"But I think that you can still hear me," Corazame said. "I only want to say one more thing. Whatever happens, I'm grateful to you both." She hugged herself and bent back her head to stare through the leaves at the sky. "I'm glad that I've known that there really are other worlds. These memories, these *thoughts* . . . they won't survive reconditioning. But I'm grateful to have had them. Thank you."

Angrily, Efheny wiped her eyes. She could not afford this kind of luxury. And this was not her function. She wasn't trained for this. She wasn't trained to feel.

Oh, Cory, why did you follow me?

But Efheny already knew the answer to that. Corazame had followed Mayazan because she was her friend, and she had wanted to protect her.

Hertome rolled onto his side. His voice came through the darkness. He sounded surprisingly gentle. "Go to sleep, Corazame Ret Ata-E. Who knows what tomorrow might bring?"

Approaching the edge of the Tzenkethi system, the *Aventine* slowed its pace to something that could be achieved by a local cruiser. They were drawing close to the net of satellites that comprised the system's outer wall of defenses. Dax watched on the viewscreen as a large silver, teardrop-shaped object appeared. A smaller silver teardrop suddenly peeled away and headed in their direction. A dark shape unfolded upon it, like an eye winking open, watching them.

"Unmanned probe," said Alden. "They'll ask for identification in a moment and almost certainly visual confirmation."

"All right, Nekelen," Dax said. "Time to find if your holo-filters work."

"I'm sure they will, Captain," Nekelen said cheerfully. "But let us not forget that this is also a test of Commander Alden's ability to reprogram flight schedules into the Tzenkethi system."

Dax glanced at Alden, but he gave Nekelen a wide smile. Throughout this tense journey, Alden had been relaxed, as if this was all in a day's work. The jagged, febrile intensity of the previous week had disappeared entirely. This was someone confident of his ability to handle this situation, sure of his own expertise. This was somebody you would send on a mission without compunction.

Along with the engine modifications making the *Aventine* appear to be a Venetan ship to sensors, the holo-filters were needed to give the same visual impression. Alden's hack into Tzenkethi traffic control provided confirmation that this ship should be where it was right now.

At a request from the probe, a channel was opened and Dax indicated that Alden should speak. His body seemed almost to shift; his posture changed, became more fluid, and yet, if it were possible, even more self-contained. She wondered how often he'd played this part. He seemed very comfortable with it.

"I am Anzegar Tor Fel-A," Alden said, "request-

ing, in the name of our exalted Autarch Korzenten Rej
Tov-AA, entry into our beloved system on behalf of
myself and our friends from the Venetan Convention."

There was a screech as the probe carried out identification checks. Then the eye winked shut, and the
smaller teardrop peeled back to its mother satellite.

The *Aventine* moved on. And that was that. They
had entered the Tzenkethi system.

"Thank you, Commander," Dax said quietly.

He turned to look at her. There was a little fire in
his eyes, dying away. The thrill of it? The satisfaction of
getting past his enemies? "My pleasure."

"You make it look so easy."

"It is easy. With practice."

Dax turned to Nekelen. "How are we doing?"

"We're making good time," Nekelen said. "It's all
down to her now. Whether she's reached the pickup
point, or whether something has prevented her from
getting there."

The ship with its cargo of Atas had long since left,
taking them back to their new postings at the building
works, so Inzegil and Artamer were staying at billets
provided by the local enforcer subsection. Plain rooms
but functional, and, besides, Inzegil didn't think she
was going to get much rest.

"I can't understand it," she said to Artamer, who
was spread out on his cot, his hands behind his head.
"How have three Atas managed to avoid us for so
long?"

"Hertome's a cunning one. Have you checked his record again? No sign of any prior declassification?"

"No, although to keep out of sight for so long, you'd almost think he was a higher grade. Perhaps not even an Ata at all."

"That would explain his erratic behavioral patterns," said Artamer.

"What do you mean?"

"I mean, if he's been misclassified as Ata, he must be bored out of his mind. What was his day-to-day function?"

"He was part of a six-Ata maintenance unit at the Department of the Outside. But he was its leader. That should be providing him with sufficient intellectual stimulation. He's only an Ata-C! Anything more would overwhelm him—"

Artamer rolled over onto his side. "Look, Inzy, I don't often say this to you, because you're first-rate. But I've been doing this for a long time, and it's been my experience that every so often one or two get stuck with a wrong grade."

"That shouldn't happen. The Yai scientists are very skilled at what they do. They'd be picked up through testing and recalibrated."

"But sometimes that doesn't happen. Sometimes they're missed. They're a kind of genetic wild card. No," he said quickly, seeing her frown, "I don't think I'm saying anything inappropriate."

"But the Yai scientists know what they're doing."

"Yes, and I think these wild cards are intentional.

Part of the design. I'm not a Yai, but I think a random element helps. Why else are there irregularities? Why else does our whole function exist?"

Inzegil sat down on her cot. A random element intentionally introduced into the great screening programs? If what Artamer said was true, that meant the Autarch was wiser and more far thinking than she had ever imagined. Humbly, Inzegil ducked her head. She gestured in gratitude from her chest up at the sky, and gestured her contrition too. The Autarch was all-wise, and he was not bound to explain his ways to her. She felt ashamed ever to have thought that his intentions might always be clear to her. But the thought that her function had a deeper purpose in his plans, one that she did not fully understand, moved her deeply. She was indeed blessed to be under his protection. Blessed and humbled.

"Anyway," said Artamer with a yawn, "there's nothing irregular about the Rets Corazame and Mayazan. They'll soon give themselves away." He turned his head away from the shuttered window and sighed. "At least I hope so."

Picard, Worf, and Crusher gathered in the captain's ready room to hear the admiral's response to Alizome's offer.

"Tzenkethi scientists on a Federation starbase? Captain, have you taken leave of your senses?"

"Then let us arrange a different location," Picard urged. "Outpost V-4, perhaps, if Rusht can be persuaded to step back from her statement that Starfleet will not be allowed there again. It may at least delay the arrival of those ships—"

Akaar shook his head. *"No. Not good enough. The ships have to stop first. We've always been clear about this. What exactly is this offer when you look at it closely? They'll come to Starbase 261, have a good look around, and then say, 'Thank you for the offer of the supplies, but no, thanks.' Dax's solution will have been rejected, and the Tzenkethi ships will still be on their way. No."*

Crusher leaned forward. "Sir, I must stress the significance of this offer—"

"I don't care about Tzenkethi body issues, Doctor. What about our issue with bioweapons on our borders? No, they stop those ships and then we'll talk about the Tzenkethi inspecting the supplies we're offering. I want you to speak to Alizome. This will be better coming from you—"

"Admiral," Crusher said in alarm, "I don't think that's a good idea—"

"Nonsense, Crusher. You're a fine officer and you've obviously impressed Alizome. So go back in there and emphasize once more that we're serious about those ships. Tell her that either she stops them, or we stop them." He gave Crusher a fierce smile. *"I knew I was right to send you on this mission, Crusher. Akaar out."*

The screen went blank. Worf growled softly under his breath. "I have never heard the admiral speak so stridently," he said. "Am I alone in sensing some deeper purpose at work here?"

Picard slowly shook his head. "You are not alone, Commander. But ours not to reason why . . . Beverly, are you ready to speak to Alizome again?"

"Oh, I'm ready, Captain. But I don't agree with what I have to say to her."

And in her mind's eye, Crusher saw Madame Ilka smile at her.

Welcome to my world, Beverly.

16

1 DAY TO WAR . . .

FROM:
A syndic formed to consider the effects of fear

TO:
The people gathered under the Venette Convention

MESSAGE:
Do not let fear make you forget what is most important in life.

Love your nearest neighbors. Love their fear, love their foibles, love them as they are. They will do the same for you.

Keep heart. Stay strong. A life led in fear is a half life. Trust that this will end.

LT. COMMANDER SUSAN HYATT
SHIP'S COUNSELOR'S LOG

It's the little things that have the biggest effects. Cumulatively, I mean. Oh yes, Peter Alden is thriving right now—he's back in the thick of things and he's loving every moment that he's causing trouble for the Tzenkethi. But what will the cost be? Because I'll bet my commission that Peter Alden is storing up more trouble for himself. And that one day, something very small will cause him to crack. That's all it takes. Something very small. And what I can't understand is why he's here. If I can see it, then so can the people who are giving him orders. So why have they sent him here? What do they think they're doing? They're supposed to be responsible for him. They're supposed to care. But he's here, and he's damaged, and he's panicked once already, and that's not going to be the end. Living only to outwit your enemies is not enough. Not for a full life. And unless Peter Alden sees this lack for what it is, and fills it with something more meaningful, he will never be a well man.

Crusher sat before the viewscreen in her office and prepared to speak again to Alizome.

"I'm sorry that you've found yourself in this position," Picard said. "We have to trust that Akaar knows what he's doing—but can't as yet share his reasons with us."

Crusher gave her husband a dry look. "A higher authority, Jean-Luc? I wonder what Dygan would say if he could hear you."

"I hope he would understand that sometimes we have to take people on trust." The comm chimed. Picard moved out of sight. "Remember that you've beaten her once already. But she's still ahead. Even the score, Beverly."

Alizome appeared on-screen and Crusher relayed the news that they would not accept the Autarch's kind offer of inspectors on Starbase 261, and that further discussions were dependent on the ships that were now approaching the Venetan border stopping and turning back.

Alizome pondered this reply for a while. *"That . . . is a matter of some regret, Doctor,"* she said slowly. *"I must ask, did you understand the full nature of our offer? Did you convey that full understanding to your superiors? We have said that we are willing to accept medical supplies from you.* Medical *supplies."*

"We do understand the full nature of your offer."

"Then how can you—"

"How can I? Because I am *serious*!" Crusher said. "I don't know how we look to you, Alizome. I don't know what stories you tell yourselves about us. I imagine that from a certain angle we look dangerous—unbalanced, even. Constantly bringing worlds under our banner, integrating them into our Federation. We're chaotic, disorganized in your eyes, we don't police ourselves properly and, worst of all, we're right on your borders.

Well," Crusher continued, "we're not monsters, any more than you are. I know that when the threat of bioweapons is being used, I react with revulsion. You keep asking me whether we understand the full nature of your offer. But do you understand the full nature of our refusal? Stop your ships before they enter Venetan space. You threaten our lives, the lives of our children. We will never allow that to happen ever again. Stop your attempts to militarize the Venetan border."

She cut the comm and fell back into her chair.

Well, that certainly felt *convincing. But I hope our superiors know what they're doing.*

Efheny was woken in the dead of night by Hertome shaking her.

"What?" she mumbled. "Are they here? Have they found us?"

"No, they haven't found us," he hissed. He dragged her out of the hollow, ignoring Corazame's pleas. "There's nothing to find, is there?" he said, pulling her around the hill. "You've lied to me, Mayazan! I've looked everywhere. I've searched this whole damn hill. There's no transporter, is there? You're going without me, aren't you? You're going *without* me!"

"Hertome," she whispered, "calm down. There are enforcers everywhere. Of course I haven't lied to you—"

"You're lying even now. I'm not staying. I'm not staying here for them to take me."

You don't have much choice in the matter, Efheny

thought, but then he pulled her to her feet and started searching her.

"Get your hands off me!"

"Where is it? Your implant? I'll tear the damn thing out of you with my bare hands if I have to."

They fought. Corazame, huddled in the hollow with her arms wrapped around her cold body, begged them to stop, but they didn't. They couldn't. Only one person was going to get away, and neither of them could allow it to be the other.

Kicking Hertome's legs from under him, Efheny brought him to the ground. He pulled her down after him, and she fell, heavily, on top of him. She slammed one arm into his chest, winding him, and, with the brief window of opportunity that this gave her, picked up a nearby stone and smashed it repeatedly against his head. He screamed for a little while, but very soon all Efheny could hear were her own grunts of exertion. So she stopped beating him, and there was nothing to hear from Hertome. There was only her own breathing, Corazame's weeping, and the faint *chik* of an air car.

Corazame scrabbled out of the hollow on hands and knees and came toward them. Reaching out one finger, she touched Hertome on the cheek. She began to wail.

"Oh, Maymi, what have you *done*? You've killed him, an Ap-Rej!"

Efheny leaned over Hertome's body and grabbed Corazame by both shoulders. "Be quiet! He wasn't an

Ap-Rej. You know that. He was an alien. A human, they're called. He lost his nerve and nearly got both of us killed!"

Cory's wailing, thankfully, subsided at the shock of what she was hearing.

"Now listen to me, Cory," Efheny said quickly, "because this is important. You're about to go on a long journey, and there are some things I need to tell you before you go."

Corazame stared at her uncomprehendingly. Efheny shook her, hard.

"Cory, *listen*! This is important, much more important than you or me. You're about to meet a man with ridges on his face. Do you understand?"

Cory, mesmerized, whispered back, "Ridges. Ridges on his face."

"That's it. Ridges. Believe me, you'll know who he is when you see him. You're to give him this." Carefully, Efheny reached above her eye. Digging her fingernail deep, she dislodged the tiny implant embedded just below her skin. She pressed it into Corazame's palm. "Hold on to that, Cory. Hold tight."

Corazame gripped her hand around it.

"Give it to the man with ridges on his face. Nobody else. Do you understand?"

Corazame was bewildered, but she nodded. "The man with ridges on his face."

All of a sudden, Efheny felt completely free. She burst out laughing.

"Good-bye, Cory! Good-bye! You don't know how

wonderful it's going to be. You're going away. You're going to be free. It'll all be beautiful, and different, and dazzling. Oh, Cory, you're in for the time of your life!"

The homing beacon activated, Corazame was transported away, and Efheny was left alone on the cold hillside.

She reached over to Hertome and searched his rapidly cooling body. When she found his heat shielding, she turned it off. She did the same for herself. It was no more than a few heartbeats before the *chik-chik-chik* of the enforcer air car turned her way.

"Wait!" said Inzegil. "I'm getting two readings! Two life signs. No, wait, one of them's very faint and getting fainter. Artamer, hurry. In the name of the Autarch, hurry! I think those two girls are about to run out of time."

"Captain, this is Spon. She's aboard."

"Thank you, Chief," Dax said calmly.

She turned to address her flight controller. "Lieutenant Tharp, you heard that. Get us out of here, warp nine point six. Back to the Venetan border. I think we have a war to stop."

There was a man with ridges on his face bending over her. His face was gray. Gray and ridged.

"Neta?" he said uncertainly.

His lips were gray too, but his tongue was pink, as pink as the pearl of the Autarch's palace.

Oh, my beloved Autarch!

He was saying over and over again a name that she didn't recognize.

"Neta? Neta? Are you all right?" He blinked. He had bright blue eyes, wide open, as terrifying as an open sky.

"Neta," he said again, "you're back now. Don't worry if you feel disoriented. Coming back suddenly can be like that. Everything's going to be fine. Trust me. Everything's going to be fine. Have they hurt you?" He reached out a gray hand to touch her face. "Neta?"

Corazame, she thought. *This one is Corazame.*

"You," she whispered. Her voice sounded weak and lost. She *was* weak and lost. "You. She said I'd see you. The man with ridges on his face." She looked around the room. There were other people there too, and they all looked different: different from her and different from each other. That one had blue bulges across his forehead and chin, with one hand on a weapon. That one had three arms. And this one, standing close by, had dark hair, pale skin, and was staring down at her with steely enforcer eyes. She was terrified, looking at those eyes.

"Oh, please!" Corazame cried out, not knowing to whom she was making her plea. "Help me! Please!" She rolled her arms and legs around herself. "Please. Take me away from here." Where did she mean? Surely she did not mean her home, beneath the Royal Moon, under the Rej's protection? So did she mean this place, this little gray room where the air smelled like metal and there were all these different people with their different faces and everything was so different and not everything was kind?

"Please," she cried. "Somebody help me. Oh, my most beloved and exalted Rej, help me!"

The man with ridges made a hissing noise. "It's not her!" he said. "It's not Efheny!" He leaned in. The blue of his eyes was very cold now. He put his alien hand upon her shoulder and grasped hard. "Where is she? Where's Efheny? What have you done with her?" Turning his head to address the dark-haired man, the enforcer, he said, "We've got to go back for her—"

"You," Corazame whispered. "She said I'd meet you. She said I'd meet a man with ridges on his face." She lifted her clenched hand and brushed her knuckle across the indent on his forehead. "Here." She opened her palm to show him the small black device that Maymi had entrusted to her. "She said to give this to the man with the ridges on his face." She laughed a little, teetering on the edge of hysteria. "I think she meant you."

The man with ridges on his face looked down at her palm. He took the device and stood up.

"This is it," he said. "The last of the data. This is what we need."

The one with three arms looked at him uncertainly. Its arms were hovering over a display of flashing lights. "What about your operative?"

"Too late," said the ridged man. "We have to go.

We can't wait. Besides, she's probably dead already. Why else would she have given it to this one?"

"Mayazan!" Corazame cried. "Maymi! She gave it to me. She said to give it to the man with the ridges. She let me go. She saved me from the enforcers." She looked wildly around the room. "You're aliens, aren't you? You're all aliens. You all come from different worlds." Suddenly everything became too much, and a great empty fear washed over her. Her hands began to gesticulate, as if they would somehow instinctively know the right moves to make, the right signals to send. The colors of her skin began to flare out of control. "Oh, help me! This one begs for help. This one assures you of her gratitude, her loyalty, her devotion. Oh, please, do not hurt her. Do not send her back!"

Her fear turned to terror when the enforcer kneeled down beside her. But when she looked into his eyes, she saw the same kindness that Inzegil had shown when she had placed her hand upon her head. He took hold of her hands, but she didn't feel the same charge. *I will never feel that again. I will never feel the fullest touch from a friend . . .*

"Ret," the enforcer said, "everything's fine. Look at me. Look right into my eyes. Everything's fine."

He touched her chin and gently lifted her head up so that she could not help looking at him. He reminded her of Hertome. Hertome, who had been good to serve.

"My name's Peter. Do you hear that? Can you say it? Peter?"

"*Peteh.*"

"Good! Well done! Now tell me your name. Your full name."

She stared deep into his unblinking eyes and obeyed what she saw there. "This one is called Corazame. Corazame Ret Ata-E."

"Corazame," he said. "Cory. It's okay. You'll be fine. I'll look after you, Cory. You don't have to be afraid." He kept his eyes steadily upon her. She thought that he looked very kind. He said, "Trust me."

I do, she thought, grasping his hand as if it was the only link left to life. *I always will. I* must.

Week 3

Blink

FROM:
Civilian Freighter *Inzitran,* flagship, Merchant Fleet 9

TO:
Ementar Vik Tov-A, senior designated speaker, Active Affairs, Department of the Outside

STATUS:
Estimated time to border: 0.25 skyturn
Estimated time to destination: 4.5 skyturns

We are monitoring high levels of activity on the border. Cardassian *and* Starfleet vessels are present. What are your instructions? Repeat: What are your instructions?

Detrek, joining Picard, Jeyn, and Crusher in the observation lounge on the *Enterprise*, was a new woman. There was almost a spring in her step. Crusher didn't blame her. She was feeling pretty pleased with herself too.

"Negotiator Detrek," said Picard. "I assume explanations are forthcoming?"

"Indeed they are," Detrek said. "The agent that the *Aventine* was sent to collect has, for the past two years, been in deep cover at the Tzenkethi Department of the Outside—their foreign affairs office. Through the information collected by her, our intelligence bureau became aware of irregular relationships between officials at that department and several attachés at our own embassy on Ab-Tzenketh. You know how it is," she said. "People go native. They start to see the possibility of friendship—"

"That's no bad thing," Crusher said.

"No," acknowledged Detrek, "except when they begin to lose sight of why they were sent to a world in the first place. They are there to look after the interests of their own people rather than the people of the world with which they are enamored."

"So some of your embassy staff on Ab-Tzenketh had become overly friendly with Tzenkethi officials?" said Jeyn. "Doctor Crusher's right, Negotiator. This happens. This is the risk we run when we send embassies to other worlds. To some extent it's what we hope will happen—that these links will turn into friendships, and these friendships will give us pause before we go to war."

"These friendships went farther than the usual sparring and bonhomie at diplomatic functions, Ambassador. Two of our attachés were discovered to have links to a splinter group unhappy with our alliance with you and keen to forge closer links with the Typhon Pact. These same two have a great deal of influence over a number of rising politicians."

Picard was appalled. "If they'd established themselves and their agenda, that might in time have put Cardassian membership of the Khitomer Accords into danger."

"You understand our concerns, Captain," Detrek said. "And the concern of your president. And so I hope"—she looked at each of them in turn—"that you will forgive the performance that I had to give on Venette. I wanted them in an uproar, Captain. I wanted these conspirators terrified. I wanted them to make mistakes."

"A little warning might have been good," said Jeyn.

"Or might have been enough to make Alizome more cautious," Detrek said. "Alizome did not think she could lose. But, if I understand your Earth legends correctly, hubris is often followed in short order by nemesis."

"Pride comes before a fall," said Crusher. "So your agent? What was this crucial evidence she had? How is it going to help? I assume this was why the *Aventine* was dashing to the border."

"You're correct, Doctor. What our agent saw should be enough to undermine Venetan confidence in the Tzenkethi."

"How?" said Crusher. "What does it matter to the Venetans if the Tzenkethi have been trying to influence Cardassian foreign policy? Isn't that simply your

own concern? My apologies, Negotiator, I'm just trying to understand."

"No, it's a good question, Doctor." Detrek smiled
around at the three of them. "I think you're going to
like my answer. The Tzenkethi, you see, couldn't help
taking out a little extra insurance policy. It wasn't
enough simply to *persuade* our staff to their side. They
tried to blackmail them. Imagine the meeting: 'So
often we've met! So many good times together! What
do you think your superiors will think of that?' That's
our winning move. *That's* what our agent saw—even if
she didn't know what she was seeing."

"Ha!" said Picard, with barely suppressed delight.
"One scheme too many. Game, set, and match!"

"Sometimes you can prepare too carefully," Detrek
said with a sly smile. "Blackmail, Doctor. I believe that
Rusht will be *very* interested to hear about that."

But it was Vitig who spoke to them. Rusht, she told
them, was too ill to participate further in discussions.

"So you see, Vitig," Picard said, "the court of the
Autarch has been trying to undermine Cardassian foreign policy, but not through gestures of friendship or
even through solid debate. Covertly. Suborning staff
at the Cardassian embassy on Tzenketh, attempting to
place them at the heart of the Cardassian government,
and then blackmailing them to ensure their compliance."

The Venetan woman considered the evidence that
had been presented. *"This is troubling information,"* she
said. *"This is not the Venetan way."*

"We don't ask you to like us, Vitig," Picard said frankly. "You have no reason after all that has happened between us. But we ask you to consider whether we are better or worse than your friends. We ask you to consider whether Tzenkethi untrustworthiness might not also extend to what they say about those ships that are still en route here."

"I shall speak to Alizome," Vitig said. *"I shall ask for explanations."* She cut the comm.

"That's it," said Crusher. "We've got her. Explanations? Alizome can't give any. None that will satisfy the Venetans."

- - - - - - - - -

FROM:

Ementar Vik Tov-A, senior designated speaker, Active Affairs, Department of the Outside

TO:

Civilian Freighter *Inzitran,* flagship, Merchant Fleet 9

Stop.

- - - - - - - - -

"They've stopped," confirmed Worf. "They are turning back."

An audible sigh of relief passed around the bridge of the *Enterprise.*

"Thank you, Commander Worf." Picard relaxed and sat back in his chair. "Well, it seems there's to be no war."

"Not today," said Worf.

Dax was pleasantly surprised to see the sweet silver face on the viewscreen in her ready room.

"Heldon! How can I help you?"

"I hope that I may be able to help you, Dax. We did some tests here, during the blockade. Took another look at that explosive device we found."

Dax's stomach sank. "Oh, yes?"

"I think you should know that it's possible—only possible, mind you—that the bomb was of Tzenkethi origin."

"What?" Dax fell back into her chair.

"Although I'm not sure exactly how to interpret this information. Your people could have intended me to discover this in the long run." She gave a wry smile. *"Do you see, Dax? I'm learning. I'm starting to think your way."*

"I'm sorry about that."

"So am I." Heldon sighed. *"But the doubt is there now. Was it your people, in desperation, or with some scheme in mind? Or was it our Tzenkethi guests, with ample opportunity and good reason to want to make us doubt you? I imagine I'll never know."*

"I'll never know either."

"Life is uncertain, Dax. But we can choose how to live with that uncertainty." She leaned forward to cut off the comm. *"My best wishes to you. I hope you pass*

this way again in more certain times. I hope we have the opportunity to meet in friendship."

She was glad that Inzegil Ter Mak-B was the one to take her. She had liked this young woman with the authority and sense of certainty she carried with her. She had been comforted by her. She trusted her. The young enforcer strode toward her, taking in the scene—the body sprawled on the ground, the Ret kneeling before her—and ordered, "Speak. Speak quickly. You have permission not to address me as your Ap-Rej."

"He came in the middle of the night," Efheny whispered, gesturing down toward Hertome. "He threatened us. He made us come with him, all this way. We were so afraid!" She looked around the bare hilltop and shivered. "It's so lonely out here!"

The other enforcer, not Inzegil, said sharply, "Both of you? Where's the other one?"

"Let her explain in her own time," Inzegil said. She knelt in front of Efheny. She was grave and kind. "Carry on, Ret Mayazan. Tell me what happened."

"We got here," Efheny said. "Then Cory, Corazame . . . Oh, I don't understand what happened to her! She changed. She turned on the Ap-Rej and she killed him. It was so horrible. And then . . . Please, forgive me, but this is true. In the Autarch's name, this is true. She *disappeared*, Ap-Rej! Her body rippled, and she disappeared." She looked unblinkingly into Inzegil's eyes, willing her to believe her words. "How can that happen? How can that *happen*?"

"Be quiet, Ret Mayazan," Inzegil said gently. "Do not distress yourself." Slowly, Inzegil helped her stand. "You have been brave. Now you are safe again." Her voice was so very kind. "You must not trouble yourself further," she said. "You did all that could be done by one like you. My colleague and I will take your story to our superiors, and they will judge what should be done."

She put her arm around Efheny's shoulder, guiding her away from the body and down the hill. Her colleague gripped Efheny's arm. "Inzegil's right," he said, and his voice was kind now too, much kinder than before. "You need not concern yourself with these matters anymore."

"We are going to take you back to the boat," Inzegil said in a clear voice, using plain words. "After that, we will take you back to the city. You can complete your restorative leave there. We will find you a peaceful place where you can rest for a while longer. You have earned it. You have been very brave."

Late that night, a small boat arrived to take Neta Efheny away. Inzegil and the other enforcer boarded with her. They led her to a small cabin at the back and sat on either side of her. Their silver glow filled the space.

Efheny sat between them, her hands folded quietly on her lap. She knew she was not going back to the city. A Ret Ata-E could not be allowed to continue to know about other species and other worlds. She was not going to continue her restoration, whatever her kindly captors said. She was going for reconditioning. For how long? She did not know. How long before you forget everything you have once known? How long before you are taught not to think? She hoped it would not be very long. Not because she feared the process, to which she would willingly surrender herself, but because when it was done, they would send her back, back to her life as a Ret Ata-E, back into the unthinking bliss she craved. Neta Efheny's old life would be over. She would be far, far away from the trials and uncertainties that were tightening their grip upon the quadrant. She would be free to live among her beloved Tzenkethi, and she would never have to worry about anything again.

Beyond the window of the little boat, the sun set and the moons rose over the lagoon. Efheny shifted forward in her seat, and her two guards laid gentle, restraining hands upon her. The shuttle shot out into the open expanse of water. Inzegil Ter Mak-B reached out to draw a cover across the window, but before she did, the person who had been Neta Efheny lifted up her eyes and caught a shimmer on one moon of the luminous outline of the Autarch's palace, pristine and unreachable, high above a world that she would never now leave. She twitched her hand to show her gratitude. The blind closed. Mayazan Ret Ata-E shut her eyes and listened to the low hum of the boat cutting inexorably through the water.

"Is she asleep yet?" Inzegil Ter Mak-B said to the other enforcer. She had switched to her own dialect, a

Mak variant of Tzikaa!n that Neta Efheny had studied in depth before taking up her posting and could speak fluently.

"She should be. I doubled the dose."

"Little fool." Inzegil's voice was full of pity, as one would have for a child who has found itself caught up in a situation beyond its understanding. "They never learn, do they? Never stop thinking they're somehow special." Her grip upon her charge's arm softened: still firm, but protective. "Well, I guess you can't blame them. What a drab little life."

"What? Kept safe and warm and happy? Not a care in the world? They should be grateful!"

"So you'd swap with this one, Art? Swap life as a Mak for life as an Ata?" Inzegil sounded amused. "It could be arranged, you know. A little reconditioning and you'd be a whole new person."

The other enforcer chuckled. "Not my purpose, Inzegil. Not my purpose."

The Ret Mayazan stopped listening. Surely this was not for her to hear. Instead, she filled her head with thoughts of how tired she felt and how she would soon be at peace. She was going for reconditioning. She was going to be remade. And when this one was fit for use once more, they would let her return to her station, to her tasks and the custody of Karenzen. Soon, she would kneel again beside her workmates, and bow her head, and sing with them the songs, soothing as lullabies. Soon she would be free to sing with them forever. And their Autarch, their most exalted and beloved Rej, would look down upon his servants and smile.

Dax oversaw the collection of a large supply of emollients from Starbase 261 and then turned the *Aventine* back toward Outpost V-4. *Will they ever even be used?* Dax wondered. *Will we ever know whether this whole business was bluff after bluff?* Still, the emollients had to be delivered. Nobody was going to lose face.

The door to her ready room chimed and, on her instruction, Peter Alden entered, sitting when she gestured toward a chair.

"How's the Tzenkethi woman?"

"So-so." He jiggled his hand up and down. "Still very frightened. She didn't know aliens existed until today. Can you believe that? Most people make first contact only with a single species. Not poor Corazame. A Cardassian, a Takaran, a human . . . I think Spon was the real shock, though."

"Is Nekelen still insisting that she go back with him to Cardassia?"

"I think I've talked him out of that. Mostly Cory's doing. She won't speak to him, except through me. I persuaded him she might enter a catatonic state without me, in which case they'll never get the full story about their agent. I've promised to share whatever information I learn." He looked past Dax, at the bulkhead just behind her. "My superiors are very pleased about that, of course. They think in time she'll be a valuable asset."

"After all she's been through? Peter, we couldn't use her like that!"

"Well, we don't know yet what she's been through. She might be a perfectly happy Tzenkethi E grade who has somehow found herself mixed up in a very confusing scenario and is eager to get back home as soon as possible."

"Would Starfleet Intelligence *let* her go back?"

He looked at Dax, rather sadly. "When I remind Cory of what's likely to be waiting for her if she does go back, I think she'll choose to remain an alien in an alien land. But she's got some tough times ahead. They're damaged, the Ret Ata-Es, in particular ways. Damaged by their conditioning and the rules that they have to obey. They're taught to be helpless, to suspend judgment and let others decide—one of the worst things that can be done to anyone." He sighed. "Who knows how she'll cope out here? But perhaps, with care, she'll learn. Given time, and space, she might even flourish. If I can get her to stop thanking me for everything."

"What about the agent that died on Tzenketh? Did you know him?"

"Yes, I knew him well. Poor Alex. No partner or children, thank goodness."

"And what about the rest of the network operating on Tzenketh? What's the news on them?"

"A lot of arrests. We've arrested a lot of theirs in response. There'll be an exchange at some point. Not soon. Poor sods." A frown crossed his face. "Poor Alex. You know, I'm not so sure he was in danger of arrest.

Tzenkethi counterintelligence isn't as good as it thinks it is." He gave Dax a narrow look. "I shouldn't have said that. Forget I said that."

"Of course. But . . . if you're in the mood for confidences—"

"Oh, dear. Here it comes."

"The bomb, Peter."

"Ezri, do you really think I could have done that?"

"I'm going to take a leaf out of the Venetan book here and be completely honest with you. I don't know. I don't know whether or not you could—"

"Ezri," he chided her softly.

"Peter, you're a *spy*! You're trained to do that kind of thing. You're trained to look at a particular situation, and weigh the odds, and decide whether the ends justify the means. That's your *function*. So don't pretend to me that it's something you couldn't do."

He looked at her thoughtfully. "I know what you're thinking. That I've changed. That once upon a time I was somebody you could trust. But you can trust me. You can trust me to have the Federation's interests at heart."

"You do know that hearing you say that doesn't help?"

"No?"

"It just makes me more afraid of you. Makes me even more afraid of what you might be able to justify to yourself."

"And you understand, don't you, Ezri, that we're living in dangerous times? The days are gone when we could look benignly out across the universe and explore it in peace. There are people out there that hold us in contempt, whole systems of worlds that fear us and hate us because of what we are and what we stand for. They might even fear us enough to want to destroy us. I'm not going to let that happen."

"For Alex Gardner's sake?"

"That's one reason, but it's not the only one. What we have is good, Ezri, and it's worth fighting for."

"But isn't it always the same, Peter? We say these things, and then what we do corrodes the very values we claim we're trying to uphold."

He smiled enigmatically. "You might say that. I couldn't possibly comment."

Dax left it. She wouldn't get any more answers. She would never know who had planted the bomb on Outpost V-4.

She stood up and went to look through the port at the myriad stars. What was Corazame Ret Ata-E making of such a view?

"You know," Dax said, "I can't begin to imagine what it's like. To be confronted with a universe so vast . . . It reminds you of why we are here." She looked at her old, changed friend. "At least, I hope so."

The admiral was on the line. Crusher eased out of her seat and came to stand behind her husband.

"I assume," Picard said, "from the involvement of the *Aventine* in extracting the Cardassian agent, that that was your priority even before the crisis began."

"*Yes. I'm sorry about that, Jean-Luc. The fewer people who knew about it, the better. But the alliance with Cardassia had to come first. The Andorian secession's been a terrible blow to our status and prestige. If anti-Federation sentiment—or even plain ambivalence toward us—takes hold on Cardassia, we run the risk of seeing much less friendly people in charge there than the current administration.*"

"And we can't afford to lose such an ally?"

"*Oh, it's more than that. I want that alliance set in stone. I want people thinking about Federation and Cardassian ties as a special relationship. So natural that hardly anyone remembers we were once at war. I want war with Cardassia to seem like an aberration, something that could have happened only in fiction.*"

"Close friendship is a good thing, Admiral," Picard said. "But, as the past few weeks have proved, that surely gives the Cardassians a great deal of bargaining power over us—"

"*I think it's a good deal, Jean-Luc. I'll take it.*"

"What about the three Venetan bases?" Crusher said. "Will there be a Tzenkethi presence there?"

"*There will,*" said Akaar, "*but there'll also be observers from the nearest Khitomer powers present.*"

"The Venetans agreed to that?" Crusher asked in surprise.

"*The Venetans are lucky their civilization is still intact. They'll accept what we and the Tzenkethi tell them to accept.*"

"Not quite in the spirit of self-determination," Crusher said.

"*If the Venetans didn't want to play ball in the galactic playground, Doctor, they should have stayed in their own backyard. They put themselves in the firing line. Now they have to live with that. Sad, but true.*"

"And what do we get out of all this?" Picard said. "I assume a deal has been made with the Tzenkethi somewhere?"

"*Very perceptive of you, Jean-Luc. Yes, we've agreed to the presence of Tzenkethi observers in the Maqbar system. Starfleet has just leased four bases from the Maqbari.*"

A deeper game indeed, thought Crusher. Something had occurred to her—something which she didn't like much at all. "Admiral, why did you send me to Venette? It wasn't because of my prior visit or my medical expertise, was it?"

Akaar had the good grace to look embarrassed. "*No, Doctor. I wanted our delegation off-balance when Detrek became unreasonable. We had to ensure that Tzenkethi attention was diverted fully toward Venette and not anywhere near the Cardassian agent. I'm sorry, Doctor. But that's the truth.*"

"I see," said Crusher. "Thank you for being honest with me, Admiral."

She moved out of his eyesight and did not listen to any more of the conversation between Akaar and her husband. *So,* she thought, *I was set up. Not only was my mission nonsense, but even when my role expanded, I was intended to fail. All those conversations with Alizome— the heartbreak, the worry, the fear of failure—and my superiors didn't want me to be successful. Or, if I was, it didn't matter. I was a distraction. What mattered was to keep Alizome busy wasting her time with me for as long as possible. What mattered was happening elsewhere.*

She heard the comm channel close and turned to face Picard.

"Beverly," he said cautiously. "I know you're upset—"

"Upset? Jean-Luc, I'm not upset. I'm furious."

Later, in their quarters, Crusher watched over René until he fell asleep.

Her husband hovered worriedly behind her, uncertain how to handle her in this mood. Eventually she took pity on him and sat beside him on the couch.

He took her hand, awkwardly. He cleared his throat. "You saved the day, Beverly."

"Hardly."

"Your handling of Alizome was superb—"

"Don't patronize me, Jean-Luc," she said—firmly, but not unkindly. "I understand what happened and I understand why. People like me, and Ilka, and Dygan—we don't count. Not really. We're here to carry spears. We're here to obey."

He started. "Beverly, that isn't true—"

She put her fingertips upon his lips to silence him. "I made a mistake forgetting that," she said. "I won't make the same mistake again."

After Jean-Luc went to bed, Crusher sat awake for a long time, tired but far from sleep. A message had arrived from her sister-in-law. She watched it with relief, reveling in the domestic detail, far away from her own situation.

"I'm just so relieved to know that all three of you are okay. Hey, a strange thing happened yesterday. I was contacted by a Ferengi merchant looking to import wine to Ferenginar! No idea how he found me . . ."

Crusher silently saluted Madame Ilka. *To friendship,* she thought. *To difference.*

To trust.

Acknowledgments

Thank you to Margaret Clark and Ed Schlesinger for support during the writing of this book, and to David R. George III and Dave Mack for correspondence and help during revisions.

Grateful thanks to the contributors to the online *Star Trek* wiki sites.

My love and thanks as ever to Matthew, who didn't let a house move disrupt my writing.

About the Author

Una McCormack is the author of three previous *Star Trek* novels: *Cardassia—The Lotus Flower* (which appeared in *Worlds of Star Trek: Deep Space Nine, Volume 1*), *Hollow Men*, and *The Never-Ending Sacrifice*. She has also written two *Doctor Who* novels, *The King's Dragon* and *The Way Through the Woods*. Her short fiction has appeared in *The Year's Best Science Fiction 2007* (ed. Gardner Dozois), *Dark Currents* (ed. Ian Whates), and *Glorifying Terrorism* (ed. Farah Mendlesohn). She lives with her partner, Matthew, in Cambridge, England, where she reads, writes, and teaches.